TUNISIAN

DREAMS

TUNISIAN

DREAMS

A NOVEL

IVOR RAWLINSON

Matador
9 Priory Business Park,
Wistow Road, Kibworth Beauchamp,
Leicestershire. LE8 0RX
Tel: (+44) 116 279 2299
Fax: (+44) 116 279 2277
Email: books@troubador.co.uk
Web: www.troubador.co.uk/matador

ISBN 978 1780882 031

British Library Cataloguing in Publication Data.
A catalogue record for this book is available from the British Library.

Typeset in 11pt Aldine401 BT Roman by Troubador Publishing Ltd, Leicester, UK

Matador is an imprint of Troubador Publishing Ltd

Cover image from an original painting "Coastal Shelf" by Val Archer based on a Roman mosaic.

For Catherine

Foreword

We remember what we want to remember and easily forget the rest. Lest we forget what life was like in Tunisia before the Revolution of 2010 - 2011, this novel stands as a humble record. It was completed just before the Revolution began. You will hear the distant rumble of thunder. The underlying issues with which it deals are unlikely to go away, though today they would be approached rather differently. Even in the most pleasant countries, such as Tunisia, unpleasant things happen. That they do, is not a reflection on the place or the people, for both of which I have the highest possible regard and admiration.

Ivor Rawlinson
January 2012

TUNISIA

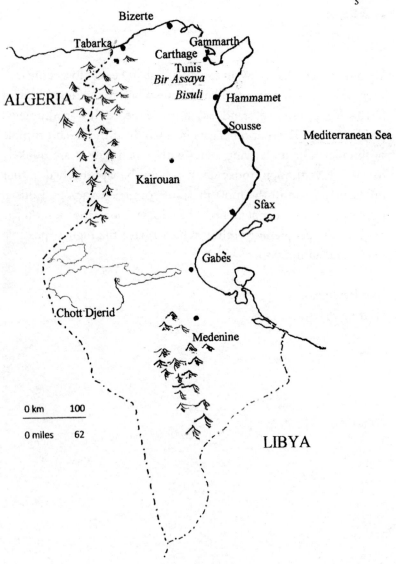

Place names in italics are invented

CHAPTER 1

Carthage, Tunisia, September 2009

"**S**top! Photography forbidden! *Arrêtez! Pas de photo!*"
The guard waved his rifle fifty metres away in the shade of
a sentry-box. Fallen pillars and broken arches littering the
site did not obstruct his voice which sounded close. Celia lowered
her camera and peered beyond the sunlit ruins into the shadow
beyond. She hadn't noticed the soldier and didn't know what he was
guarding. But by narrowing her eyes she could make out a long,
white wall, dark trees behind it and the red and white Tunisian flag
quivering on a flagpole.

"Why shouldn't I?" she shouted back. "I don't understand."

To her alarm, the guard walked directly towards her, holding his
rifle with one hand and glancing backwards to see where the other
guards might be. She did not recognise the uniform but assumed it
was Tunisian army. Her heart began to thump as he lengthened his
stride. She switched off her dictating machine and put it in her
pocket. She turned round hoping to see other visitors to the
Antonine Baths in Carthage behind her. There were none.

She wondered whether she should run back to where she had
left Rafiq, her guide. She was fit and might be able to outrun
someone in boots, carrying a rifle. But then he would have reason
to suspect her. So running was not an option.

She wished she'd brought her phone with her. Foolishly she'd
left it behind in London when she'd been told that in Tunisia she'd
have to change the SIM card.

"You take too many photographs," the guard said, rolling the "r"

1

in the last word. Beads of perspiration lined his forehead where dark, curly hair peeped from under his cap-band.

"Did you not see the notice? *Vous n'avez pas vu le panneau?*"

"What notice? No, I did not."

"It is prohibited to photograph the Presidential Palace. I could arrest you. Your papers, please."

Reading from her passport, his attitude perceptively softened and Celia detected the faintest of smiles.

"Celia Purchas. British," he said.

He was now looking for entry stamps and a visa perhaps. She was tempted to offer to delete her pictures, to apologise if she'd done something wrong. She remembered Rafiq saying the President of Tunisia lived next door to the site. She vaguely remembered him talking of political tensions, increased nervousness and suspicions of outside interference. She had genuinely seen no notice about photography. Her mind was on the splendours of the Roman Carthage of 370 AD and how it would have looked to a first-time visitor.

"So what are you doing?" the guard asked.

His features were relaxing, his fingers were off the trigger guard and the barrel was pointing firmly towards the ground.

She should have known better. Had he noticed her dictating, she wondered? That must have looked suspicious. But she always dictated notes whilst impressions were fresh in her mind. Otherwise she forgot them.

"Researching for a film. Looking at locations. This might be one." Her gesture took in the whole archaeological site, a maze of massive reddish walls, waterworks and heating ducts.

"A political film?"

The guard was still unsure what she had been photographing.

"No. Not at all. It's a film on the life of St Augustine of Hippo. An amazing man who lived here in Roman times. It's for the BBC."

"You work for the BBC?"

"Not exactly. But I used to. I haven't for a year now. Why do you want to know?"

"Ah. But you know people there? You are in contact?"

Celia's mind continued racing. It was over a year since she had quit the frenetic world of journalism so that she could be more of her own mistress in films. She didn't answer straight away. Warm wind from the sea, a stone's throw away, puffed dust across her sandals. She looked above the foundations of the Roman baths to the indigo Bay of Tunis, darkly sparkling in the September afternoon sun, then back at the face of her interrogator. His smile had developed and his eyes definitely sought contact with hers. Who was this man?

"Yes. I still know people at the BBC. But my work here is nothing to do with them."

"Something very serious happens. Very serious."

He looked around him once again then held Celia's gaze. If expression alone could convey sincerity, his did.

"It is urgent that the right people will know. But at any time the patrol will see I have not returned and will come to look for me. Listen, can I meet you when my duty is finished, later today?"

"Who are you? Where are you from? Your English is good."

"My name is Khaled." He lowered his voice. "But it is not important. I am in the army – temporarily. Normally I work in the university in Tunis. I am with an army unit reinforcing the palace guard over there. When they ask me what I was doing, away so long from the patrol, I will say I was interrogating you."

"But, it's ridiculous. I was not photographing the palace walls. I was photographing the site of the baths…"

"It is prohibited…"

Just then, the radio at his belt startled Celia, who hadn't noticed it. It spluttered *"khamsa, khamsa"* (five, five) then cut out. The man in uniform motioned to Celia to stay where she was. He lifted the radio from his waist and gave a brief reply. She noticed he had a ring on the small finger of his right hand. He must have been about thirty. But his eyes looked older.

"They want to know where I am. I do not have long. Can I meet you to tell you what is happening? In two hours my duty is finished.

We can meet at the ruins over there, a basilica, called Damous el Karita." He indicated the direction with a nod of his head.

"Can you remember the name? Damous el Karita."

"O.k. I'll be there. Perhaps."

She was shocked to hear herself saying this. Yet it was a considered reply. The "perhaps" gave her time to reflect, gave her room for manoeuvre.

"Of course," he was almost whispering now, "what I am doing is illegal. We were told not to speak about it to anybody, *"jamais"*, not even our families. I must return, quickly, otherwise I will be in trouble. Thank you. Thank you sincerely."

"At six this evening, then," Celia confirmed.

"You must be alone. Please. I cannot trust anyone."

Curiosity was what had made Celia a good journalist at the beginning of her career. What turned her away from the profession was dissatisfaction: she constantly felt she was just scratching the surface. She was never given time to explore her stories deeply enough. At first she blamed the market-place atmosphere, the budget-driven agenda; then she blamed her editors; but finally she convinced herself it was the public that didn't want to know too much of what lay behind the headlines. It didn't have time and it probably didn't care.

Celia made her way back to the centre of the site, looking for Rafiq. The sun was surprisingly hot and there was not much shade in the ruins of the third largest baths in the Roman world. Two grey, granite columns stuck up to the blue sky like the remaining teeth in the wreckage of a giant's jaw. All the other columns holding up the roof thirty metres above her had gone, plundered, leaving just their bases and intricately carved capitals, mute testaments to the opulence of Roman Africa's chief city.

She tried to imagine the virile young man that was Aurelius Augustinus coming to this colossal complex for the first time. No wonder he was overawed. He would have met his student friends in the meeting rooms, looked at the shops, exercised in the gyms, sweated in the sweating room and swum in the huge pool. The cavernous baths would have echoed to shouts and splashing from the privileged bathers. Light from the sea and sky would have flashed off the wet, white marble.

Celia had spent the morning at Tunisian TV with Rafiq and Ferid, the two film production assistants she was using, discussing studios, equipment and costs. In the afternoon, Ferid had gone to search for countryside locations (straight roads between wheat-fields, a Roman bridge and orchards) whilst Celia and Rafiq came here.

She would have preferred to have been alone. Reconnoitring film locations was something she liked to do in her own bubble, without distraction. But Rafiq was an ideal guide – discreet and sensitive.

After twenty more minutes of meandering, Celia came to the conclusion that a full-scale mock-up of the baths would be impossibly expensive. She would ask the experts whether there were ways of conveying the size of the complex without a life-sized model. Perhaps with computer-generated techniques based on the ground plan, making full use of sound and light? Whilst the nudity at the baths would be a problem for some, it fitted well with the message in this part of the film – the decadence of a Carthage that Aurelius Augustinus called a cauldron of carnal love.

As she sat at his table in the little café beside the site, she was amused to see that Rafiq had been button-holed by a Swedish couple at the adjoining table. Celia guessed they were honeymooners, from the way they regularly held each other and took pictures of themselves. They must have heard Rafiq's good English and thought he was a site guide. Rafiq would have been flattered. He'd learnt his English in the States, at the same film school as Ferid. Anyway, the Swedes were spell-bound by the carved stone Roman latrines sitting side by side in two graceful monumental arcs.

"When first discovered they were thought to have been part of a theatre," Rafiq was telling them.

The Swedish bride was incredulous.

"How could they! All together. I mean it is so public, one beside the other."

"The Romans were less inhibited about the human body than we are. Less prudish perhaps." Rafiq was getting into his stride.

"Have you visited Dougga yet? No. Well, it's a couple of hours' drive from here. They've discovered a communal latrine there for twenty-six people at a time!"

"Really?" said the Swedish groom, not quite sure what else to say.

Looking towards the sea just a few steps away, she noticed a black cormorant on a post on the beach. It flapped up and out to sea before folding its wings to make a steep dive. It punctured the calm water like an Olympic gold-medallist and emerged with a quivering fish. A formerly free fish. A symbolic Christian fish perhaps. Was this another idea for the film, she wondered? Finding a cormorant to perform to order would be a further test for the production crew! But they enjoyed a challenge.

Artistically and financially Celia was in an unusual position. On the one hand she had her film treatment more or less ready. She had Alfred Feldstein's personal word that Malwood Films were extremely interested, as was the BBC. But on the other hand, Feldstein wouldn't put anything in writing resembling a financial commitment. "Saints are high risk," as he had quaintly put it to Celia in his London office. Yet she was more than ever certain there were good audiences for Augustine's extraordinary life, his deep friendships, his illegitimate child and his long-suffering mother, Monica. The time was right for his ideas, too: pointers towards how a decadent civilisation could save itself. So this trip was at Celia's own expense. If she didn't take her chances now, would she ever, she asked herself?

She had decided, she wasn't sure why, not to mention her strange meeting with the soldier to Rafiq or Ferid. Something Rafiq said in the car earlier stuck in her mind. He'd been asking her about TV in Britain and how free it was. Was nothing off-limits, he asked?

"We could report pretty much everything. Very rarely, the

lawyers would tell us that we'd be breaking the law if we said such and such – you know, during a criminal investigation or during a trial. Or if we said something that put lives in danger. Why do you ask?"

Rafiq kept his voice down, even though they were in a car with the air-conditioning working and the windows up.

"The media here is completely…" He put the fingers of one hand to his mouth as if clamping his lips together.

"They say nothing about what is really going on. And the foreign press is not interested. If a French paper prints anything critical about the President or his family, it is banned, copies simply do not go on sale. We rely on rumour, on whispered conversations with people we trust."

"So what is going on?" asked Celia.

"Plenty," said Ferid. "Especially…" Rafiq ostentatiously turned and stared at him, effectively silencing him.

Celia wondered if the soldier was a stooge, if she was being set up. It was odd that he had made a bee-line for her, almost as if he was expecting her. She was conscious about her ignorance of the political scene in Tunisia beyond that the president ruled the country with a rod of iron, that he tolerated no dissent and that resentment was simmering under the surface. She could still change her mind about meeting the soldier if she wanted to. She composed herself.

Returning to the café table, Rafiq asked questions about the film project, where she had the original idea, whether there was a copy of the treatment to see or even the outline script. Celia was happy to chat about all that. She told him it was to be a film about Augustine's personal quest for happiness, about guilt and how to hang on to personal values in a degenerate society.

When they had finished their drinks and there was still no sign of Ferid with the car, Celia strolled over to look at postcards and souvenirs being sold under a large, red and white sun-shade. The seller's wares were spread out on a couple of upturned cardboard boxes and on a small rug on the ground. Leather belts and cheap scarves hung from the spokes of the umbrella. Normally she did not stop to look at this sort of thing but now she had time to kill.

"You want something special?" the fez-wearing old man asked from his position sitting cross-legged in the shade on the pavement.

"Maybe," Celia replied.

He turned his head towards her but didn't stand up. Celia thought there was something dignified about him. She smiled whilst pushing her collar-length auburn hair back round her ear in a characteristic gesture revealing a clear, pretty, strong English face.

"My son found it. In Carthage."

He looked up and down the street before beckoning Celia down to his level. She squatted beside him. He pulled a cigarette packet from his cream coloured tunic, his "djellaba". Pushing it open with an arthritic thumb, he carefully took out a coin and gave it to her. It looked old enough to her untutored eye. It seemed to be bronze and she saw the letters SEV with the outline of a laurel-wreathed head. There was a good image on the other side but before she could examine it, a black Mercedes came into view and the old man became nervous.

"How much?" Celia asked.

The old man shrugged.

"You make a price," he said.

Celia looked in her purse and produced a crumpled, twenty dinar note. The old man saw its colour and nodded before Celia had second thoughts. She knew she only had low denominations in her purse anyway, so both parties were happy. She returned slowly towards the café. Half an hour later, Ferid arrived with the car and they all climbed in.

It was her journalist's sixth sense that inclined her to make the rendezvous with a soldier she had only met for a moment. It was, of course, crazy. On any purely rational reckoning, the risks were unreasonably high. One just didn't make assignations like this in unknown places with unknown people for unknown reasons. On the other hand, Rafiq and Ferid would be with her, so it would be alright.

What was pushing her towards keeping her word was her

conviction that the man in uniform was genuine. He did not seem to be a career army officer at all. He had said as much. The way he spoke, and his good English, backed that up. The impression of urgency he gave, in very few words, was striking. The context was credible, too. In the army, he might well be in a position to learn or see things which others did not. Perhaps it was connected with the palace? Was there to be a coup? Was the President dead?

Was it reasonable, she finally asked herself, that he should have insisted that she come alone? She was an attractive woman, after all, a foreigner, who didn't speak Arabic. She could hear her mother saying that she must be completely out of her mind to even think about meeting the man. But Celia had not become either an award-winning journalist or a director by being timid. She was a risk taker.

"I hope you don't mind, but I want to fit in one other site visit before we go home," she told Ferid and Rafiq.

"Damous el Karita. It's a ruined basilica. Augustine preached in most of the basilicas in Carthage later in his life. I have two scenes where he is preaching, scoffing at pagans for worshipping statues, telling sinners how they can save themselves. Powerful stuff. I'd like to see where this all happened. It's important to understand the atmosphere, don't you agree?"

There was no dissent. How could there be? Celia was paymaster and director.

She was thinking of the precautions she should take. If she was being set up for a robbery, she wanted to be sure she had at least some foreign currency to hand over. She had just seen she had two fifty-euro notes in her purse. And she wouldn't stray out of shouting distance of her guides.

"As before, I'd like to see it for myself first; to make up my own mind. So if you keep an eye on me from the car, I'll take some pictures then ask you for your views. Give me just a few minutes."

Damous el Karita turned out to be an evocative but isolated site on the outskirts of Carthage. It was surrounded by fields on three sides and what looked like a cemetery on the fourth. There was no car-park or even a sign to say what there was here – at least she couldn't see one. A mass of broken pillars and partially restored, knee-high walls clearly outlined a large church with many aisles. An evening breeze waved the weeds growing between the pillars. A dog barked in the distance. There wasn't a soul about. It looked as though the rest of the world regularly passed it by.

As Celia stepped out of the car at six precisely she noticed how quickly the sun had dipped in the sky. In an hour, night would be falling. She hoped this meeting would be quick.

"Are you sure you don't want us to come with you?"

"No thank you. I want to take it in alone. I'll call you over in a few minutes."

She walked thirty metres or so across the road and towards the entrance. Graffiti in Arabic and French scarred the limestone on the first pillar inside the ruins. The proportions were handsome. This had once been a very substantial church. She imagined what a service must have been like in those early days. Much longer, so she had read: all morning, with more ritual and much more religious fervour. And she imagined the effect Augustine's brilliant sermons must have had on his devout listeners.

There was still nobody there though. She kicked some pebbles to make a noise and coughed. She walked through the grass to the end of the ruin where a few steps led down to a circular room again lined with pillars. It must have been a sort of subterranean rotunda. The low sun slanted through the open space above. There were prickly bushes of some kind which caught on her trousers before she had gone even a few paces inside. She stooped to free herself from the thorns and as she did so was aware of the shapes of two men rapidly closing in on her from behind.

CHAPTER 2

Celia didn't even have time to scream. She felt a large, wet hand press across her mouth, her chin and her nose. The noise she made was more like a muffled grunt. She raised her arm thinking she might knock at least one of them down but the two men were behind her and no sooner was she ready to turn and hit out than both her arms were gripped firmly. Though slender and slightly below average height, Celia was surprised at the ease with which she was lifted and carried by her arms and elbows back up the steps. It took her a few seconds to coordinate her thoughts. She tried to jerk away and she twisted round so that she could see her attackers. She partly succeeded but tripped to the ground. She opened her mouth to scream but again the wet, dark hand whipped up and stopped her. One of the men raised his finger to his mouth and said "sshh."

She rose to one knee and saw that she had scratched her forearm and it was bleeding slightly. Her back hurt too. She saw where she could run to but before she could prepare to do so, she was held by the arm on either side and propelled forward. The men were extraordinarily strong for they ran with her to the opposite side of the ruined building from where she had parked and onto a path of sorts. She felt vulnerable and extremely frightened. Two buttons of her short sleeved, white blouse with two front pockets had become undone and was in any case riding up over her breasts because of the way she was, quite gently, being half-carried, half-lifted.

She twisted round one last time both to see the face of the man behind her and to escape. It was Khaled. Her twisting did no good. She'd pulled a muscle somewhere in her back and it was hurting with each jolt as she was led away. She couldn't escape yet. Surely

11

Ferid and Rafiq would have heard her grunt or seen something, she thought. Then again, she had told them not to follow her but to wait by the car. What a fool she had been.

Behind some thorn bushes, was a white, well-cleaned, new looking Renault with the sun-visors down. It looked incongruous in this untidy, desolate spot. The man she didn't recognise on her right, opened the driver's door, looked at Celia and smiled. He again put his finger to his lips, urging silence. Celia made no noise. She thought of making a run for it but she knew she would be caught within seconds and might then be given rougher treatment. She was reluctant to get into the car and showed it. Khaled turned round to face her. His face was so close to hers that she could see marks on the bridge of his nose made by his sunglasses and that he had extraordinarily good skin texture.

"I said you must come here alone. You have not. This is my brother, Omar. He's a doctor. You will be safe with us but if you make noise or try to run, we will have to tie you."

Khaled lowered his voice.

"Go into the car. *Allons-y*."

As soon as the three of them were in, Khaled and his brother closed the doors quietly and Celia heard the central locking system go "clunk".

"Keep your head by your knees. More down. More. I will tell you when we have no danger. I am sorry it is like this. I am really sorry."

She felt the car racing over bumpy terrain, then over grass, then onto a surfaced road. At this point Khaled indicated Celia could sit upright in the back seat and she did. Noticing the blood on her arm, Khaled produced a folded, white handkerchief from his pocket. She used it to clean the blood and then held it in place. They were driving fast in gathering darkness on a road that Celia didn't recognise. Her heart was pounding and her mouth was dry. The full realisation of what had happened began to register. She was very, very scared. When at last she was able to speak, she was surprised at her restraint.

"What on earth is all this about? Is this necessary, all this secrecy and drama?" she asked, wiping the hair back from the front of her face.

She felt better once she was able to speak. Her anger was now bubbling up. She tried to regain control.

"Listen. We agreed to meet at that place – that ruined church or whatever it was – because you had something to tell me. Something important, you said. And you thought it would be of interest to me because I used to be a journalist. I can't understand, I absolutely cannot understand, why you two think you can carry me off – kidnap me – like this. It's true I didn't come here alone. But the two men who were with me have been with me all week. They are in the film business, like me. There is a big project to make a film here in Tunisia about Saint Augustine."

"Who?" said Omar.

"St. Augustine."

Celia, whose mother was half French, pronounced the name again but this time the French way. *"Saint Augustin."*

Neither brother reacted.

"Charismatic," Celia continued, "passionate, frank. An intellectual brought up by a Christian mother and a pagan father. He described life in Roman Africa in detail, like no other. We have a lot of work to do for the film. I have commitments all day tomorrow. Those men will be looking for me now. So why don't you stop right here, tell me what you have to tell me and then we can go our separate ways?"

"No. We are going to Omar's house at La Marsa. We want to show you documents and explain what we know. It would be too dangerous to do this anywhere else."

"If it is about military secrets, I'm not interested. Let me tell you that straight away."

"No."

"Ah," Celia said. "Of course. You were guarding the President's palace. So you've information about him – or the dissidents perhaps?"

13

Only that morning at the t.v. offices, Celia had picked up a rumour about unrest at two different universities outside the capital. The people she was talking to seemed to think it was significant that it was not in Tunis but in the provinces. And she remembered how her Tunisian contacts that morning had all been trying not to laugh at some sort of joke about the President's wife.

"Not military secrets. It is about the lives of hundreds of ordinary people…"

Khaled stopped when he heard Omar in front gasp, then shout something in Arabic that Celia supposed was "Watch out." They had all noticed a police patrol car and a police motorcyclist waiting in a clearing beside the road just the other side of an intersection. There was nothing unusual about this; police were everywhere around the presidential palace. Many had little to do and were bored. They were a visible presence, a deterrent. Whatever was motivating these particular policemen didn't interest Khaled or Omar. The unpleasant fact was that the patrol car and the motorbike swung out of the clearing, accelerated and came right up behind them. Omar slowed slightly but was still travelling well above any speed limit.

"*Merde, la police.*"

Typical of so many educated Tunisians, Khaled switched effortlessly between Arabic and French. To Celia's surprise, his English was good too.

"Omar, tell them you are a doctor and you are taking this English lady for urgent treatment. Slow down or they will force you off the road."

He turned to Celia.

"*On n'a pas de chance.* We have no luck. It will be o.k. if you help us."

Celia already knew what she would do. The policeman on the motorbike roared round Khaled's car, waving Omar to stop with a white-gloved hand signal. He wore a dark leather jerkin covered in badges and insignia, black boots, an outsize pistol in a white leather holster and sinister Rommel-type goggles. His bike was equally huge, or so it seemed from the back seat of the Renault, and was laden with radio, loudspeaker, panniers, lights and mirrors. Indeed

14

it was so heavy that he had to have two attempts at heaving it onto its stand before taking his gloves off and walking over to Omar. The other car had closed up and stopped behind.

The policeman saluted Omar and spoke surprisingly calmly in Arabic whilst pointing back to the crossroads. Omar spoke equally calmly back, turning to point to Celia and tapping his watch. The policeman then saw that Celia was holding her stomach and rocking back and forth in pain.

"Miscarriage," said Khaled, first in Arabic then in English, "miscarriage," presumably for Celia's benefit.

Celia then slowly pulled out the handkerchief, spotted with fresh blood, from the cut on her arm. The policeman seemed to freeze. Celia grimaced and lent forward again, this time holding Omar's shoulder.

"For God's sake drive on and quickly, Doctor. I am losing my child."

Two other policemen came up and there was another conversation in Arabic. The motorcyclist looked as though he was in shock.

In French, the policeman asked Celia whether she would like to go to hospital in the police car. Khaled intervened, thanking them but saying that his brother's clinic was closer, his brother was a gynaecologist, the lady should not be moved more than necessary but that they ought to get moving quickly. With that, Omar manoeuvred the car back onto the road and they drove off, leaving the police in a huddle behind them in the gathering darkness.

As they drove on, Celia realised that she had virtually signalled her capitulation to these two men. They were clearly not criminals. Far from it. One of them had given her his handkerchief. Their body language was confident. They kept looking to see that she was alright. The men seemed to have an understanding that she was not going to try to escape. Mentally, Celia too had accepted this.

After a moment's silence, she said,

"You know, I could easily have told the police that I was being kidnapped."

"I am very grateful you did not. You are a good actress," said Khaled.

"Are you really a gynaecologist, Omar?"

"Just a boring doctor, I'm afraid." Omar's English was as good as his brother's.

"Would a boring doctor have such a thing as a bandage for this cut on my arm? It doesn't seem to want to stop bleeding."

"At home I have everything. We'll be there in fifteen minutes. Hold the handkerchief round it. I could even put in a couple of stitches if necessary. Do you feel o.k?"

The approach road to their destination in La Marsa was rough and pot-holed. It was a substantial, old house, white, with two domed roofs. A solid house for a solid family, Celia thought. A development of new, small villas pressed around it. As far as she could see, few of the villas seemed to have been completely finished. Several had not had their roofs tiled but instead had tarpaulins stretched across the top. Alighting from the car, she saw the ground all around was a sort of rocky, ochre grit. A heavy scent of jasmine came from the garden, now cooling down after the heat of the day.

The family house was protected by the family dog – an alsatian – that was bounding around barking, clearly delighted to see the men but perhaps not so delighted to see Celia at whom he growled. Omar took him firmly by the collar.

"This is Foudre. He won't hurt you. We called him that because we had a *"coup de foudre"* – love at first sight – when we found him, abandoned, a couple of years ago. Most people do not treat dogs well here. They're thought to be dirty. The local authorities occasionally go around shooting stray dogs. We also call him Foudre because he is as fast as lightning. *N'est-ce pas, Foudre? N'est-ce pas? Du calme, du calme, voilà.*"

Khaled reached into his pocket for his keys and undid the lock on the front door.

Celia was surprised that there were no women or children present, though quickly saw evidence in the hallway that both were normally there. She was reassured. Half a dozen headscarves were hanging next to a child's denim jacket in the blue-tiled entrance. The fridge door had images of farm animals stuck to it with the wrong French words under each one. Someone had put *"le lait"* under the chicken and *"l'oeuf"* under the cow.

Sensing Celia's puzzlement, Khaled said, "This used to be our parents' house until they moved to Tunis. Now Omar and his family live here. His family is at the beach in Hammamet this weekend. The sea is still warm in September. Omar has to cook for himself."

Omar looked at Celia, then at his brother, smiling broadly. There was obviously an in-family joke about Omar's lack of culinary prowess.

Within a few minutes Omar had produced antiseptic and a dressing for her arm, had cleaned the cut and put a large plaster on it. Khaled meanwhile had placed a copper tray, inset with enamel chain designs, with a jug of squeezed lemon juice, ice, sugar and mineral water on the low table in the vaulted living room. He pulled away the dog's rug and invited Celia to sit on a comfortable green sofa. He drew the dark red curtains then took out a briefcase from a locked drawer in a desk covered in family photographs.

"Twelve months of military service is obligatory in this country for all men reaching the age of twenty. You saw me in uniform this afternoon, guarding the palace. I feel more comfortable in normal clothes like this. Our unit was suddenly told to guard the palace last week. I think it's a sort of punishment.

"Previously, I had been sent to a place twenty-five kilometres south of Tunis, an empty army camp called Bir Assaya. You would not notice it unless you were looking for it. It is not far from the Zaghouan aqueduct."

Omar poured lemon juice for the three of them and sat at the other end of the sofa.

Khaled paused then leaned forward. Foudre settled at his feet with his head on his paws, as if ready to listen too.

"Mademoiselle…"

"Please. Just Celia."

"Thank you. I am sure you know," he continued, "that hundreds and hundreds of African migrants from the south are all the time trying to come to the coast here to – how do you say – to flee to Europe."

"Of course I do," said Celia. "There are often reports of them drowning trying to cross over to Italy or Spain. Or being picked up by the Italian authorities from overcrowded boats. It's sometimes on the news in Britain."

"They are people totally desperate who have nothing to lose. If you can see them as we have seen them. It is pitiful. They have great determination to succeed somehow, somewhere; they have great courage. Most of them have walked hundreds of miles when they reach our territory. Their sandals are sometimes held to their feet by bits of cloth or even string. They have had to suffer for weeks in order to get here."

"Where do they come from?" asked Celia.

"Some have come from as far away as Uganda. Many from Sudan and Chad. And many are West Africans who believe it will be easier for them to get to Europe from Tunisia than from Morocco to the Canary Islands for example. Because many of them are reluctant to say where they have come from – too frightened to say – and because most of them have no papers at all, we sometimes have to guess from language, from tribe, from dress in the case of women. Especially in the hot months they are suffering from dehydration – oh and so much more. Omar will tell you in a moment."

Celia took out her notebook and a pen and smoothed over a page with her hand.

"Are there many women? Do whole families make it here?"

"Mostly it is men, young men. There are fewer women, because they do not want to abandon their children. They know they would not survive the terrible marches across the desert, the lack of good food, and the extreme temperatures. The women, of course, have pitiful stories to tell, though few of them want to speak about what they have suffered, for example, in Darfur."

Celia nodded, made a note, and looked again at Khaled.

18

"It is extraordinary that these desperate people usually have, somewhere, hidden in their clothes, many dollars, sometimes several hundred, which they must pay to go from the African coast to Lampedusa, the little Italian island half way to Sicily. These dollars are unimaginable riches for them – several years of income for a poor farmer from the south – yet somehow they manage to find the money. By selling cattle or camels or jewellery; by borrowing from the extended family; by a gift from abroad from someone who has already successfully fled."

As Khaled spoke, Celia couldn't help looking at the silver-framed photos on shelves and desks of the obviously successful, old-money family in whose house she found herself. The contrast between them and the desperate individuals Khaled was describing was striking.

"For years they are coming to the North African shore, to 'les passeurs'. I do not know what it is in English?"

"People-traffickers," said Celia.

"They operate in the ports and fishing villages, sailing north in boats of all sorts, any sort of boat, little like this, broken, old engines, from our beaches by night. There are so many of them and the crossings are very frequent."

"How dangerous is it?"

"It is difficult to exaggerate the risks. Those waters look nice from the tourist beaches but they are very different at night in an overcrowded rowing boat out there where the currents are treacherous. As you said, many do not make it. They are lost at sea. The traffickers do not care at all about the conditions; or the state of the boats; or food and water for the migrants, or the fact that there are sometimes women – nothing except their profits which are hundreds of dollars each time."

"I had no idea it was on such a scale," said Celia.

"We suppose in Tunisia that many migrants reach southern Europe every night," said Khaled.

"We can only guess at the true scale of what is going on," his brother added.

"Yes, I remember reading," said Celia, "that in Italy, the army was mobilised to round up illegal immigrants and send them back."

"I think it is true. There is surveillance in many more places in the Mediterranean," said Khaled. "Navy ships now try to stop the migrants from landing in Europe. So the sea crossings have become more difficult and the costs have risen. Boats, mostly fishing boats, are becoming scarcer. And more migrants now have to wait by the coast. It is a big problem in Libya. Local people have become very angry. Incidents were happening."

"What sort of incidents?" Celia asked.

"Racial incidents. People with black skin and not speaking Arabic were being humiliated by local people, pushed out of the towns and villages. They were suspected of every crime. They were given no peace. Some were being attacked. A few migrants were living in abandoned houses. They were becoming squatters."

"I can picture the problem," said Celia, "but it isn't new, is it? It's being going on for years hasn't it? Why are you personally so concerned?"

"Because now more migrants are dying and nobody knows about it. Omar will explain. His English is better than my English."

"The army was ordered to set up a temporary camp for the migrants," Omar said. "The authorities wanted it to be well away from the towns and coastal resorts and indeed out of sight, so they chose these barracks at Bir Assaya. Nobody goes there, and the entrance is well hidden."

Out of the corner of her eye Celia saw a lizard dart along the wall under the open window. Foudre saw it too and opened his eyes wide but did not lift his head from his paws. A whiff of warm wind blew into the room making the curtains shiver.

Omar relaxed back into his chair for a moment.

"It's quite interesting," he continued. "When the engineers moved in, to make the camp habitable again, they discovered the remains of a British military storage place."

"A dump is what they called it," said Celia.

"Yes. A dump, dating from the Second World War. They first

found a lot of barbed wire, many rolls of it, all rusty, which had been pushed into an old quarry. The wire had not been touched for years. The British must also have kept fuel there. There were about a hundred, empty, green-painted petrol drums neatly stored, with a broken pump. There were corroded caterpillar tracks, spare wheels and masses of rotting old tyres in an overgrown pit where no one had gone for nearly seventy years."

What sounded like a cat screeching outside, followed by a scrabble of falling stones, silenced the three of them. They all turned their heads to the window. Foudre pricked his ears forward and jumped to his feet.

"Cats," said Khaled. "It's nothing."

Foudre, however, didn't think it was nothing. He moved towards the French window, listening intently.

Omar continued. "Those tyres were in the wrong place at the wrong time. I remember our grandfather telling us he saw the British arriving in Tunis in May 1943. There were many German snipers hiding in the town and they shot away the tyres of the British scout cars. The drivers kept going nevertheless. They were often driving on their wheel rims and as they accelerated along the cobbles, they sent up showers of sparks."

Khaled quickly returned to the present day.

"The camp is remote and new barbed wire has been put all around it, so it is more like a prison than a camp for migrants. No local people know what is going on."

"Really?"

"Absolutely. Perhaps you have not been here long enough to understand. It is by keeping people in ignorance that the regime keeps total control over us."

"Or," added Omar, "simply by lying. Telling us that everything in Tunisia is wonderful."

He leant forward. "There is so much lying by the authorities, by the government that we give up trying to find the truth. In Tunisia we live in a web of deceit."

"We have problems in Britain. We call it spin."

21

"No. From what I know of the West – and I am lucky to have travelled – your problems are nothing like ours in Tunisia. Here lying begins at the very top and continues down to the applicant for a job when he has to say he's a member of the party if he's to be successful. Nobody believes anyone in government any more. We don't believe the national statistics; we don't believe the newspapers. And we don't believe the election results. They are so false, it's a national joke. I tell you, I don't even believe the weather forecast sometimes!"

Khaled smiled. But he wanted to return to the camp story.

"As soon as the engineers moved out of the old barracks, migrants were rounded up and installed there. More and more arrived in lorries and buses and police vans every week. The whole place is run by the army but we were told never to mention it, even to other officers or soldiers."

Celia asked if she might help herself to more juice. To do so, she stood up. With a full glass and as she moved towards a hard chair, which would be more comfortable to write in, she looked through the gap in the curtains at the French window. She saw the unmistakeable glimmer of a cigarette in the gathering darkness. There was no moon and certainly no street light, so she could see no more than that. She turned to Khaled. She spoke softly, almost a whisper, because the glass door was half open.

"Do you have glow-worms, *'vers luisants'* in your garden?"

"Why do you ask?"

"Because," she whispered, "there's something over there in your driveway. Wait. Now it's moved behind the car. I think it's a man with a cigarette."

Omar quickly moved to Celia's side, but remained behind the curtain. Khaled came too. For several seconds they could see nothing. There were the usual night noises of insects and a football match on a neighbour's television. Until, unmistakeably, all three saw wisps of cigarette smoke from behind the Renault. Khaled pointed his dog at the car, slid the window fully open and let him go. Foudre needed no second bidding. He bounded the five metres to the car, first looked under it, barking loudly, then ran round behind it. He growled as he bit into a leg and didn't let go. The man shouted a profanity in Arabic. Ten seconds later, there was a loud shot. Celia saw a dark clothed figure with a white belt running back towards the road. He said something to a companion as he jumped into a car which sped off, spraying stones and sand as it did so.

Celia's first reaction was to jump aside from the open glass door. The shot shook her. She couldn't make out what was going on. Omar and Khaled took cover momentarily, too. When it was clear that their visitors had gone, the brothers ran out of the door and onto the drive.

"Brutes! Quelles brutes!" Khaled shouted, standing over Foudre as blood oozed out of the side of his fawn-coloured head. Omar crouched down to feel the dog's heart and looked up at his brother. No other words were necessary. When Celia arrived, Khaled and his brother had picked up the lifeless dog and put him on a piece of sacking at the side of the garage. As they he did so, she noticed the cigarette still burning beside the car in the dirt.

"Why were we followed by the police?" Celia asked, as Khaled washed his hands under the kitchen tap.

"I don't like it," Khaled replied. "I don't like it at all. We're going to have big trouble."

It could just be the bored policemen problem," Omar said. "They followed us here because they had nothing better to do. They didn't like the fact that we turned down their offer of escorting you to hospital."

"Perhaps we should have been more diplomatic," said Khaled. "Why did they shoot our beautiful dog? We shouldn't have let Foudre go for him."

Omar put his arm round his brother's shoulders.

"We did the right thing. Foudre died defending our property. That idiot knows he had no right to be eaves-dropping, otherwise he wouldn't have run away."

Omar led them all back to the living room.

"I am really worried. That policeman will have to explain to his bosses later tonight at the commissariat why he discharged his pistol. Those men will be scared. They might well invent some crazy reason for having followed us here. Depending on what they invent, it's quite possible the commissariat will want to follow it up."

"Alternatively," said Khaled, "it is worse than that. They know what I have discovered at the migrants' camp. Already I could be under surveillance. You know how paranoid the authorities are about the camp and everything to do with it."

"So what have you discovered?" asked Celia.

Omar brought his strong-looking hands together in front of his chest as if about to splash his face with water. It was to make a point.

"There are now about one thousand migrants packed, like this," he looked down at his hands, "into a place designed for half that number at most and unfit for human habitation anyway. What is terrifying is that over a dozen have died this month alone,"

"How do you know?" asked Celia. "Did you see the bodies?"

"The army doctor told me. The commandant confirmed it. There are a lot of sick people there."

Omar paused, then shrugged his shoulders. Celia wondered whether the matter-of-fact way in which doctors always talked about death was simply an emotional safety device, a way of separating out the sentiment.

"Some of the sickness is typhoid fever. I have had proper pathological examinations carried out and there is no doubt about it. Here are the test results."

Omar took a bundle of papers in a plastic folder from the top of the pile beside his brother and handed them to Celia.

"It is spread through contaminated food or water. If they treated the water and had proper sanitation, there would be no problem. But they will not listen, or do not want to listen, to me."

She looked through the papers quickly. One was in French which Celia could read easily. She took it out and turned to the conclusion.

"I don't understand how you, two brothers, one in the army and one a medical doctor, are involved in this together."

"I was involved in setting up the camp from the beginning," said Khaled. "We were never told who the camp was for. Or why there was such a rush."

"Really?" said Celia.

"You cannot imagine the secrecy surrounding all this."

"Why are you in the army if, as you told me, you are normally at the university?"

"For various reasons, I was allowed to defer my military service until now. My father is a judge and, how do you say, had some – influence – when I was in my early twenties. I wanted to finish my studies in France. Then I found a position with an international water company in Paris. But in the end, I couldn't avoid military service, so at the age of thirty, I am in uniform. I am even a lieutenant," he said, smiling.

Omar took up the running.

"The commander of the camp is a major who will not take advice from anyone beneath him. He thinks that his subordinates are all against him. Particularly he does not like me because I have more experience of the world than he has and he thinks I come from a more privileged background. His army medical staff numbered four people – one doctor, one paramedic and two nurses – and we could see that they were fighting a losing battle."

"How did Omar come into the story?" Celia asked.

"It was a miracle that I persuaded my superiors, including the major, that my brother, who had worked in Uganda, would be able to help, quietly and without publicity. It is my fault. I brought him into all this," Khaled said.

"Without fuss. Yes. Now I see," said Celia.

"The major began to panic when he saw how many migrants died and when he saw that we were too late in dealing with the typhoid. Unfortunately, he overheard part of a conversation Omar and I had when we agreed that we had to do more for the sick. It was unbearable, intolerable what we were witnessing. And extremely dangerous. The major called us to his office an hour later and said he would charge us with refusing to observe secrecy as had been demanded by the highest authorities, of making a plot behind his back and of spreading false rumours. He had arranged for me to be transferred temporarily and I was to leave first thing next morning. Omar, as a civilian was asked to leave more politely. The camp's medical staff would be able to manage on their own, the major said."

"Khaled, I'm puzzled. You're pretty well-connected, after all. Your father, you told me, is a judge. Your brother, as a doctor, has great standing in the community. You must know people in government and in the ministries. You must have access to them, surely? Why haven't you both gone to your own senior authorities?"

Khaled did not say anything but looked for some time directly at Celia. Omar, too, was strangely silent.

"Well, why not?" Celia said again.

"It's not the government or any politician that counts here," said Khaled. "It's money. It's Abdelaziz Ayeb."

CHAPTER 3

It was at an International Tourism Conference in Geneva that Abdelaziz Ayeb spotted Samuel Glover. To an afternoon audience of travel professionals, blonde, curly-haired Sam was explaining exciting developments on the English heritage scene, the attraction of London's free museums and how their unrivalled riches were now better displayed than ever. Sam was an inspired choice by the Tourist Board. Few speakers on the other days had been able to keep listeners awake in the so-called graveyard slot between three and four p.m. But Sam's blend of humour and genuine enthusiasm for contemporary museology, overcame the insidious effects of lavish lunch-time hospitality. His confidence, good looks and eloquence ensured applause – and serious enquiries – at the end of each of his talks.

Abdelaziz Ayeb, North Africa's biggest tourism investor and operator by far, was always curious to see how rivals marketed themselves. He had dropped in to the British workshop on a whim but was soon mesmerised by Sam's pitch. His argument for maximising the interest of archaeological sites, for widening the audience, for appealing to visitors from the new Asian market who had not the remotest idea of, say, the legacy of the Roman Empire, impressed Ayeb.

"Dr Glover, I was intrigued by your references to the Romans," Ayeb said after the lecture. His English was perfect. "Are you a historian of the period?"

"Not quite. I'm an archaeologist by training and it remains my first love. My focus has always been on the Roman empire."

"I did not realise the Romans were such a draw for foreign visitors to Britain," Ayeb said.

"Not enough of a draw. We could make much more of what we have, of the collections in our museums – models of towns, replicas of artefacts and so on," Sam said. "But my generation has to battle with the heritage old guard who often control the purse strings. We don't have a single Roman town to show people in Britain. They've all been built over or covered up. And our wet climate does us no favours either from the preservation point of view or for holiday visitors."

"Sometimes in Tunisia we would give anything for a bit of your wet climate," Ayeb said. "Do you know our country?"

"Yes. Quite well, actually. I spent many summers excavating one Roman site in particular as part of an Oxford University team. You may have heard of Bisuli?"

"Interesting," said Ayeb. "I have often wondered whether something could be made of that place. There are no tourist facilities there. No public transport. No reception once you arrive."

"No signs or audio guides. Nowhere proper to eat," added Sam. "Yet it is relatively well-preserved and an absolutely enchanting location."

And so began Sam's friendship with an entrepreneur from a very different background.

Talking to the press, Abdelaziz Ayeb ascribed his business success to his lineage. Tunisians, he maintained, couldn't fail in the commercial world because of their racial mix. It was no accident, he used to say, that the corner shops in Paris were so successful. "*Le Tunisien du coin*" worked hard, was good value and stayed open late. "Our heritage says it all. The Phoenicians who settled in Carthage were consummate traders. The Romans were ruthless builders. The Jews were brokers and bankers. The Arabs were clever fighters. The Ottomans were the devious fixers. And the French provided a market."

But what really drove Ayeb on, was his need to escape from a childhood of poverty. He was born in Sfax, the cradle of entrepreneurial business in that part of the world, but it was in the slum behind the port. His father was a docker and casual labourer.

His mother had eight children to look after. Home was a series of run-down flats or shacks without utilities. He ran around barefoot until he was six. When he was put into his first pair of shoes, he couldn't stand up in them. He shared beds with his brothers until he was ten. In the room he slept in for five years, he could make drawings with his finger in the grease on the wall. Love was divided by eight. None of his siblings died but they were all stunted emotionally.

The young Abdelaziz Ayeb learnt more in the street and in the docks than at school. Somehow his father used to get him through the dock gates as a dependent urchin, later as a tea-boy cum water dispenser. In the hot, stinking warehouses, on the quays slippery with spilt diesel, fish slime and olive oil, in the lethal loading bays, with the fighting, foul-mouthed dockers, he grew up fast. He learnt how to defend himself. Luckily, he was well built – square shoulders, narrow hips and enormous hands. His father got him his first job as a bricklayer's apprentice at the age of sixteen. As soon as he had enough money for the bus fare, he left Sfax and the depressing family home for Sousse. Here there was an abundance of work in the seventies as new hotels multiplied like amoebae. Diligence and a lot of brass-neck saw him rise through the building trade until he had enough savings to move to Tunis. For ten years he speculated cleverly in property.

It was a small step then to the purchase with a French partner of a distressed civil engineering company, then a lorry and bus business, then a small hotel. He started to find barriers being put in his path once he left construction. He saw bigger profits available in the booming tourist industry. But much of it was controlled by joint ventures with foreign companies who played by the rules. Or by respectable local families with villas in Gammarth or Carthage. Or by Arabs richer than himself from Saudi Arabia and the Gulf. Abdelaziz Ayeb had to learn to be more subtle. He first of all acquired an obscure financial services company which he smartly turned into a bank. A small one but a bank nevertheless. With this he had undreamt of leverage. Other hotels were acquired as well as, much later, an airline. It was logical that he should also want to build with the help of his bank the new airport for his airline to service his hotels and his golf courses and spas. He had two guiding beliefs: that every person on the planet had a price and that transparency was fatal for concluding a business deal. As soon as any sort of negotiation began, Ayeb would swear the players to secrecy. He would quickly become the only person with the whole picture, the only person holding all the strings – the puppeteer. He was a past master at fabricating lower rival bids and sowing seeds of suspicion amongst rivals.

Power and those who exercised it attracted Ayeb. He had an uncanny knack of spotting ambitious politicians. He cultivated them assiduously. They came to his luxury spa and golf hotel in Djerba for free holidays like moths to a flame. There was an added incentive. Ayeb had become first a sponsor then an office holder at the World Economic Forum in Davos, the Mecca for the truly ambitious and power hungry. As the global economic crisis worsened, so the influence and power of the Davos inner circle increased.

Sam saw Ayeb as an interested potential investment angel. Over many meals and many conversations he described his plans to produce software bringing satnav and museum audio guide technology together. Tomorrow's tourist, with a couple of touches on his mobile phone, would be guided round any city, archaeological site or museum in the right order with on-screen instructions in any language. When Ayeb came shopping in London, as he did twice a year, Sam was each time invited to Ayeb's hotel, with its top-hatted doorman and Russian-speaking receptionists, a stone's throw from Hyde Park Corner.

To rebuild a Roman town in Tunisia in its entirety and on its original site was an idea that Sam had been nurturing for several years. It would, he was sure, be a significant contribution to scholarship as well as widening the appeal of archaeology. It would, of course, horrify the conservatives. It was an irresistible challenge for a showman archaeologist like Sam. From an early age he had always been fascinated by artists' impressions of Roman sites. German, Italian and

French scholars since the nineteenth century had been making drawings, paintings, wood and plaster reconstructions which were now in forgotten guides and old coffee table books or tucked away in museum reserves and depositories. Town models, in particular, had involved much inspired guesswork because there had usually been so much overbuilding. Computer aided design, new software, the i-Pad and GPS technology had transformed archaeological surveying in the past few years. Recreating a working Roman town was an idea whose time had come.

There was no denying the site of Bisuli was outstandingly beautiful. It occupied the side of a relatively steep hill overlooking a river. It had a well-preserved amphitheatre, aqueducts, baths, temples, villas and a forum. With their Tunisian counterparts, archaeologists from France, Italy and Britain were regularly working there. Marketing, visitor numbers and operating profit were Ayeb's interests in Bisuli.

Celia had known Sam since her BBC days when she had covered the new discoveries at the Roman villa in Brading in the Isle of Wight. Sam Glover, who used to live nearby, gave a brilliant description of the significance of the finds straight to camera which impressed Celia immediately. He was undeniably very handsome in a wind-blown, outdoor way. She guessed his blond hair had never seen a brush which made her instinctively want to put her fingers through it. And there was something irresistible about his intoxicating voice. They kept in touch and a year later in London, Sam invited her to a classical guitar concert in a new auditorium near King's Cross. The English virtuoso, probably the best player of his generation, floated his audience to that rarely visited musical space somewhere between trance and ecstasy. Celia was spellbound. The dinner that followed in Islington was even more memorable. She felt the energy radiating from him as from a sun-baked wall. When their hands touched, picking up her fallen napkin, she earthed him like a lightening conductor. Only one conclusion to the evening was possible. Thus began the most meaningful relationship in her life.

It was hugely important in Sam's life, too, although Celia sometimes thought he was playing a longer game. She was sure that at the end they would be together. Getting there would not be straightforward with him. His energy was not confined to his work. She knew he had many admirers, particularly since he had been selected to present a TV series on his beloved Romans. The viewer ratings were extraordinarily high for a post-watershed history/archaeology series.

It was ironic that when the BBC was falling over itself to sign Sam up for more, Celia was deciding to quit the organisation and journalism. She discussed her dilemmas at length with Sam. He fully understood the risk Celia had taken. He encouraged her to follow her dream and move into the film industry proper. Without his support she might never have taken the step. Her admiration for him grew steadily throughout their first summer. But she never came to terms with Sam's lack of discrimination as regards his friends. So many were odd and too many were downright unscrupulous, like Abdelaziz Ayeb.

Celia had met Ayeb twice, both times in London, and she took an instant dislike to him. For one thing, she could feel that Ayeb did not rate women highly and could not disguise it. He wasn't interested in Celia's work, her project, or her opinions. For another, he never stopped talking about business, or rather money. And it had rubbed off on Sam.

The evening before Celia had made her fateful visit to the Antonine Baths, she was clearing away the table after an early supper in the small villa Sam had rented in Gammarth, a couple of miles from Carthage, on the coast. It was another balmy evening and they had eaten on the terrace with its view of the sea. Birds that Celia couldn't recognise were having a last insect snack on the wing. Sam had, as usual, been excited by his day at Bisuli and by his talks with the superintendant there, Tahar Haddad. He believed the superintendant was at last coming round to the idea of increasing the visitor footfall at the site.

"Sam, I sometimes worry that you are trying to go too fast,"

Celia said, standing still with two plates and two glasses in her hands, to make her point.

"What do you mean, too fast? The word isn't in the Culture Ministry's vocabulary. Even the idea of building a toilet for visitors at Bisuli is too fast for them. It's been discussed for five years but still nothing's been done. It's taken even longer to agree on the location for a proper car-park. Sometimes people have to be prodded by outsiders like myself and Ayeb."

"But aren't you going to need their cooperation? Can you afford to antagonise the Ministry of Culture?"

"Listen. As they begin to understand the huge commercial possibilities, they'll all want to start moving faster. The cleverer officials will soon see the advantages of a makeover, of agreeing to upgrade the site."

Celia put the dishes back down on the table, frowning and shaking her head.

"Upgrading the site? Is that the phrase you are using with the Ministry? With Tahar Haddad? 'Upgrading the site.' What a laugh! Sam, you're not being honest. You're taking them for a ride. What you really have in mind is a theme-park, isn't it?"

"No. We intend to recreate Bisuli as we think it was at the height of its prosperity, to show visitors the daily life of a successful, grain-exporting market town. Warts and all."

"I don't see much difference, frankly," said Celia, annoyed that she was not getting through to Sam. "Bisuli is a historic site, a fragile site. Future generations will not thank you for destroying it."

"Destroying it? Who said we were going to destroy it?" said Sam, raising his voice.

"I did," said Celia. "I'm sorry but I have to say it. I think your project is going too far, too fast. It's vulgar. You're only concerned with turning the site into a money-making venture, aren't you? Money, money, money! You should listen more to Tahar Haddad. He knows…"

"He knows nothing about creating a visitor attraction, which is what we shall do."

Celia picked up the plates and noisily loaded the dishwasher in the kitchen.

"Tahar is learning more about the commercial realities every day. And more about Ayeb." Sam paused. "Money talks."

"I never thought I'd hear you say that. I suppose I'm not surprised. You're always on the make."

"That's rich, that is," spluttered Sam. "Aren't we all trying to make money? Isn't that what you're in the film business to do?"

"No. I mean only partly. It's not my be-all and end-all." She paused but then couldn't prevent herself adding "I've always thought Ayeb was dodgy. It's not normal that one guy should have accumulated shed loads of cash like that. I've never liked him, never. And I think he's having a dire influence on you, Sam. He's just using you. You'll live to regret it."

"You don't know what you're talking about. You're totally and utterly wrong," shouted Sam.

With that, Celia collected her film project papers and maps from the living room and swept into the bedroom.

Twenty-four hours later, whilst Celia was being told just outside Tunis what was happening to migrants reaching the coast, Sam was dining with Abdelaziz Ayeb at a first-floor hotel restaurant in Tunis itself. He had been on the verge of cancelling the dinner thinking that he should remain at home in case Celia came back. But the meeting had been fixed long ago and was to take decisions about the Bisuli project. Celia knew about it: indeed it was probably why she gave Sam a piece of her mind before she disappeared.

Sam had scarcely slept the previous night because he was so worried about Celia. He had quizzed the two film production people who were with Celia and he had gone with them to where she was last seen. Even if she had been more upset than he thought by the row they had had, this was an extreme reaction. But it was also true that the spark had gone out of their relationship ever since coming to Tunisia. After a year together the passion had certainly diminished. He thought it was turning into something more durable. Maybe, Sam told himself, as he saw dawn breaking and she still hadn't returned, maybe he had been taking her too much for granted. Maybe he should have taken more interest in her search for locations. Maybe he had bored her by talking so much about Bisuli. Celia was surely cooling off somewhere. She was proving her independence. He felt sure she would come back in a couple of days. He shouldn't panic.

Lack of sleep and anxiety showed on Sam's face which was illuminated by an unflattering Scandinavian-style light in a burnished copper shade over the middle of the table. It hurt his bloodshot eyes. Rubbing them made it worse. He hoped a drink would relax him. He tried to slacken the muscles round his neck and jaw but couldn't. He fidgeted instead with his fast-emptying glass of white wine.

"Dr Glover, if I may say so, you look preoccupied."

Abdelaziz Ayeb rarely made personal remarks to Sam or showed more than perfunctory interest in his private life.

"Do I? Well, I suppose I am. In fact I'm very worried about Celia. You met her in London."

"Yes. I remember. Why are you worried?"

"She's sort of disappeared."

"Sort of disappeared?" Ayeb cocked his head slightly to the side.

"Well, she didn't return home last night. Nor did she come back today."

"What about her mobile? Can't you contact her on her mobile?"

"No. She hasn't got her mobile with her. She left it in London."

Sam was not so tired that his brain had slowed down. Indeed it was functioning fast. He knew Ayeb would want to know more about Celia but he knew too that it would be courting disaster to say that their row the night before was about Bisuli.

"We had had an argument." Sam paused. "She has been stressed about her film, finding locations and good people to work with."

Ayeb seemed satisfied. But Sam was as agitated as before because he did not know whether to seek Ayeb's help finding Celia. Ayeb was a fixer if ever there was one. He had contacts everywhere.

Something held Sam back. Ayeb was too big a gun to fire, at least for the moment. Their relationship was a business one and nothing else. And Sam didn't want to come across as someone who panicked.

"Couples have their ups and downs, don't they," Sam said, trying to smile. "She's probably trying to test me. You know what women are."

Ayeb had no time for women but nevertheless responded with a nod of the head and a mumbled "Oh yes, women."

Sam quickly turned to the Bisuli project and within a minute was elaborating on the sequence of rebuilding the Roman town.

"We should re-use as much of the original material as possible. As you know, more than half the stonework has been stolen over the centuries. It was a cheap quarry for local builders. One can understand. The stonework that is left and is scattered all over the site needs to be cleared up. The first task will be to restore the roads so that we can bring machinery to the centre. Then we'll need to remove hundreds of tons of topsoil and sand which has layered the site over eighteen hundred years since the town was abandoned; abandoned very suddenly, so it seems. The foundations of most of the public buildings are exposed so it shouldn't be too difficult to move on quite fast."

Ayeb carefully brought his knife and fork together on the right of his plate in the French fashion, but with a noise so as to stop Sam's flow.

"When can this be started?" said Ayeb.

"When we have the blessing of all the authorities," said Sam.

"We will have that without any problem," said Ayeb.

"Mr Ayeb, there is a fly in the ointment."

"What do you mean?"

Sam hesitated. He should have come clean with Ayeb long before this.

"All the archaeological teams who have worked at Bisuli have naturally concentrated on the best preserved monuments these past twenty years. The capitol, the amphitheatre, the baths and above all the wonderful mosaics from the private houses. They have picked the low-hanging fruits. Fantastic progress has been made. We are so lucky to have a site which has never been built over. But the experts, including myself if I may use the term, have tended to overlook the forum."

"Come to the point, Dr Glover."

"I believe…I have a little evidence to suggest there is something most unusual, not just a temple, but a more important structure, built into the side of the slope beside the forum. I can't be sure. I just wonder whether our plans to rebuild the forum on the classical African model will not need rethinking."

"You are not suggesting that we stop our project, I hope. It is unthinkable after I have gone to so much trouble…"

"No, no. Quite. But the superintendant at the site, Tahar Haddad, is an old-fashioned archaeologist and fears…"

Conveniently, something was happening in the restaurant which enabled Sam to collect his thoughts about which direction to take with Ayeb. If Ayeb pressed blindly on, rebuilding Bisuli at speed, the chance of a proper, scholarly investigation of a critical location in the heart of the town would be lost forever. If the project stalled, however, Ayeb would lose interest and Sam's once in a lifetime chance to make serious money would disappear.

Both Sam and Ayeb turned to look at a middle-aged man, impeccably dressed with a purple tie, sitting alone at a table near the door. Champagne was on ice beside the table which was adorned with red roses in a red glass vase. He was sitting strangely erect and looking straight ahead when the head waiter quietly laid before him, a small, square semolina cake glistening with honey. It was adorned with a single lighted candle. As the waiter stepped back, the man leant forward and silently blew it out. The waiter refilled his glass with champagne and withdrew in silence.

Ayeb leant forward, having seen Sam's puzzlement, to explain.

"That is, or used to be, one of the cleverest men in the country. A former minister." Ayeb's voice dropped to a whisper. "But he's no longer in favour. Too much of an intellectual." He looked across at him again. "He went to Paris to write another book about democracy. Nobody saw him for a whole year."

"Ah. Perhaps it's something I should read."

"You would not want to," said Ayeb, firmly. "The book was a complete failure. No bookshop here stocks it. Nobody quite knows what happened to him in Paris. Some sort of breakdown perhaps. When he came back from France, he was given a big pension and told to take it easy, to keep quiet. Now he's lost his mind, completely lost his mind. Sad really."

At times, Tunisian politics mystified Sam. He would like to have known more about his fellow diner solemnly savouring his sickly sweet. But Ayeb was warning him off.

Sam continued. "As I was saying, about Tahar Haddad. He could delay things for us. He has the ear of the Minister of Culture."

"I too have a little influence there," said Ayeb. "Nothing special. But I once helped him sort out an embarrassing domestic problem."

"Oh really? What sort of a domestic problem?"

"A private domestic problem. But I don't think he would wish to hold up our project, let's put it that way," Ayeb said confidently.

"There might not be a problem at all," Sam lied. "But if a new structure is discovered, something really significant and it's right in the middle of the site, there will be huge interest in the archaeological world."

Ayeb quite liked it when his mobile rang at meetings or meals. An audible demonstration of his status, how his empire never slept, of how much he was in control. So when it vibrated on the table, he made no apology but answered it with a flourish.

"*Assalama.* Hello."

"*Missa el khir.* Good evening. This is Habib Takrouna from the commissariat. You remember? Apologies for disturbing you so late."

"Habib. Go ahead. I'm sure you have a good reason for calling. You always do."

"You said you wanted to be informed personally should we discover any leaks of information about Bir Assaya."

"Yes."

"Well, two of my men, two of my best men in fact, have reported – unfortunately the report's only just reached me – that two individuals from La Marsa who know everything about Bir Assaya were seen talking to a woman, a foreigner, in English and she was taking notes. They heard the word BBC."

"Who are they? How can they know everything?"

"Omar and Khaled Ansari, sons of Judge Ansari. Omar is a doctor. He went to the camp at Bir Assaya a week ago to give assistance. Khaled is doing his military service. He's an officer in the army. He has been involved with the project from the beginning when the army set up the camp."

"If she's a journalist, why hasn't she been under surveillance?"

"She caught our eye at a road block. But she gave us the slip. She has not been easy to follow. And she doesn't use a mobile phone."

"Fools," he hissed.

Sam looked up from the file on Bisuli that he was reading. He was nonchalantly picking up small breadcrumbs from the starched white table-cloth and putting them in his plate. Ayeb realised Sam might be listening, so turned in his chair and changed the mobile from one ear to the other.

"Where are they now?"

"We think the woman spent the night at the Ansari's house at La Marsa."

"Think? Don't you know for certain?"

"Unfortunately my men had a small problem. They had trouble with a guard dog at the house. They were close to an open window, using a directional microphone. The dog leapt out of the window. One of my men was bitten. They had to leave the house in a hurry."

"Bitten. Bitten? You say these men are your best? They sound incompetent to me. Listen."

He walked a few paces towards the restaurant window. Outside and below he saw his driver chatting to two other drivers whilst all of them leaned against Ayeb's Mercedes. Beyond them, a group of young men had gathered round a park bench where there were some girls. They were laughing, joshing, bouncing a football.

Ayeb looked down at the floor as he spoke. "Keep them under

surveillance. Under no circumstances should information about Bir Assaya become public. This is a vital matter. Very, very important. You understand? I want to know who else the woman is seeing. Above all, I do not want her sending anything about Bir Assaya to the BBC or anywhere else. I leave it to you as to how you stop her."

"There is something else that our surveillance team picked up before they had to leave the Ansari house."

"O.k. Tell me quickly because I'm with someone at dinner here."

"The doctor talked of deaths at Bir Assaya. My men couldn't quite catch all he said beyond the mention of typhoid. Several deaths apparently."

Ayeb's face went rigid, his mouth half open, his eyes fixed unblinking on the middle distance where waiters were scurrying about.

"Hello. Are you still there, Mr Ayeb? Hello."

"Yes, I'm still here. Typhoid. May God preserve us. Are you absolutely sure?"

"Yes."

"Don't mention this to anyone else, do you understand. Nobody. I don't want your men writing this in their reports; I don't want them to repeat what they heard to anyone, anyone at all. Alright? Keep me informed regularly."

"I understand, Mr Ayeb."

"By the way, thank you. I'll show my appreciation to you and your organisation in the usual way. Goodnight."

Ayeb snapped shut his phone and stood still for a moment lost in thought. He then moved back to the table to rejoin Sam Glover.

"No problem, I hope?" said Sam, smiling.

"Oh no. No problem. What were we talking about?"

"This man at Bisuli, who could spoil things for us."

"Yes. I need to know whether your theory has any substance. Then we can see whether it is really likely to hold things up or not. To be honest, Dr Glover, what you think is significant might not be what I think is significant. Another mosaic floor for example I would not think at all important. We already have so many mosaic floors on display in Tunisia, do we not?"

"True. And we have a dozen superb mosaic floors in Bisuli already uncovered."

"I want to know rather more, Dr Glover. What more do we know about the site superintendant, Tahar Haddad? What about him?"

Ayeb leant across the table once more, a patently false smile revealing heavily re-worked teeth. He tapped the tablecloth in front of Sam with an index finger.

"You have work to do if we are to clear obstacles from our path, do you not? We don't have long. I want to start the project before the presidential election next year. Who knows what the political climate might be afterwards? My wife and I will be in London in a few weeks' time. Airport business. Construction business. Hotel business. A little golf if the weather allows. We'll meet at the usual place. Oh yes, and my friend Bill Wells is giving a party for me at the Foreign Office."

"I saw that he was all over the English papers the other day. He was saying that there's no political problem in the world that couldn't be solved with money."

"My view entirely. He was my guest at a little dinner in London when he said it, sitting right beside me. He's a Foreign Office minister now."

Sam smiled.

CHAPTER 4

It took Celia less than a minute to decide that she could not turn away from a news story as important as this. The easy course would have been to have thanked Khaled and Omar for having confided in her, to have put them in touch with the World Health Organisation or one of the embassies in Tunis and then to have returned to her film.

There was nothing, nothing at all, in Celia's background to indicate, at least to the casual observer, that she would ever do anything courageous. It was true that she had a strong physical presence: she was direct, she was extrovert and she reacted best with people who came quickly to the point. Her parents were more concerned about respectability than anything else. "Don't rock the boat; time to keep your head down; put it on the back burner; take a back seat" were the elliptical phrases she grew up with. But there were signs for those that could read them that Celia would be her own person. Instead of an easy gap year, like most of her contemporaries, she worked at Heathrow Airport dealing with problem passengers. At university, where she read English, her chosen sport was long-distance running. Still a student, she wrote, directed and mostly shot by herself a twenty minute film on spiders. Celia had guts. It was just that it didn't show.

"I believe you. I understand why you sought me out. But I need to see for myself. Can you get me into the camp?"

Khaled was visibly relieved. His eyes creased into a smile for the first time.

"More difficult still," Celia continued, "I need to film what is going on there."

Omar said that the only way to get her in was as a medical expert.

42

He had not left the camp commandant on particularly good terms but he had said, and the major had agreed, that more medical expertise was needed.

"Major Mifsoud will not be entirely surprised to see me turn up with an English doctor," Omar said. "But not in the middle of the night. I suggest we go there tomorrow morning."

"I have to return to Gammarth to pick up my camcorder and tell my friend that I'm alright," said Celia. "He will be desperately worried already. I'll ring him to say I'm coming."

"His phone will be monitored, I'm afraid," Omar said.

"So I can't ring him from here?"

"Absolutely not."

"Well, I'd better just go there now. What time should we meet tomorrow?"

Omar looked at Khaled and shook his head.

"I don't think you understand," Khaled said. "The regime's very nervous. The country is like a bottle of cola which has been shaken for a long time. When the top comes off, the contents will spurt out. At the moment when tiny bits of gas escape, which happens more and more, the top's hammered down again."

"There just aren't enough jobs here," Omar added. "The regime tries to hush it up but if you travel with your eyes open, you can see it for yourself."

"It borders on paranoia," Khaled continued. "The security apparatus is working overtime. They are control freaks. They want to know who foreigners are talking to. They think foreigners might discover things the regime wants to hide. The authorities treat everyone who is not a package tourist as suspect. As a regular visitor from London with high level contacts, and not living in a hotel, your friend will have been under observation since arriving with you."

"I find that hard to believe," said Celia.

"It's the system," said Omar, shrugging his shoulders. "Trust us. Our father's a judge so he sees this from the inside."

"There'll be an unmarked car outside the house with two men.

Your friend and now you will be followed. If we returned you there now, we'd all be in trouble," Khaled said.

Celia's mind was racing. She had a lot to weigh up quickly. She didn't want to compromise the brothers. She badly wanted to warn Sam that he was under surveillance. And she wanted to be taken to this migrants' camp.

"I know my friend has an appointment at the Ministry of Culture tomorrow morning. He's been waiting for it for ages. It's important – with the minister, I think, so he won't want to miss it. I suppose the police will follow him, leaving the house unguarded. That's when I could slip in and collect my camcorder. What do you think?"

"Good. We were so hoping you wouldn't try to go there now. It sounds alright. Tomorrow is fine – once he has left."

"If you leave a message in the house for him, remember it could be found by the police. I beg you not to tell him where you are going. If he comes looking for you and stumbles on the camp, our lives will be in even more danger," Khaled said.

"But Sam is discreet. Anyway, I wouldn't say exactly what I was doing," Celia said.

"He will not understand the forces that are at work here. The camp is wholly illegal. But people are paid to keep their mouths shut in Tunisia. This regime couldn't care less what happens to migrants." Khaled's voice rose. He took a deep breath before continuing. "If he knew that you were about to go to a place as dangerous as that camp, to film something for which you could get into very serious trouble, he would stop you."

Celia paused. Khaled was right. Sam wouldn't understand. But nothing was more important just now than to expose what was happening.

"Alright, I won't tell him what I'm doing."

"Would you like to spend the night here?"

"That's very kind. If it's no problem…"

"Absolutely no problem, is it Omar?"

"Of course not."

"If you could take me to his house by mid-morning tomorrow, I could be in and out within ten minutes."

"Before we go any further, there's something you both ought to know," Khaled said.

Omar turned from tidying up the table. Celia stood still beside the door.

"The army will be looking for me tomorrow. I had no authority to leave the palace. I told my colleagues I had to do some interpreting for the Commanding Officer and would be back in a couple of hours. I had no such appointment and I knew no one would query my story. So I am absent without leave from my unit."

Omar looked shocked. *"Mish fehem.* I don't understand. I imagined you had agreed your leave. What will you tell them? Will you go back?"

"I don't know. I've been thinking about it a lot. This little act of defiance might be the trigger for me to pluck up the courage to do something."

"What do you mean?" his brother asked.

"Meeting the boys in the Army has been quite an experience, a revelation I suppose. The ones from the south especially. I had no idea what life was like for a nineteen year-old in Gabès or Medenine. No jobs, no money, living with their parents, nothing to look forward to, corruption everywhere. They had difficulty in the Army from day one because to them everyone in authority stinks."

"I guess we all know that, Khaled, but you need to think about your safety now. You can't just quit Presidential guard duties without consequences," Omar said.

"I know there are consequences. But there comes a time, surely, when we have to start taking risks. We have to follow our consciences, don't we? For me, that time is now."

He stood up and turned towards the window. Then, turning on his heel, he said, "What worries me most is what's happening to people dying in that camp. Nobody's doing anything about it. They're dying because one man, Abdelaziz Ayeb, wants to pretend the migrants don't exist because they will hurt tourism and his damned businesses."

"Technically then," said Celia, "you're a deserter. What's the penalty for deserters here?"

"Ten years."

Khaled was up at five-thirty next day to find another car. His white Renault could easily be on the stop-and-search list for the whole security network in Tunisia for all he knew. His childhood friend, Lotfi, lived ten minutes away and had an electrical business with a sideline in TV aerial installation. Best of all, he had always dabbled in the second-hand car market. Khaled walked there quickly in the clean morning air. Lotfi, he knew, was an early riser. He was attaching a bracket to the back of a satellite dish on a bench just inside his workshop. Incongruously, a few metres away to the side, a donkey was munching a small heap of weeds which Lotfi had obviously just given it for breakfast. The donkey looked up briefly then concentrated on breakfast again. The two men greeted each other in the Tunisian manner with a double hand-shake, then an embrace. Khaled put his hand on Lotfi's shoulder.

"Lotfi, how long have we known each other?"

"Since we were nine-year-old kids together. That's when my parents moved close to yours. But why do you ask?"

"Have we not always been like brothers? Have we not always tried to help each other? Have we not always trusted each other?"

"Yes, Khaled. Well, wait a minute – except where women were concerned. You stole my beautiful Salma when we were both only, what, twelve years old!"

They both laughed and Khaled squeezed Lotfi's shoulders again.

"Lotfi, I hope you can trust me again like a brother – and this time without even asking questions. I have an urgent journey to make first to Gammarth and then on to another place and I cannot use my car. Can you do me a big favour? I need one of your cars for the day. I would bring it back either tonight or tomorrow morning."

"This is unlike you, Khaled. Only one of these lovely looking cars is really roadworthy. What's the rush?"

"Lotfi, look at me. Have I ever asked a favour of you like this before? And at this early hour?"

"Well, yes, once actually. When I had to drop everything to help you rescue your wife who had reversed into the trench outside your house last month. Remember?"

"That doesn't count. Today is really important, Lotfi. Please. I can't tell you why but I need a car for just a couple of days, maximum."

Lotfi looked Khaled right in the eye for several quiet seconds. Khaled held his gaze. The donkey looked up with a large bunch of weed falling out of either side of its mouth; it blinked then bent its neck down for more breakfast.

"I will never forget how you helped me when my son was sick last year, when he couldn't breathe that night. Your brother the doctor was here in no time." Lotfi wiped his hands on a cloth beside a huge tool-box. "Ok. We'll say you are just trying it out. You'd better have that one. Keep it as long as you like. It's taxed and insured," he said pointing to the one furthest away, with a typical collection of scratches and dents.

"How much do I owe you?"

"Don't be daft," said Lotfi, throwing him the keys. "I don't want your money. But if I find it scratched when you bring it back, I won't be pleased!" he said, laughing.

"May God bless you! May He make more men like you," said Khaled in Arabic, putting his right hand first on his forehead, then on his chest. Lotfi wasn't to know that he wouldn't see his car again for six months.

There seemed to Khaled to be many more police around than usual on the road to nearby Gammarth despite it being before seven o'clock. But then again, there were always masses of police there. After a while they were unnoticed, like lampposts, unless, that is, you had a guilty conscience. Then you noticed everyone in a uniform. Men ostentatiously doing nothing also put you on your guard. People speaking into mobile phones suddenly became suspicious. And since twenty percent of the population seemed to be talking into mobile phones that morning, Khaled was jumpy. He drove carefully so as not to attract attention with Omar beside him and Celia in the back. Khaled was wearing stained jeans and a jean jacket with screwdrivers in his top pocket. To cover his military haircut, he had found a greenish coloured baseball hat. He had loosened the strap at the back so that it pulled low down over his forehead.

Celia did not expect Sam to be out and his villa empty till at least eleven o'clock. Since they were slightly early, she asked if they could make a short detour to the echoing Roman water cisterns at La Malga. Khaled agreed. It might throw any surveillance vehicle off the scent. They left the car briefly and brushed past grazing sheep. They were standing beside the aqueduct which used to bring fresh water to these cisterns for Carthage from a spring in the mountains at Zaghouan, so far away it was invisible. In the growing heat, swallows chattered as they fluttered in the shade of the arches. She wondered if the birds had come from England. She suddenly felt nervous. But only for a moment. A couple of giggling lovers were playing hide-and-seek in the ruins. They stopped on catching sight of Celia. She felt conspicuous and was glad to return to the car. Khaled was by now sure they were not being followed.

They approached Sam's villa, a couple of kilometres up the coast, with the utmost caution. If Sam saw her, the likelihood was that he would physically restrain her and certainly stop her from investigating a typhoid epidemic. Khaled parked the car in the shade of a thorn tree twenty metres from the villa. Had he seen the surveillance car earlier, he would never have stopped. It was cleverly parked in the shade between two other cars opposite the villa. The two men inside were supposedly looking together at a catalogue. As if men did that sort of thing in a parked car in mid-morning. Khaled had come into the street right behind a lorry so with luck had not been seen. Celia had found a faded blue cap at the Ansari brothers' house and used it to hide at least part of her face. She looked in her handbag for the key. Panic. She couldn't find it. This was not entirely unusual however. She was constantly losing things there; it hadn't been emptied for months. To her surprise, the key was in the zipped pocket inside the bag. As she fished it out with her two fingers, she also withdrew the antique coin she had bought the day before. This was the first chance she had to look at it more closely and she was surprised at what she saw. One side was perfectly ordinary – a laurel-wreathed head with an illegible inscription around the edge. But on the other was an inclined, three quarter profile head and shoulders of a woman, a goddess she supposed, holding a wand. She could make out the letters "FE..IS." Was this Febris, goddess of fever? She remembered that there were several temples to Febris in ancient Rome, venerating a goddess who might protect believers from epidemic diseases.

The noise of a slamming door caused Celia to look up. She was able to peep through the climbing plants to see Sam jump down the two steps from his front door, cross the gravel driveway to the open garage and get into his car. Unusually, he was wearing a suit. He dropped a cardboard tube on the gravel in his rush. As he stooped to retrieve it and put it in the back of the car, he looked towards the gate as if he had seen something. If he had, he didn't reveal it for he reversed the car fast out of the garage, turned the wheel hard and accelerated out of his drive into the road. Sure enough, the tail followed him.

As Celia skimmed round the villa, she debated again as to whether she should leave a note. But she couldn't think of what she would say that wouldn't alarm him. And anyway she would only be gone for the day. It might actually do their relationship some good. She treasured her independence. She did not see why she was obliged to tell him that she was following up a story. Sam did not control her life. She was still a free spirit. It might even add spice to their lives. A bit of irresponsibility now and again, so Celia thought to herself, was actually quite a good idea. Keep him guessing.

In their bedroom she had second thoughts. Just one night without her and the room was a mess. The bed hadn't been made,

Sam's clothes were on the floor and there was half a cup of black coffee on the bedside table next to a pile of maps. As she picked up her camcorder from a side table, she noticed that Sam had been through all her papers, which had been put back in the wrong order. He had even been through her diary because the page marker had been moved.

She found the envelope with all her money in it, still untouched in the drawer of the bedside table. She folded the envelope carefully into her trouser pocket. She quickly stuffed a change of clothes into a plastic bag together with the camera. She took one last look round the room. She couldn't help herself; it was one of those silly things that she had to do. She made the bed. When she'd finished, she picked up a pencil from her bedside and was looking for a scrap of paper when she heard someone coming up the drive outside. Panicking, she put the pencil down, took the Roman coin out of her bag and placed it on Sam's pillow. She ran to the back door which she knew would be open and left the house. She would never return.

CHAPTER 5

It was that furnace-hot part of the day – one o'clock – when they reached Mohammedia. Nothing moved between the houses or in the streets of the little town save swirls of dust and the inevitable black plastic bags. Heat shimmered off the scorching metal of trucks and cars unlucky enough not to have found any shade. A tired bus was resting beside the post-office where the only sign of life was the national flag over the entrance, swaying slowly in the hot air funnelled along the main road. Celia was glad she was wearing a white cotton shirt which breathed and cotton slacks. Khaled had thoughtfully given her a headscarf which allowed her to blend in better with the women trudging home with baskets groaning with vegetables, fruit and unplucked chickens.

It had been market day and much loading of trucks and dismantling of stands was going on. Mohammedia was on the road to the migrants' camp and was a good place, Khaled thought, to have a meal before the rigours of the afternoon. Market traders and farmers were doing the same thing. Omar pointed out two parked army lorries, both with a handful of bored looking conscripts in the back. Perhaps, he said, the army does its shopping at the market. Or perhaps this was just a comfort stop for conscripts on the move. To be on the safe side, he suggested they eat at the other end of town. Choosing a restaurant in the middle of a row of shops and cafés, he cast a glance over his shoulder to see if they were being followed. Apart from a woman carrying a dozen loaves of fresh bread and a young man pumping up the tyres on his bicycle, there was no one watching them. Omar parted the plastic fly screen and ushered Celia and his nervous brother inside.

It took Celia some time to adjust to the gloom of the room after the glare outside. Her senses were assailed by the smells of grilled mutton and rose-water. The lovely aroma of wood smoke reminded her for a brief moment of her parents' country cottage and the crackling winter fires there. The sense of family and safety contrasted starkly with her present situation. The proprietor motioned the three of them to an empty table by a door which seemed to connect to a hardware store. As Omar and Khaled sat down, they noticed the young man with the bicycle casually lean it against a post outside the front door, step inside and sit on a stool by the till. A television high on the wall above the door to the kitchen was showing a documentary about irrigation. The loud background music was appreciated by the patrons. They could talk more easily. Eavesdropping became more difficult.

Nevertheless, Omar kept his voice down.

"You will find a frightened man in charge at Bir Assaya," he said. "Major Ali Mifsoud is completely out of his depth. He doesn't know how long he is meant to keep the detention centre open. He doesn't know what is meant to happen with the people there. And above all, he doesn't understand why so many of them are dying."

"How did you find out that there was typhoid fever there?" Celia asked.

"By accident," Omar said. "I was at the morgue in Tunis to certify the death of one of my patients killed in a car crash. None of the relatives could be traced. As I was leaving, the supervisor took me aside to say that he was mystified by the symptoms on a corpse he had just received from the police. The supervisor, Hedi Soukni, as it happens is an old friend. He's someone I respect. He has a terrible job when you think about it. So I agreed to have a look, partly out of professional curiosity. Challenging me to make a diagnosis is like asking an alcoholic whether he'd like a drink. Irresistible. And for the supervisor to be mystified, it had to be something unusual. So before I knew it, he had pulled open the drawer containing the latest arrival."

Omar paused. Khaled knew what was coming and turned away in his chair. But Celia didn't.

"The body was of a tall African male; Sudanese I would guess."

"Are you alright with medical details? Some people, I know, feel faint at the mere idea of blood."

"I'm used to blood, Omar. I started my career as a crime reporter before I moved to foreign assignments. I have seen all too many dead bodies, I'm afraid."

"The first thing the supervisor drew my attention to were the rose spots on his lower chest and abdomen. Then there were signs of major organ damage. I asked if he had fallen from a height or been in an impact of some sort. He had not been. But of course what was conclusive were the cultures. Hedi had been very thorough. *Salmonella typhi* bacteria were there alright."

"When the three policemen brought him in, according to the supervisor, they had an argument about completing the paperwork, about what to write. It seems they had been ordered to say by their superiors that the body had been found by the roadside. One could, I suppose, have mistaken some of his symptoms as being those found on someone who has been the victim of a hit and run crime. But not on closer inspection. The policemen wrote instead that the body had been delivered to the police-station by unidentified military personnel. This was true."

As couscous, bread and mineral water was brought to their table, Omar stopped speaking. The hubbub of dishes, diners and TV music remained satisfyingly high. Khaled noticed that the young man with the bicycle, now sitting by the till was looking at them and then out of the window. Celia noticed the man, too. Omar resumed talking, but more quietly. They all ate.

"Doctors the world over have been studying typhoid since the birth of micro-biology. When I was doing my medical training in Lyons, a good Tunisian friend of mine was working at the Institut Pasteur on typhoid. He was both repelled and intrigued by the lethal power of it, by how some people could infect others without showing symptoms themselves. We sometimes spent the afternoon at the zoo in the *Parc de la Tête d'Or* watching the primates and wondering why animals were not affected by the disease. Animals were usually not fussy about the water they drank. Or the purity of their food. It just so happens that my friend is now the Director of Pathology at a private clinic at *Les Berges du Lac* in Tunis."

Had Celia watched the restaurant cat, she would have had warning of the chaos that ensued. The cat saw that three plain-clothes police officers had jumped out of a blue estate car outside the restaurant, had run across the pavement and were parting the plastic-strip fly-screen in the space of several seconds. As it was, the first Celia realised that something unpleasant was about to happen was that the proprietor slammed a tray of salads and a large carafe of water onto their table, turned on his heel and sprinted towards the till which he locked. The cat's eyes widened with fear before it turned tail and dived into the kitchen.

The first of the three policemen had a moustache and bad teeth. The other two had several days' beard. All wore identical grey trousers and sunglasses. The first into the restaurant stopped and looked slowly round the crowded room. He did not catch sight of the informer who had been at the till because he was on the floor in the foetus position, moaning. He had just been felled by a chair thrust into his groin by Khaled. So without any help, the policeman had to make a guess as to which group it was they had come to arrest. For no less than three tables were occupied by groups similar to Khaled, Omar and Celia. The policeman happily chose the trio furthest away from Khaled's table. Fortunately, also, there were multiple diversions. Two djellaba-wearing Berbers at the back of the room scooped up the necklaces they had been bargaining over and thrust them into inside pockets. The local cigarette smuggler, seated next to the fly-screen, rolled round his table and slunk out of the doorway. Elsewhere, in their haste to leave, another couple of men knocked over their glasses of mint tea which smashed noisily on the stone floor.

Khaled, Omar and Celia wasted no time either. Khaled could see out of the corner of his eye that the informer was trying to rise.

"This way," he hissed to the other two.

He leant down on the emergency exit bar on the door beside

their table, and closely followed by his brother and Celia, pushed through a pile of empty, locally woven baskets into a hardware store. The surprised shopkeeper stood up from tying the neck of a sack, completely taken aback. There was a pungent smell of hessian, of rope and doormats, with undertones of creosote and leather. The shopkeeper didn't believe in shelves but in piles. Khaled's brusque irruption had a disastrous domino effect on them.

"Police next door," said Omar.

"Allah preserve us."

If there's one thing that unites deserting army personnel, liberal-minded doctors and tax-averse shopkeepers, it is fear of the police.

"Police, you say? What's it about? Looking for smugglers, I bet. Or fundamentalists."

The shopkeeper went to the connecting door and slammed it shut. There was uproar in the restaurant. He slid a metal bolt across the door for good measure.

Omar said "We don't know what it's about. But you know what they say. If you play with scorpions, you'll be stung. We're not going to hang around. *Bisslema.*"

As they left, Celia said, "We didn't pay for our meal."

"We didn't finish it either," said Omar. "Get in the car, quickly."

They drove south, then east in silence for the few kilometres to Bir Assaya. The road ran alongside, then crossed under, the magnificent Roman aqueduct, narrowing as it followed a railway. They passed a junction with a sign which Celia was surprised to see said "*Bisuli*".

"Interesting. I recognise the hills in the distance. I didn't realise we were so close to Bisuli," Celia said.

"Where?" said Omar.

"Bisuli. It's an important archaeological site. A former Roman town," Celia said.

"Well, it's certainly close to Bir Assaya because we are arriving now," said Khaled.

For the last couple of kilometres the land on both sides of the road was closely fenced. It looked, and was, military land. A red and white pole across the narrow track was the first indication of the army presence. Two well-equipped armed guards had obviously heard the old Toyota arriving and were standing outside their hut with their SIG 5.56 mm assault rifles at the ready. Both had two-way radios on their shoulders.

"Let me do the talking," Omar said.

Celia had already started filming. She was pleased with the establishing shot of the barrier and the guards. She had devised her own unusual camouflage for the camera which she had used successfully from cars before. It was a small, open-weave straw handbag lying on the dashboard. The lens was virtually invisible.

"Switch off your engine and get out of the vehicle," one guard said, still holding his rifle menacingly.

Celia lifted her handbag down, switching the camera off as she did so. She also picked up her shawl which she carried loosely over the bag on her wrist. She followed Omar and Khaled to the guard's hut.

"So what's your business here?" the other guard said. "Your papers?"

They each handed them over.

"English?" the guard said comparing Celia to her photograph perhaps because that was all he could readily understand on the document.

"Yes. I'm a doctor," she said in French.

First one, then the other guard recognised both Omar and Khaled once they were out of the car. They nodded when he explained that he had told the commandant he would seek special medical advice; this was why he had brought this English lady doctor. As for Khaled, he said that he had been told to report back to the camp after his special duty in Carthage. He was in civilian clothes because he had not wanted to draw attention to himself.

The guard spent several long minutes on his radio with his back turned to the new arrivals. Celia didn't know who was most at risk of being tripped up. They were all three counting on there being little if any communication between the camp and Carthage or indeed, headquarters. They were right. When orders were given to let them in, they were told to report directly to the commandant's office.

Beyond the check-point, the track turned sharply to reveal a collection of long, low buildings completely shielded by trees – evergreens of some sort. In the afternoon sun they were beginning to cast dark shadows. One could immediately see why the site was good for the military. It was well hidden, except from the air no doubt, and with just one entry and exit point it was easily defended. There was a rail link close by but not a single house or farm within sight.

Celia's old journalistic senses were fully alive by now. Once past the entrance gate, she switched the camera on again and continued to film covertly. Her first visual sweep took in rolls and rolls of rusting barbed wire arranged to make a large square. Within this were the roughly constructed huts parallel with the perimeter fence. In the centre was another smaller square area fenced off and enclosing five better built huts. Between the inner and outer fences and sitting in the shade of the huts were groups of young and not so young sub-Saharan Africans all, without exception, looking towards the car. Each moment, more and more people materialised from shady spots where they had been resting and some from inside the huts. She noticed that there were only a few women. They remained on the ground in the shade, just turning their heads. All were badly dressed and there were none of the broad smiles, laughter and noise which always used to greet Celia when she was on assignments in Uganda or South Africa. The men at least just stood and stared.

White painted stones marked out a path to the inner sanctum through a large metal gate, already unlocked by the time they reached it. They drove slowly straight ahead between the stones towards the middle. Celia stopped filming at this point. More guards, another gate and there was Major Ali Mifsoud, the commandant, standing outside the door of the main administrative hut. He had made an effort with his uniform but there was no disguising the sweat patches under his arms and the grease spots on the tunic. He was smaller than Omar and Khaled, with wavy hair and an Iberian look. The slightly paler skin framed dark, bloodshot eyes. Sweat threaded along the creases on his forehead, over his lip and all over his neck. The thumb of his right hand was hooked over his belt from which hung a leather holster with the standard issue revolver.

"I was not sure we would ever see you again, Doctor," said Major Mifsoud in Arabic.

"I have brought help with me this time, an English doctor," said Omar, switching to French and gesturing towards Celia.

"I don't know how much I can help but I'll do what I can," said Celia, also in French.

"The English are so modest," the major replied, with a thin smile. As they walked into his oppressively hot office, Celia noticed that over the windows were what looked like squares of white nylon sacking tightly nailed up where glass might have been. This lowered the light level and bathed the interior in a milky opacity. There was a trestle table in the middle with a film of yellow dust on it, one rush-seated, wooden backed chair for sitting at the table and two camp chairs on the other side. On an upturned, sturdy box sat a military two-way radio with next to it a more modern looking field radio. Two sets of earphones lay beside this equipment with military notepads and perfectly sharpened pencils. Leaning against one end of the table was a venerable US M16 rifle. There were two other rifles in the far corner of the rectangular hut together with several ammunition boxes. Flies crawled over a dirty plate and plastic cup on a folding table by the window. More flies walked round the headband of the major's upturned cap which was on what looked like a bit of a fluted column by the door.

"Lieutenant Khaled. It's a surprise to see you back so soon."

"I hope you had the message from Carthage that I was returning."

"No. But it doesn't surprise me. The paper pushers at the Ministry are determined to keep me in the dark about everything."

He turned towards Celia, obviously delighted to have a listener for his catalogue of woes.

"I have one radio contact a day with HQ. I'm told that if I start complaining again, I will be sanctioned, whatever that means. This is a fifty year-old disused barracks. There used to be a power line but it has not been operating properly since our first week here. I'm still waiting for it to be restored. I've been asking for another generator for this place for days. The original one keeps breaking down. Each time I'm fobbed off with an excuse. The latest is that there is no suitable transport. But that's rubbish. The army has scores of trucks. It's the same story with restoring the phone line. Regular promises but nothing is done."

"Do you have any electricity at all?" Celia said.

"Intermittently. We use car-batteries as back-ups for the radios, for example. Without reliable power, I cannot install water pumps, security lighting, fans – nothing. Not only that. We have no hot water. No proper clothes washing facility. Not enough bedding. Not enough cups. Can you imagine trying to keep one thousand men alive without enough cups for them to drink out of? They even have to share cups. Look," he said, pointing to a kerosene lamp hanging above the table. "That's the light I used last night. It's absurd."

Major Mifsoud unscrewed a plastic water bottle, waved it vaguely in front of his visitors as if offering some to them but then immediately put it to his mouth for a long swig. Putting the water bottle down, the major swept a pile of blister-packs of pills from the table to a box under it. One pack had been half used. Omar recognised it straight away from the distinctive logo: codeine. Harmless in small doses but the empty packs in the box showed the major was seeking a lot of relief from the opiate. Was he in pain? Was it to sleep? Before Omar could ask, the major said, "I have two problems here. First, too many migrants are dying. Second, those that are not ill are trying in every way they can to escape. We had an attempt at a break out this morning when the food truck started to leave. We do not have the men or the equipment to deal with that sort of thing."

"How many more have died since last week?" asked Omar.

"Thirteen. The medical staff here say two more are dangerously ill. The first ones we sent to Mohammedia for burial but if I send many more there, suspicions will be aroused."

"Autopsies?" Omar asked, disingenuously.

"Yes. At first."

The major looked flustered and got up, to create a diversion. He blew the dust from a brown file of papers on a corner of the table, pulled the papers out then put them back in again.

"We all know we have a bacteria problem of some sort, but perhaps you doctors can stop it quickly."

Celia's nervousness before seeing the camp was becoming more like panic. She was seriously worried. Maintaining the pretence of being a doctor when her main objective was to film what was going on and somehow send the result back to the UK was fraught with difficulty. She somehow had not expected the migrants' plight to be so desperate. This was more like a prison than a camp. And law and order was very shaky, if the major was to be believed.

She realised that she had made a fundamental error by agreeing to the doctor pretence. She wondered, even at this stage, whether she could get out of it. Yet she needed to see for herself, if she was to be a credible reporter.

It struck her in the major's office that she did not have an exit strategy. Omar's position had not been questioned. He had serious medical work to do at the camp and would need to come back and spend several days. Khaled seemed less sure of himself. Celia suddenly wanted to get back to Sam – and Saint Augustine – but she had a strange feeling that it wouldn't be as soon as she thought. There was just so much to record. She wanted to film the people, gain their confidence, hear what they had to say. She wanted to build scenes in a sequence so that the international audience could quickly understand what this was about and how bad it was. She resigned herself possibly to spending the night there. For one thing, by the time she had been taken round the camp and met the key people, the light was beginning to fade, making filming difficult, let alone clandestine filming.

"You'll find our little medical team in one of those two huts – numbers eleven and twelve over there," the major said to Celia, pointing beyond the inner sanctum to one corner of the camp. "We've had to turn them into a clinic. They are slightly removed from the other huts."

When Omar and Khaled had washed their hands in the corner of the officers' hut next to the major's office, Omar gave Celia a stethoscope and a white coat.

"I know nothing about medicine, Omar. The army doctor here will spot that I'm an imposter straight away. Then I'm finished," she whispered.

"Nonsense. You've done well so far. To look the part you just need to take a pulse here and there. You know how to do that, don't you? Then look for signs of profuse sweating, diarrhoea, perhaps a rash," Omar said.

"No. No. I'm not going to get involved with individual patients. It wouldn't be right. I'm not even sure about the stethoscope and the white coat. I could make things worse if I'm not careful by making some stupid mistake out of ignorance. Omar, there are people dying here…"

"Ok, ok. As you wish. The important thing is that you should see for yourself exactly what's happening. This is the only way I can think of for you to be able to do this."

The three visitors were objects of intense curiosity as soon as they left their quarters. Puzzled, hot guards, with rifles in hand, watched them from a distance. Crowds of men shuffled around them as they tried to walk purposefully towards the huts in the corner. Celia, of course, as a white woman in a white coat, carrying a bag, attracted extraordinary attention. Some men were desperately trying to open a conversation with her, whilst others simply tugged at her sleeve. She could recognise Swahili but none of the other languages they spoke. Sleeve tugging became a queer sort of game. They found that the harder they pulled at her sleeve, the more likely she was to turn and look at them. This is what they craved: a glance, a smile, to be looked at, to be noticed.

One tall, thin man, a Malian called Mohammed, would not be ignored. He had somewhere picked up a pair of earphones with an adjustable headpiece. The wires from the earphones joined together at a plastic and metal jack which usually swung loose around the level of his belly-button. He sometimes wore his earphones all day long. The fact that they were not connected to anything at all was entirely unimportant. Mohammed lived in his own world. Celia could not help smiling when she first caught sight of him.

She now started to take in her environment. The ground was uneven, covered in small stones and fine sand. Each footstep produced a puff of dust and a dusty haze hung over the men. So, too, did the flies. Hundreds of them. They quickly discovered Celia's neck, the back of her hands, her face. When her spare arm was not being tugged or held, she used it to brush the flies off. But it was a zero-sum game. She noticed the men around her were resigned to their personal clouds of flies. Flies lay thick on the buckets outside the doors of the huts and on the crude tables beside the huts in the shade. Flies settled on the larger rocks and stones dotted around the camp where men had been sitting.

Shade was at a premium. Cardboard boxes had been flattened out to make extensions to the roofs of the huts for shade. Grey nylon flour sacks were also being used as awnings. Rags or old clothes, mostly whitish – God knows from where – had been tied together and attached to a part of a tall post for shade but now, hanging limply in the dust, they looked like pathetic flags of surrender.

Inside the sick-bay, the air was fetid and stank of urine. There must have been forty or fifty people in the first hut but only twenty were on beds. The others lay on straw mattresses, tarpaulins, bed sheets or strips of canvas on the ground. Omar and Khaled moved confidently towards a table in the middle of the hut. Normally, Omar would have expected to find one of the Army medical staff there but there was no one. Celia remained close by Omar's side as he moved from patient to patient.

"You'll find gloves and a mask in the pocket of the coat. Put them on and keep them on," he said. "Then help me turn this man over. I want to see his back."

Celia immediately found herself helping and involved. There was no way she could stand aside or attempt to film yet, however much her brain told her she should. She had to do whatever she could as a nurse. She brought water, she wiped foreheads, and she cleaned people up. She tidied the beds, she wiped dirty drinking cups and plates and she even emptied a bedpan. She was struck by the loneliness of these people. There were so few women – wives, daughters or mothers – to be with them.

"There is a young Army doctor, called Brahim. He must be in the next hut," said Khaled.

"The next hut is where the suspected typhoid cases are," said Omar to Celia. "We are doing things in the right order. There's a huge mixture of illnesses in this hut. But most of them will never be properly diagnosed so one doesn't know what one is faced with. Let's find Brahim."

Perhaps it was just as well that the light was fading fast, for the sight that greeted them in the typhoid hut was horrific. There were about the same number of very sick people, some fifty, but their symptoms were extremely distressing to see. The most unnerving and hopeless cases were suffering from delirium.

Omar was confident that he could speak in English to Celia without the patients understanding what he said. He nevertheless kept his voice low.

Celia had heard and seen enough. But in the lecture-theatre way typical of doctors, Omar continued. "By the time intestinal haemorrhage occurs, it is usually too late to save the patient."

Brahim was delighted to see Omar and his friends. He kept his mask on but they could tell he was smiling from the wrinkles around his eyes.

"It's good to see you back again, Omar."

"And it's good to see you too, Brahim. I've brought Celia Purchas, who's from England, to see the problems we have."

"I'm pleased to meet you. I'm full of admiration," Celia said.

"What drugs have you brought with you?" Brahmin asked Omar.

"Some anti-malarials; some mebendazole for worms and more antibiotics for our friend salmonella."

"For the typhoid patients?"

"That's right."

"Any response to our requests to transfer the worst cases to hospital?" asked Brahim hopefully.

"None, I'm afraid," said Omar. Brahim shook his head.

"My messages to the military hospital are simply not answered," he said. "It's as if they don't want to know about us."

"I'm sure they would prefer that we didn't exist," said Omar.

Newest cases were allocated beds at one end of the hut whilst confirmed (and therefore usually hopeless) cases were at the other end. Like a production line, as Brahim put it. He said he was now concentrating on trying to help those who were suffering the earliest stages of typhoid. In a few cases the bacteria were knocked out or were unable to take hold completely and the infection was beaten off. Recovery, if it came, tended to be long and slow. But all too often, the doctors found the patients too late. They only came forward when they were desperate. For as long as hygiene was primitive in the extreme and for as long as there was no decent sanitation, the bacteria would continue to flourish in the camp.

Thankfully there were no very young children. But the eleven year-old, long-legged Nigerian girl with two bracelets quickly caught Celia's eye. She had attended a church school and spoke good English. She said she was called Hope. She had travelled with her uncle for over a year, stopping like so many, first in Agadez and then Tamanarasset on her way north. They could not afford to pay the traffickers in Libya so eventually had come to Tunisia. The uncle had been away looking for a boat when Hope was rounded up and brought to Bir Assaya. Now she was on her own. She had not lost her dignity and always looked clean in her too-short cotton dress.

When Celia stopped and spoke to her, Hope was sullen and shy.

She would not look Celia in the eye or say more than a few words at a time. Yet she understood everything Celia said.

"I like your grisgris, your bracelets," Celia said, indicating on her own wrists what she was talking about.

"Thank you. I made them when I was ten."

"Will you make one for me?"

Hope giggled. Celia helped her with her hair and they played noughts and crosses in the sand outside her hut. The one thing that became clear was that Hope was desperately missing her mother. She never mentioned a father. When Celia asked her what she most wanted, she said,

"A baby."

"Not yet. Not here. When you are older," Celia advised.

Hope looked forlorn. As Celia rose to leave, she saw Hope was sitting on something. It was a rag doll. The face was delicately sewn but the body showed signs of hard travelling.

"It's beautiful, Hope. Where did you find it?"

"I made it in Nigeria and brought it with me. She knows all my secrets. She brings me luck."

"We all need that, don't we," said Celia, tucking her hair behind her ear.

As Celia was debating with Omar whether to stay a bit longer or to leave, all three visitors were invited to share a simple early-evening meal with Brahim in his quarters which were as primitive as all the others. It was a couscous from a packet to which he had added some dried mushrooms which he had been keeping for a special occasion. As they were about to start their meal, the commandant knocked and entered without waiting for a reply.

Major Mifsoud was flushed. There were still large sweat stains on his shirt. His trousers were creased behind the knees.

"Apologies for interrupting. I have just had a message on the radio."

He waved a grubby piece of folded paper.

"It was graded 'Secret' which was a damned nuisance. Took a long time to decipher it with the old equipment I've got."

He paused to cough, then wiped his mouth with the same filthy handkerchief that Celia had seen him using earlier.

"It's from Tunis, from the Ministry of Defence. From the Minister's *chef de cabinet*, actually."

The major was clearly impressed by that. He straightened himself ever so slightly whilst speaking as if the *chef de cabinet* was in the room and looking.

"It says that it has been reliably reported that there are cases of typhoid at the Bir Assaya Migrant Holding Camp. Tests have apparently been carried out on bodies at the military hospital mortuary which confirmed the presence of typhoid. There's a whole lot of technical stuff about the bacteria classification and so on. Then there's a paragraph about recent outbreaks – all in central Africa. Then there is a passage about the need to apply barrier nursing techniques and another passage – very short in fact – about treatment.

"But the bad news is at the end. It says that on occasions typhoid can be transmitted by unwitting carriers. Some of the deaths, it says, are from as yet unidentified causes. I have to make a weekly, classified progress report. They have given me a special code word to use at the top of the report and I am instructed not to copy my report anywhere else. The minister has been in urgent consultations, it says, and has decided that in order to minimise all risks and to contain anything that might be contagious, Bir Assaya is to be isolated with immediate effect. No migrants, no service personnel or any persons whatsoever may leave Bir Assaya until further notice."

CHAPTER 6

November

B ill Wells MP, Minister of State for Foreign and Commonwealth Affairs, was just finishing a frustrating day at the Foreign Office much of which he had spent arguing with the "Camel Corps." The Foreign Office's Arabic speakers year after year rose through the hierarchy across the Office and occupied the key jobs. They now headed the departments dealing with the parts of the world for which Bill was responsible. Much given to byzantine argument about even the simplest development in the Middle East, incapable of being straightforward, they seemed to the minister to be deliberately obstructive. As if he had not had enough of them during daylight hours, he would now be surrounded by them at the reception he had to host for Abdelaziz Ayeb, the Tunisian billionaire. Bill Wells was therefore feeling tetchy.

The minister had been befriended by the Tunisian two years earlier when he was still new in government. Ayeb knew that ministers, especially junior ones, were not impervious to flattery. The friendship was cemented by a delightful free holiday in Tunisia, in Djerba.

"I am taking our guest of honour to see the Emergency Incident Office after the speeches, David," Bill mumbled to his Private Secretary, David Atkinson, as he turned over the cards on which his speech had been typed in large font. David knew all too well how awful the day had been, because he had shared most of it with his minister. This was not the time to make difficulties for him. But surely the minister was not serious.

"The EIO will be under some pressure, of course, following the PM's decision this afternoon."

Bill Wells made no reply. David paused, then continued, "Incidentally, Minister, I've forwarded two Immediate and Confidential e-mails to you. One's from the MOD about options for the deployment of naval assets in the Western Mediterranean. The other's from our Ambassador in Tunis who has been summoned later tonight to see the President."

"I'd better read those before I go along to the Locarno Suite for the reception," Bill said, looking at the mahogany chiming clock with gilt metal mounts on the mantel piece. "You should warn the Emergency Incident Office manager that I'll be bringing a group round at – what – I suppose seven-thirty?"

"Are you sure it's wise, Minister?" David said, as he gathered up the letters just signed on the side of his desk.

"Of course it's bloody wise. We've precious little to show visitors to the Foreign Office that wasn't here in Queen Victoria's time. I'm as proud as hell of the EIO. It's state-of-the-art as far as incident rooms go. And its present form is my idea – well, mostly mine."

"You have a point, Minister." David said. He often used this phrase to set up his target before delivering a knock-out blow after a second's pause. "But the EIO is in a secure zone and will be in the thick of discussing pretty sensitive operational questions for the whole of the next twenty four hours, as you know. The Tunisians will be alarmed if they see the true scale of the spill. There's still been nothing so far in the media."

Bill Wells wasn't surprised that his Private Secretary wanted to thwart him. After all, that's what Private Secretaries spent most of their time doing – squashing anything unconventional, making ministers toe the line. Today Bill Wells had just about had enough of irritating civil servants, diplomats and arabists in particular and was determined not to miss an ideal opportunity for a bit of self-publicity.

"Look David, Mr Average British Citizen doesn't see the point of the Foreign Office at all. For him, foreign policy comes below

Welsh Affairs and Fisheries in terms of importance. Until you tell them that we deal with terrorism and Europe, they think we only give advice to travellers – which most of the time they disagree with anyway. As for foreigners, most of them believe our foreign policy is handled by the Prime Minister."

Bill Wells paused to await the inevitable smile of complicity at this sally.

"For once we have something relevant, eye-catching to talk about – the best equipped crisis centre of any foreign ministry anywhere. No need to be shy about it. On the contrary – let's show it off precisely now, when it's got a crisis to deal with. I know all about the confidentiality and operational problems. Let's not tell our visitors the whole truth, hmm? Let's tell them that it's an exercise?"

David was not attracted by this. But ultimately it was the minister who called the shots.

"Yes. We could, I suppose. But the risks remain… our off-shore gas installations first of all, then the beaches, holidaymakers… "

Bill Wells wasn't listening.

"Then that's settled," he said. "I'd like to take, say, a dozen suitable people with our Tunisian guest. But no journalists, of course. I'll leave the choice to you, David."

"I'll just check with our press people that nothing is in the public domain yet…" the Private Secretary said.

"There have been so many oil pollution crises in the past ten years that even if the press do get hold of the story, it won't make any front pages," said Bill Wells. "Unless the rupture is worse than we thought or the weather makes containment difficult. It would be a British tanker wouldn't it."

Ten minutes and a quick shave later, Bill Wells strode down the corridor to the Ambassador's Waiting Room, alone. Abdelaziz Ayeb seemed tiny framed against the tall window looking out onto Horse Guards Parade. Mrs Ayeb was perched on the edge of an armchair away from the window. Despite the lights being on, the high ceilinged room was dark. Bill Wells closed the door and was embraced, Arab-fashion, by Ayeb. The two were soon engrossed in very private conversation on a red leather settee under the worthy gaze of a bearded Victorian statesman in an elaborate gilded frame whilst Mrs Ayeb minded her own business in the far corner.

Shortly afterwards they were greeting the large group of Middle Eastern and African ambassadors in London who took any and every opportunity to attend functions hosted by the Foreign Office. Since the budget cuts, government receptions were few and far between. Most of them knew, or correctly guessed, why Bill Wells was extending hospitality like this to Abdelaziz Ayeb. It was not so much for who he was but who he was likely to become – Secretary General of the Davos Forum. Many of the guests dreamed of being invited to Davos but never would be. With so many other international organisations deadlocked and powerless, it was now the movers and shakers in the business world who called the shots, not governments. The Forum was even destined to play a crucial role in dealing with what was becoming an issue which it had studiously avoided up to now – uncontrolled south-north migration.

The links, Bill Wells said to himself, between fine architecture and good policy making were worthy of study. If the State Department had been in a better building, perhaps U.S. foreign policy would have been more refined. These thoughts drifted in and out of the minister's mind as he stood near the four metre high hardwood doors of the superbly appointed Locarno Suite greeting his guests. The magnificent reception room spoke volumes about Britain's nineteenth century history, her place in the world as she once saw it. The space, the lofty gilded ceiling, the heraldic emblems, the velvet drapes, the rare woods all said "look at who we are; take note of what we are about to say; no messing." Of course, the *Quai d'Orsay* strove for the same effect in Paris but in Bill's view was not so successful. Sir Gilbert Scott's architecture encouraged Great Britain to punch above her weight. God help us, Bill thought, if the iconoclasts ever had their way so that the Foreign Office had to work out of a soulless tower block in Docklands. Or Croydon.

Bill Wells had decided to be innovative the day the Prime Minister had appointed him. Before he had set foot in the Foreign

Office he had somehow convinced himself that it was bound to be stuffy, living on its past. He had been surprised to discover that the Diplomatic Service was well switched on: state of the art IT, quick thinkers, smart operators. He had been bowled over by the speed of the place.

He had asked that guests for receptions or dinners that he was to host should come from a wider pool than the somewhat stagnant ones usually fished in by his predecessors. Country desk officers and research analysts were urged to be imaginative. This resulted inevitably in numerous noses out of joint, particularly amongst the free-loaders from the press.

Certainly Alison Grainger was astonished to receive the crested invitation card, correctly addressed (Alison with one "l"). She was in no way part of the diplomatic scene in London. Her Tunisian credentials had obviously come to someone's notice in the FCO. She was intrigued enough to accept. But another motive for accepting was that the reception gave her the excuse she had been waiting for to buy the purple designer dress that she had had her eye on for weeks at Tempest. Which in turn meant she had to buy a pair of shoes. Whilst she was at it, she had a hair makeover too.

The result was that she looked and felt at her stunning best. Her swept-back, chestnut hair exposed an elegant face with clear, wide eyes. At twenty-eight, she was considerably younger than most other guests. She was delighted to see that she wasn't the only singleton. There were several FCO staff present without wives. She could spot they were staff because of the security passes on ribbons round their necks. She was surprised to see the Irish poet whose name she never remembered and anyway couldn't pronounce.

The intelligent eyes of a confident, thirty-five year-old man engaged Alison's attention after just ten minutes at the reception.

"A beautiful colour, your dress. Purpura."

"Thank you. You know about purple?"

"The finest and most costly dye of the ancients. Made from two kinds of Mediterranean shell – the rather ugly murex or trumpet shell and the pelagia, the true purple shell. The shell juices were placed in salt (one pint of salt to seventy five pounds of juice) and gently heated in metal vessels. An extraordinary range of scarlets, violets, mauves and blues were made by mixing the juice of these shells with other matter including, I'm afraid, urine."

"I rather doubt whether the dye used for my dress is a natural one. But I'm curious to know how you acquired your information... I'm afraid I don't even know your name."

"So sorry. Of course. Glover. Samuel Glover. Museum of London."

"Alison Grainger." She made a theatrical delay before adding "Oxford."

When her father died suddenly, leaving her just over twenty million pounds, Alison's first reaction was anger at having an unwanted responsibility dumped on her. Her second was to create quickly a defensive mechanism to repel gold diggers. This had had an insidious effect on her previously fluffy, open nature. In a matter of weeks she developed sharp edges where none had been before. Perhaps it was instinct. Perhaps it was her bank manager turned mentor. She had inherited him along with the fortune. He shared a passion for collecting Leica cameras as did her father. He was brutally frank about the heiress hunters, the rip-off merchants and sticky-fingered financiers who would dog her at the beginning. Alison did not withdraw from the world as some would but became prickly and assertive instead. She had the confidence that money and beauty bring but there were many chinks in her armour.

Glover continued: "Trumpet shells were always exciting to find on archaeological digs because one knew that if they were there in quantity, dyeing went on nearby. Purpura was a discovery of the Phoenicians. The best and dearest purple was always the Phoenician, especially that from Tyre."

"Yes, I know," said Alison. Taking a sip of her wine allowed her to look more closely, over the rim of the glass, at the man from the museum. He was a bit taller than her, well-built with deep smile creases. She didn't want to stare, though. She suddenly understood the value of the eighteenth century hand-held mask. You could eye a man up without embarrassment.

"Crushed murex," she continued, "has been found in what was assumed to have been an industrial area of Carthage, near where I lived as a child."

"And at Kerkouane on the other side of the Cap Bon peninsula from Tunis, piles of murex shells were found."

Out of the corner of her left eye Alison could see an official wearing a green, shot-silk tie edging towards her, or perhaps Sam Glover. The official had a list in his hand.

"Good evening. My name's David Atkinson. I'm Bill Wells' Private Secretary. Would you be Alison Grainger by any chance?"

"Indeed I am. How clever of you to know. This is Samuel Glover."

"Yes. I know your face from television," said David Atkinson. "'Sex and the Romans'. I missed the first part, but I caught the second."

"What did you think of it?" asked Sam, keenly.

"Well, to be honest it was much more interesting than the title led me to expect. The cult of the body, the way it was copied by twentieth century fascists and so on. Beautifully filmed. The orgy murals were an eye opener too. But I found some of it hard to believe," said David.

"Every single event depicted was authentic, as I explained on camera at the beginning. I stuck scrupulously only to what can be verified. Of course, the emphases were mine as well as my focus on bisexuality."

"I didn't see the series," said Alison. "But I read the reviews and was struck by the one which said that you made too much of Christianity making people feel guilty about sex."

David Atkinson, sensing that this was straying into deep water, took advantage of a waiter's arrival offering more wine, to change the subject and return to his real task. He ostentatiously looked at his list again. "Bill Wells is extremely proud of our Emergency and Incident Office and wants to show it to his guest of honour at around half seven. He asked me to choose a dozen other people so as to make up an interesting group and I had chosen both of you. Would you be prepared? It will only take twenty minutes or so."

So it was, that after Bill Wells' speech, which was unusually short and to the point, Alison found herself looking for the promised signal from David Atkinson to make for the doors at the far end of the room. But she had not counted on Abdelaziz Ayeb exercising his right of reply in order to deliver a five minute discourse which was embarrassing and elegant by turns. When he called Bill Wells a visionary and far-sighted friend of the Arab world, guests were too polite to blink. This was balanced by equally extravagant praise for British entrepreneurs who needed to grasp what Ayeb called the unique opportunities in his country, using it as a stepping stone for North Africa as a whole.

As cocktail party incidents go, the one that occurred immediately after the speeches was spectacular. The beginning was banal in the extreme. The very tall, distinguished but now elderly former Permanent Under Secretary, best known for his command of seven languages, choked on a grilled cheese *canapé*. It was an accident waiting to happen, for nothing burns quite like melted cheese when it sticks to the roof of the mouth. The tragedy was that he spluttered, completely unintentionally he later maintained, from his considerable height onto the head of the beautifully coiffed wife of the Dean of the Diplomatic Corps. As she turned away from the shower of hot cheese and spittle, she raised her arm in an instinctive gesture of self-defence which unfortunately loosened her wig. Her husband, standing beside her, equally instinctively sought to move the wig back into place before anyone would see what had happened. His movement was too rushed however and his well-intentioned gesture resulted in his putting his index finger in his wife's left ear. She screamed loudly dropping her loaded glass of white wine, clutching her wig with her right hand and her ear with her left. A second after the scream, what many guests saw was a well-known foreign ambassador, a renowned philanderer, grabbing the former Head of the Diplomatic Service by the lapel and shouting

74

"Pig!" The insult is bad enough between Anglo-Saxons. To the phalanx of Arab ambassadors, who all heard it quite clearly above the cocktail party hum, it was galvanising. Most assumed there was a Jewish cause.

The distraction had the advantage of allowing Bill Wells and David Atkinson to lead Mr Ayeb towards a rear door. A handful of others, primed by David Atkinson, understood it was time to form a group and go on the Wells tour. Alison and Samuel Glover found themselves walking side by side through a maze of corridors flanked by pillars and arches. Alison's new shoes clopped on the polished tiled floor so much that she felt she ought to walk on the balls of her feet to make less noise. But she didn't. If her high heels drew attention to herself, on this occasion, so be it. In any case, her virtually perfect figure attracted looks from men everywhere. Sam was intrigued by Alison's background in Tunisia, her interest in archaeology and the fact that she was now at Oxford. Alison was actually slightly annoyed with herself for talking to the same man for more than half an hour. The room, after all, had been full of unusual people. Yet it was so much easier to go with the flow, to let herself be monopolised by one interesting person. She liked curious intellects and was attracted by Glover's confidence. There were also the eyes.

Alison's theory was that eyes and how they were set in the face, told her all she needed to know. She not only saw mean eyes and bedroom eyes but also creative, spiritual and musical ones. Tilting eyes, set a couple of degrees off the horizontal like Glover's, were a sure sign for her of intelligence. Shakespeare understood.

"There's language in her eye, her cheek, her lip,
Nay her foot speaks; her wanton spirits look out
At every joint and motive of her body."

One day she would spend time in the National Portrait Gallery, with its computerised archive, pursuing her theory. Someone, she felt, should start systematically analysing genius' eyes.

Sam and Alison brought up the rear of the little group which walked along the gallery above the desks of the L – shaped

Emergency and Incident Office. They both told each other days later that there was something uncomfortable about the place. They were apparently in the middle, so Bill Wells said, of an exercise. There were some twenty officials at work, in four or five groups when they walked in. There was the unmistakeable smell of new electronic equipment. They all looked up at the sound of the Minister's tweedy Scottish voice and soundlessly moved to their work stations, as if in a ballet, like seaweed moving with the surface of a ruffled sea. Forty hands logged off twenty screens within ten seconds.

To Alison's untrained eye, the place looked no different from what she had seen in innumerable TV programmes about the police; maps, monitors, mugs of coffee or tea. Looking more closely, she noticed the staff had earpieces for phones and that there were video-conferencing cameras at every workstation. There were what looked like electronic whiteboards around the walls captioned Log 1, Log 2 and so on. Such papers and files as there were – not many – had been turned over and could not be read. But Alison saw the heading "Winchester Star" in bold type on a document in a soft plastic folder on the desk immediately below her at one point and thought that it was perhaps to do with a gunman on the rampage.

Sam's interest was in the technology. If he leant over the balustrade of the walkway, he could just see a cluster of monitors showing what looked like CCTV pictures. He hung back from the group to get a better look. One monitor was labelled CO and focussed on someone giving a briefing using large scale maps. He strained to see the detail but only saw what he thought was the Mediterranean.

The wiry, serious-looking director of the EIO – Alison was sure he was a cross-country runner – was anxious to herd the little group into a meeting room so that business could resume. Bill Wells, on the other hand, was basking in the tide of compliments from his visitors, especially those from his principal guest.

"Most impressive, most impressive," murmured Abdelaziz Ayeb. "And you say that it is staffed round the clock?"

"Only when a crisis has been declared or is imminent," said Wells.

"This is now not a genuine crisis but only practice?"

"That's right. They have an invented scenario…I don't know what it is," said Wells in a quieter voice.

"I can tell you," said Mr Ayeb, unfolding a piece of paper, only slightly crumpled.

CONFIDENTIAL

SIT REP: 1900 hrs. Summary.

1. Cargo details; heavier than expected
2. Slick assessment; rate of spread recalculated
3. Sea conditions off Tunisia's coast; weather forecast
4. Cooperation difficulties. Malta, Cyprus assets
5. Distant locations of booms
6. Satellite monitoring update
7. First dispersal attempt result 48 hours
8. Parliament
9. Media

Like many red-haired people, Bill Wells had suffered from blushing since his teens. He had tried beta-blockers, anti-histamine creams and hypnosis without success. The excess adrenaline which brought on a blush was the problem and controlling adrenaline was, according to the experts, extremely tricky. Usually Bill wore a light foundation cream, especially if he was to be on the front bench in the House, but he had washed before his quick shave this evening, so had no make-up protection.

The blushing began well before his North African guest had finished reading the confidential situation report. Shock, embarrassment, anger and surprise combined to produce the reaction to his skin colour.

"This is indeed a frightening scenario," said Ayeb. "Extremely

77

worrying. But why are you not working closely with your Tunisian friends? We are the principal interested party."

"Of course we would. But this is just an exercise, an invention to test our systems and so on," said Bill Wells still flushed. He did not like lying, he was a poor liar, but there were circumstances – and in his view this was one of them – where an untruth was necessary for reasons of state. Of immediate importance, though, for Bill Wells, his Private Secretary and the Director of the EIO was how to recover the piece of paper Mr Ayeb had in his hand. If that document left the building that night in the hands of any outsider, the repercussions were too awful to contemplate. For a start, Bill Wells would lose the job he was just beginning to enjoy.

Asking to have the document back would have been the simplest thing to do and it might have worked. But the longer Mr Ayeb looked at it, the more interested he became.

"My wife leads the Red Crescent in my country. She is trained in crisis management. You have meetings like this, don't you?" Ayeb turned to his wife, a consciously chic, sleek-haired lady with expensive shoes and ear-rings and waved his hand round the desks below. He spoke to her in Arabic, softly but with unmistakeable authority. He folded the paper again and handed it to her.

David Atkinson not only watched the transaction but understood the Arabic instruction. More than a simple diversion was needed. The paper had to be recovered and recovered fast. David looked at Bill Wells and realised he was not in a good position to do anything physical. Nor was the Director. His options were limited inside the EIO. If he could get the party to the adjoining meeting room he could possibly rig a blackout and in the confusion attempt to spirit the paper away from Mrs Ayeb's bag. But, technically, organising a blackout for the whole corridor was difficult and, more seriously, would affect the EIO's work. Alternatively, David considered activating the water sprinkler system and the fire alarm. Again, it would be essential to disorient Mrs Ayeb, pulling her perhaps out of harm's way and grabbing her bag. A successful outcome was far from guaranteed with this plan. There was another which occurred to David which would work if he could set it up in time.

As the Wells group left the raised walkway in the EIO, David touched his still slightly flushed minister on the arm.

"Can we have a quick word, Minister?" David steered Bill Wells three steps away from the group in the corridor outside the nerve-centre.

"If you can delay the group ten minutes before they get to the King Charles Street exit, I can get the paper back."

David spoke rapidly and softly in the minister's ear as he had had to do at so many meetings in the past few weeks.

"I'm going to tell security to hand-search every single person leaving the Foreign Office for the next half-hour including ourselves. Ayeb and others will protest like hell. Whatever you do, don't let Mrs Ayeb get away with not being searched. Tell them it's a terrorist alert. Profuse apologies etc. It's the safest way to get that bit of paper back."

Bill Wells said nothing, then nodded. David slid off down the corridor, only breaking into a run once he was out of sight.

Bill Wells had always disliked the huge murals covering three walls at the top of the Grand Staircase. The image of an imperial, war-mongering Britannia implausibly dressed in a plumed brass helmet was risible. The naked, pubescent girl handing her a broken sword, flanked by scantily clothed young men was equally offensive. But his guests had to go past the ghastly murals and they were certainly eye-catching. He would have to disguise his feelings. Holding them back for ten minutes would be a challenge.

"You would not want to leave this extraordinary building, Mr and Mrs Ayeb, without seeing our heroic murals." The minister switched into museum-guide mode. "Over here, a mythical Britannia is teaching her children the arts of peace and war. The murals take some getting used to as you can imagine. Successive Foreign Secretaries have worked in the office over there and have been inspired by them. They were painted between 1914 and 1919, by a British artist who, ironically, was of German origin. The subject matter – which is nothing less than the greatness of the island empire that was Great Britain – can be understood better if one remembers the date of its creation."

Desperately, Bill Wells looked round to see if any senior official was there to help him out. There was none. Hopefully, David would by now be priming the security guards at the front door. Bill Wells felt uncomfortable as he pointed first to "Britannia Nutrix" then "Britannia Bellatrix," drawing attention to how Germany had been painted out of the scenes. He struggled to hold his guests' interest. He thought he would inject something personal into his improvised explanations.

"As a Scot myself, I am just slightly put out by the reference here to "an earlier and ruder race" where I take it the artist is talking about us Celts. Earlier than the Romans we certainly were, but ruder I'm not so sure. You see, all the descriptions of the Celts in those far-off days were made by our oppressors."

Sam found it hard to hide his embarrassment.

"What on earth does he think he's saying," he murmured to Alison.

"I don't know," said Alison. "But my new shoes are killing me and if I don't sit down soon, I will swoon." The archaism seemed in keeping with the murals. He smiled.

"Would dinner in Chelsea make you better? The Collector's Club has the most comfortable dining chairs I know. We could be there in half an hour."

The invitation seemed somehow quite natural. Alison remembered thinking that there must have been an unspoken dialogue between them from the moment they met, leading up to this. It was obvious that she would accept.

It seemed to Alison that Her Majesty's Minister for State for Foreign and Commonwealth Affairs had had, in newspaper language, a long and tiring day. He was not slurring his words but why else would he have spent a quarter of an hour with his distinguished guests, describing some absurd murals when it was clear he did not like or understand them anyway. There was an almost unseemly rush for coats and scarves from the makeshift cloakroom at the bottom of the staircase when he had finished.

Guests who had hoped to be able to make swift and painless exits from the Foreign Office that night were sorely disappointed. Not only guests, but staff too, were put through what both Alison and Sam thought were unnecessarily rigorous searches in the windy tunnel under the archway exit into King Charles Street. A besuited, cold looking but very young man repeated, as if it were a recording on a loop, "Extremely sorry for the inconvenience. We have a Red Security Alert and are searching all incoming and outgoing personnel." Two men and three women in addition to the two uniformed security staff were being insufferably zealous. What looked like a large blanket had been erected as an extension to the x-ray apparatus. Another piece of cloth extended to the side, big enough to examine a trunk or shield an operator even. Two extra tables end to end enabled several peoples' belongings to be searched at once. Most tiresome of all – was it really necessary Alison asked herself – was the painstaking hand-held metal detector search. The machine beeped at the slightest provocation which meant that virtually everyone had to empty their pockets for inspection. Alison could actually see Mr and Mrs Ayeb being searched like everyone else at the front of the group. They both remained remarkably calm as if this was standard practice in London. The serious-looking lady looking through Mrs Ayeb's bag emptied it of everything, picked out the folded Confidential paper, then carefully put everything else back.

"All clear, Madam. The classified paper cannot, of course, leave the premises. Thank you for your patience."

Alison and Sam turned into the street a few yards behind Mr and Mrs Ayeb. They seemed to be looking for their car. Sam said something to them. When he drew alongside Mrs Ayeb, she dropped her bag on the pavement. He bent down to pick it up and as he did so, Alison saw him slip a mobile phone into it. She could even see that it was the same model as hers, with a built-in camera.

CHAPTER 7

There had been Glovers in the Isle of Wight for three centuries at least. A churchyard nestling under the rounded downs running along the centre of the Island bore testimony to it. Samuel had a copy, beautifully hand-printed in India ink, of the family tree which showed that in each generation the daughters married mainlanders and left the Island whilst the sons mostly brought their brides to their farms under the downs. The truth was that the soil was so rich and the climate so good that farming there was a joy. Even bean poles sprouted in the ground, they used to say. Glovers had prospered for generations from milk, tomatoes, new potatoes, salads and flowers.

It was in the seventies that Samuel's father started to call farming a mug's game. The five children, of whom Sam was the youngest, were shielded from the worst of the household's financial turmoil. But the children all saw the damage to the farm following the rock festival on the downs above them. Sam would never forget seeing "his" barn go up in flames with its vital hay and grain. And the children were all too aware of the foot and mouth tragedy the next year. When the livestock was slaughtered, Sam saw his father shed tears for the first and only time. Sam was a teenager.

They were standing side-by-side outside the cowsheds as the vet was taking his brown bag out of the back of his Land Rover. His grim task was to put down, one by one, the whole of the Glover's Jersey herd, lovingly reared and tended on the farm since Sam could remember.

"It's strange Sam," his father said, "but I don't think I can watch this."

"It's not only our herd, though, is it? It's everyone with cattle on the Island, isn't it?"

"Yes. You're right. We're not alone. But it breaks my heart. Not one of those cows is sick. Not one. But because that single farm in West Wight has it, we all lose everything. It's not fair, is it?"

"Don't fret, Dad. It'll be alright," Sam heard himself saying, lamely.

The vet's voice was sombre and business-like.

"Mr Glover, I'll begin now if it's alright with you. Are you coming to give me a hand?"

Sam's father looked towards the house. He could see his wife standing at the kitchen door, shading her eyes from the sun, looking at both of them. Sam looked briefly at his mother, then up at his father who was gripping the metal topside of his trailer, which was beside the vet's vehicle. He was gripping it so hard his knuckles had turned white.

"No, I don't think I will, if you don't mind."

"Suit yourself. I'll manage on my own. There's paperwork to sign when I've finished though."

The vet slid back the bolts on the cowshed door and walked in to do his mortal business. It was then that Sam looked at his father again and saw the tears in his eyes. "I'm not normally sentimental but I know each of those animals by name. I gave them their names. I reared some of them with bottles. They're almost part of the family for me. Poor sods."

He wiped one eye with the back of his hand.

"Why did God send this disease to us? Do we deserve it?" said Sam.

"Of course we don't. But disease has been with us since the beginning of time. At least, that's the way I look at it. We have to live with it."

"It's as though we're being punished," said Sam.

"As if we hadn't been punished enough as farmers."

"Come on, Dad. You've nothing to blame yourself for," said the boy.

The wind blew cold off the tree-bare downs and ruffled the hair of both of them. The farmer turned towards the gangly teenager and hugged him. With an arm still on his son's shoulder, they walked towards Sam's mother and her warm kitchen.

The belt tightening was imperceptible at first – no more skiing, no new car – but by the time Sam was sixteen, "we can't afford it" was a daily refrain when he was at home. School friends had sailing dinghies of their own, ponies or motor scooters, but not the Glovers. The older children in the family appeared to have more pressing financial needs. Everything was more expensive for them; they seemed to get a bit more of everything always. Sam noticed little things. His two older brothers had leather shoes with hand stitched uppers and leather soles. He had black shoes with welded rubber soles. His two older sisters, both sporty, had new graphite tennis racquets from Piccadilly. Sam had to make do with his brother's battered racquet, as loosely strung as a trampoline.

Sam's parents tried to ensure that, as the youngest, he did not feel in the shadow of his siblings. But it didn't work. It was a family of high achievers. The pressure was easier for the elder children because the money problems were less. When he was seventeen and a half, Sam was told Cambridge was only going to be possible if he won a scholarship and worked in the vacations. He actually did both. Before then, to be noticed in a family as large as his, it needed something special and Sam found it. Even as an eight-year old, he realised he could have attention by playing the fool, by being funny. He put all his sisters' dolls onto one end of a see-saw, and then jumped on the other end. He gave extraordinarily realistic imitations of an orang-utan. He mimicked his sisters dressing, doing their hair and making-up in front of a long mirror. When he was twelve, he learnt to do a one minute mime, without any props, of a golfer choosing his club, elaborately addressing the ball, driving, straining to see where it went. It helped that after a childhood on the farm, he had the physique of a rugby player and a broken nose to match.

It surprised and alarmed his hard-up parents that he opted for classics at Emmanuel. How, they worried, would classics get Sam a job? What earthly use was Latin and Greek in the twenty-first century? When they learnt, after the event, that Sam had switched to archaeology, their fears were in no way assuaged. Of all the five children, Sam became the one over whom the parents had least control. Sam himself needed to escape the pressure at home, so kept communication to the minimum.

The first Sam's parents knew that he was a stand-up comic at the Edinburgh fringe was when they lighted on a review in their newspaper. It was headed "Sam, bam, thank you ma'am" and had a close-up of him showing he'd had his hair streaked and was wearing eye shadow. Sam guessed they would not have approved. In fact, they were as proud as anything and bed and breakfast guests at the farm were regularly shown the cutting.

Sam's archaeological interests were always Roman Empire related. Over the past ten years, he had found himself at digs in Turkey, Provence, Sicily and Tunisia as well as at the Roman villa at Brading in the Isle of Wight. Commercial archaeology at various sites in the City of London led later to permanent work at the Museum of London, which is where he still was. His speciality was commercial life in Roman cities but his particular gift was interpreting history, telling it as it was. He had an instinct for illuminating the obscure. He had deepened his learning of the Roman world hugely during his five years in London. He was involved in re-assessing the Lime Street excavations, as well as the Shadwell and Billingsgate projects. He was the moving spirit behind the museum's computer-aided design work, reconstructing Roman buildings in increasing detail as excavations progressed.

During a week-end in Paris, a spilt glass of mint tea at the *Café de la Grande Mosquée*, not far from the *Jardin des Plantes*, led to Sam meeting Tahar Haddad, the curator of the little known Roman site at Bisuli in Tunisia.

"*Pardon. Pardon. Excusez-moi.*" Sam was trying to negotiate between the tables of the packed café towards a vacant red cushion on the wall-seat. Three older men were huddled over bubbling *chichas* – hookah pipes – and playing draughts. Undulating *malouf* musak, violins and lutes, lent a definite North African air to the place.

Sam had already been poured his tea and was moving to a better spot with his glass in one hand and a pastry in the other. *"Pardon,"* he said again as he shuffled sideways. He inevitably tripped over a briefcase lying in the middle of the only passageway between the tables. His tea-glass emptied itself over the briefcase and the shoes of its owner.

"Je suis desolé. I'm so sorry," Sam said.

"My fault. My apologies," replied the surprised, trim, bespectacled North African in jacket and tie, rising and shaking the tea off his shoe. "I shouldn't have left it there."

The illustrated book on Roman coins lying open on the table caught Sam's eye.

"I can't help noticing your book," Sam said, nodding towards the table.

"Oh, yes," the Tunisian said. "There's an excellent shop in Rue Daubenton just round the corner where I found this. It's terribly out of date but the illustrations are good."

"I'm also interested in Roman coinage," Sam said. "Especially from the provincial mints such as London."

"The short-lived Carthage mint," said Tahar Haddad with a smile, "is what fascinates me. Did you know one can sometimes identify the precise man who produced the coin from the mint marks on the reverse?"

"I did actually," said Sam. "The mint marks are sometimes to be found underneath the design, below a specially drawn line. We guess it was so that the official or worker responsible could be traced if the coin was underweight."

"Roman Africa's my passion, too," said Sam. "By the way, my name's Sam Glover, Museum of London."

"Tahar Haddad. Superintendant of Bisuli, Tunisia. I'm pleased to meet you."

"I thought I recognised you. We must have met in Tunisia…"

More tea was ordered. The hubbub of the busy café subsided as the two archaeologists discovered their common interest.

What Tahar considered his carelessness with a briefcase put him in the position of feeling that he should make amends. He invited Sam to Bisuli during a part of the following summer when he knew other foreign archaeologists would not be there. And so began Sam's *affaire de coeur* with a sprawl of ruins on a scrubby ridge fifty kilometres south-west of Tunis.

At the Collector's Club, after they had settled into the soft stuffed chairs in the dining room, Alison managed to refrain from quizzing Sam about his bizarre behaviour outside the Foreign Office. Instead, "You are here alone, in London, now, I mean?" Alison asked awkwardly.

"Is that your oblique way of asking whether I'm single?"

"I suppose so," Alison replied.

"I suppose I am," Sam said.

"You must know whether you're married or not. No, I mean whether there is someone else in your life."

"There might be. But I'm losing faith. I had a partner – we'd been together for a year – but three months ago she disappeared." Sam paused. Did he want to bring all this up so early?

"It was in Tunisia, actually. In September. I had been there for three weeks already, living in a house near the sea in Gammarth, re-visiting various sites and talking to Tunisian friends about a project. She joined me there for what was due to be another three weeks. She's a film director and she was looking for locations for a film about St Augustine of Hippo. She had the help of two local experts, two young men, Ferid and Rafiq, well-known in the local film world. They both spoke excellent English, well American, because they had trained in the States at a film school somewhere in California. That strange day, they came back at nine o'clock at night, when it was already completely dark, in a state of great agitation.

"I was in the sitting room with a drink. I was surprised to hear the doorbell ringing because Celia had her own key. They said they had lost Celia. It took five minutes for them to get the story out. They had gone, as planned, to the TV station in the morning and the Antonine Baths in the afternoon. Ferid had gone off on his own, searching for another location with wheat-fields and a Roman road. At the end of the afternoon Ferid came back to the Baths and was about to bring Celia home when she apparently said she wanted to make a detour; she wanted to go back to see the ruins of a church, the Damous el Karita, not far away, on the outskirts of Carthage."

"I know the place," Alison said. "Crumbling remains of a basilica and a monastery."

"Well, it seems Celia specifically asked them to stay in the car. She then went into the ruins – and disappeared. Ferid and Rafik had hung back because one wanted to relieve himself and the other wanted a cigarette. When they followed Celia into the ruins, after what they said was no more than four or five minutes, she was nowhere to be seen. They assumed she had found something special to photograph, or was just exploring on the perimeter of the site, and said nothing for a minute or so. Then when she didn't appear, they called her name, more and more loudly and started clambering around the walls, the masonry and the scrub looking for her. They went back to the car in case somehow she had doubled back, unseen to them. They then thought she might have fallen and knocked herself out or something. So they started a really systematic search which became more and more panicky."

"Didn't she have a mobile phone?"

"She found hers wouldn't work in Tunisia unless she changed the SIM card and she said she couldn't be bothered. So no, she didn't have one."

"And the young men accompanying her; why didn't they phone you?"

"Because they were frightened. Because they kept thinking that she would turn up. They hung around for an hour. They then went to the nearest café in case someone might have seen her. But the locals said they hadn't. Anyway, I threw a fit, shouted, and screamed at them, telling them how stupid they were and so on. When I'd recovered, I asked them to take me to the spot where they had last seen her. They were not best pleased, but then neither was I.

"I made them slow down every time we saw anyone or even

groups of people on the road. In case she was walking back. I pumped them for information the whole time without learning anything new. By the time we reached the place it was pitch dark. They showed me where they had parked and where she must have gone in. It's a creepy place, at least at night. I had a torch but it was pathetically weak. We stumbled around. I had actually been to the site a couple of times myself, years ago. As you know, it was a large church and there are the remains of dozens of pillars. I looked down a well which must have been deep once but is now full of rubbish – a suitcase, rags, God knows what. It stank to high heaven. We looked especially in the sunken rotunda beside the church." Sam stopped. "But there was absolutely no sign of her."

"No point in telling the police, I suppose," Alison said. Having lived in Tunisia, she knew full well the problems that would cause.

"Everyone advised me not to, particularly Ferid and Rafiq." He paused again. Sam was finding this painful.

"We had had an unpleasant argument the night before, it's true. So I figured she just wanted to show how upset she was by staying out. In the early hours of the morning when she still hadn't returned or even phoned, I went through her things at the house. There was a briefcase full of film notes, e-mails, pages and pages of information about St Augustine, sketches by her and letters from people at Malwood Films. I didn't realise the amount of preparatory work that she had been doing. Even pen pictures of minor characters. It took me a good hour to read it all but nothing seemed odd. I didn't find any names or phone numbers because I presume, I'm sure, she had them with her in her shoulder bag. I went through her clothes. That was much easier because she travelled light. I found nothing to indicate where she might have gone."

"What about her passport, her money, credit cards that sort of thing?"

"She always had her passport and credit cards with her. She picked up all her remaining money, though. But here's the odd part of the story. I had an important meeting at the Culture Ministry that day. It went on for ages and I didn't get back to the house in

Gammarth until late. The house looked perfectly normal at first. But as soon as I went to the bedroom, I saw that Celia had been there. The bed had been made and made in the way that only she does it with the pillows on top of the duvet. On my pillow was a coin, a denarius with a figure of a goddess on the reverse. The letters of the inscription are indistinct. There's an "F", an "E" and an "I". I think it's probably Febris, goddess of fever."

CHAPTER 8

November and December were supremely happy months for Alison and Sam. The meeting of minds was evident to both and Alison was soon entranced by the Promethean energy of the man. His extraordinary skill-set was one thing; but the way he deployed those skills, together or singly, was another.

The back extension and side return of his terraced house in West Hampstead had started life as a contemporary kitchen. Sam was using it as a studio and thinking space. Leaning against the side wall were two front doors with runs of coloured wiring going in many different directions from a device above the letter-box.

"I didn't know you were an artist too. Are these doors part of a series?" asked Alison, admiring the symmetry of the wiring.

Sam laughed.

"They are models for an intelligent front door. It will open by finger-print recognition. No keys. No handles. Motor controlled. The print recognition software is too expensive though and I'll have to wait till the cost comes down, which it will."

"Is it infallible?"

"Nearly. During the tests we found that even with a finger half-covered in mud, it still worked."

"Who are you working with?"

"Stephen Morton at Imperial College. Only at weekends unfortunately. Funnily enough, opening the door is easier than closing it. I'm now wondering whether we can't use voice recognition."

"Oh Sam, that's really going too far!" said Alison.

"Not at all. We've got much further to go. We need to think about grocery deliveries, accepting mail and larger packages. And access for pets."

"Now, if it could do something to stop junk mail…"

"We haven't cracked that, but we're working on it."

The glass-topped kitchen table at one end had half a dozen headphone sets and ear-pieces. Alison's hand moved towards them and the microscope in the middle.

"Don't touch! Sorry to shout. But the circuit board isn't completely soldered yet."

"What is it?"

"Something I've been working on for a year now. An electronic guide app for museums and outdoor sites of all sorts."

"Doesn't it exist already?"

"Not as I'm intending. With the latest technology, your phone will know where you are with even greater accuracy than before. My app will begin along the lines of "From where you are standing you can see in front of you…" or "You are now standing on the spot where two thousand years ago…" And so on. At first I thought of incorporating sound effects as well. Or appropriate music. But I now think that would lead to sensory overload. Imagine how useful the app could be at the outdoor Tunisian sites, for example."

"Won't it put human guides out of business?"

"Good ones are few and far between," said Sam, "and people prefer to visit sites at their own pace. My device doesn't ask for a tip at the end, either!"

Emotionally, too, they were perfectly attuned one to the other. Sam wanted to put his strangely finished relationship with Celia behind him. She had not turned up in London, nor had Sam gone looking for her. He had grieved. He felt alternately angry and sad. But life would go on. Alison came into his life at just the right time. He desperately needed someone like Alison to talk to, to confide in. Besides which, there was the inevitable animal attraction. Alison was seven years younger than Celia and ridiculously beautiful. Where Celia was cerebral, Alison was tactile. Even in jeans with no make-up she was perfect.

The first few nights he talked obsessively. He talked romantically, he talked about compassion and its role, he talked about the language of flowers. His house was always full of fresh flowers, highly unusual for a man, Alison thought. Equally unusually, he liked dancing and danced well. To dance became their secret expression. Alison read the geography of his body like the blind read Braille – with the tips of her fingers. At those times there was no talking.

They had a magical week-end in Seville to escape continual rain that November. For the first time, Sam understood the difference money makes to travelling. Quiet, comfort and courtesy were attributes he had forgotten during his years of budget flying. In the front of the aircraft he did not feel like a date in a date-box. There was even room for his knees.

Stepping from the hard street to their soft boutique hotel, a converted Andalucian town-house, was a treat. At the reception, tasselled cushions in cadmium red and burnt umber taunted travellers to flop and feel enfolded. A polished walnut chest carved with scenes of chivalry and courtly love, incongruously supported fashion magazines with covers of pouting mannequins. Gently lit portraits of Spanish grandees glowed on the drawing room walls. As Sam and Alison moved upstairs after dinner, the only sound to be heard was the water splashing into its white marble basin from the fountain in the covered courtyard.

Annoyingly, the heavily brocaded couch, the ancient smooth cornered tiles, the cool terracotta floor reminded him of North Africa and Celia. Why had she not contacted him after all these weeks? Had she found someone else? Had he missed a signal that their time together was at an end? When did she decide her future wasn't with him? He'd had no hint that a permanent break was to come. It was so sudden. Then again, perhaps she was waiting somewhere for a sign from him. He had left messages for her at her London flat. He had made discreet enquiries at Malwood Films. The one thing he did not want to do was to contact her parents. They had never approved of him and he was sure they would delight in telling him that their daughter never wanted to see him again even if it wasn't true.

To forget Celia, to deal with his nagging feeling of guilt, to stabilise himself, Sam thought it positively helpful, necessary even, to allow himself to fall for a younger, equally fascinating woman who was rich beyond his wildest dreams. To a large extent he couldn't help himself anyway. He was infatuated with Alison and Alison with him. Sam banished his thoughts about Celia to another part of his brain. Seville had cast a spell. It was Alison who drew the curtains round their four-poster bed to enclose their ecstasy.

By day they revelled in Moorish splendour, in luxuriant gardens, in orange sun. There were few tourists and it was still agreeably warm. Sam experimented with a digital camera to make photos in the round. Alison bought a black dress with a flamenco echo which Sam said he liked so much that she wore it every evening for a week.

On returning to London, they were invited to the opening of an art gallery by an old school friend of Sam's. It was a big place, a converted bank, and there was a flower display worthy of the Chelsea Flower Show. He never normally went to those sorts of things but since the TV series, he was in demand. Amusing, articulate archaeologists were not so common in public life. Really handsome ones were even rarer. Alison was surprised to see paparazzi recording everybody who went in and out. She was mortified to be told the next day that their pictures were in the papers, with their names and something about Alison being an heiress. Sam was not bothered.

"It's grossly unfair," Sam told her one Saturday night as he was browsing the internet for museum gossip. "You know more about me than I know about you."

"It's because you talk too much in bed," said Alison.

"Emotional blackmail, is what I'd call it," said Sam. "You have a way of making me talk. I should by now know more about you, where you're coming from, but I don't."

"It all started with shoes," said Alison. "My father's business was making shoes. But the businesses in Leicester and Nottingham became increasingly unprofitable first because of cheap Italian shoes and then because of the change in fashion from shoes to trainers. I think Dad started to switch to trainers but there was no way he could compete with the Asians."

Sam looked at his feet, which, as usual in his house, were shoeless.

"Could the problem not have been that people like me simply bought fewer shoes?" he asked.

"I'm not sure," Alison said. "Dad stubbornly maintained there was always going to be a market for well-made shoes – as long as costs could be kept right down. He hated closing his businesses in England. The factories especially. He apparently looked at half a dozen locations before choosing Tunisia. I think he was partly influenced by his hobby."

"Which was?"

"Photography. Serious stuff. He did his own developing and so on."

"Anyway," continued Alison, "We all moved to Tunisia which is where I did all my secondary schooling. Dad drove himself hard. He was constantly travelling. The business grew. But he was away so often. He was a week-end father. It was my mother who took the strain."

"Was she a beauty, like you?"

"Sam, don't keep saying that. You know it flusters me."

"Sorry, but it's true."

"The fact is that it was my mother, I now realise, who had the greater influence on me. I was an awkward adolescent. But she absorbed all that and, well, shaped me, I suppose. She did all the difficult motherly things like nursing me through glandular fever when I was so weak I couldn't get out of bed for days."

Sam looked up from his laptop and stretched his hand over Alison's fingers on the table-top.

"My mother it was who forced these fingers onto the piano to practice, when all I wanted to do was play the guitar," Alison said. "Until she saw that the piano teacher – Harold he was called – couldn't resist holding my knee, supposedly to show me how to use the pedal. I was only twelve or so. My mother went ballistic. Told the neighbourhood. In fact, it was my mother who taught me…" She paused, then outlined her silhouette from head to waist with one hand six inches from her body. "…that being pretty…"

"Beautiful," interrupted Sam.

"…can be destructive if a girl isn't careful. Harold, for example, not only lost a piano pupil but his reputation. No one would have him near their children ever again"

"Being very attractive is a mixed blessing?"

"Yes. From the beginning at the French lycée, boys always seemed to be looking at me."

"I'm not at all surprised. Were you precocious?"

Alison ignored the question but said,

"My parents used to have friends for drinks in those cool Carthage evenings on a terrace facing the setting sun. I would dutifully hand round the nuts. I would be so embarrassed when they said "How pretty you've become." I suppose I should have just said "thank you" and curtseyed or something, but I found it difficult to handle because it went on and on."

Sam sought Alison's fingers again on the tabletop. But she withdrew her hand.

"You wouldn't understand, being a man. Going to the beach was a trial. Men on the beach behave quite differently from anywhere else. They were a pain. Even on guarded, hotel beaches at Gammarth or Hammamet. In the end I would only swim in the sea in a big group, preferably with my parents."

"Perhaps girls behave differently on beaches, too," said Sam. Alison shrugged her shoulders.

"How did your father react to all this?"

"Violently, sometimes. I remember when he took me to the annual Florence footwear show, there was a reception on the opening night. I was sixteen, I suppose. A good looking guy, who turned out to be Swiss, started chatting me up. He said he was looking for people of my age for a clip or a commercial or something. About clothes and shoes, he said. I was flattered of course, but I knew there was something dodgy because he stroked my head as if I was a cat. My father saw him doing this and lost his rag. The Swiss guy was shoved to the floor, everybody looked at us and I went back to the hotel in tears."

"At university, what made you start with medicine as a subject?"

"Well, it wasn't in the family, that's for sure. I guess I wanted to do something meaningful. Actually, my interests were more linguistic than scientific. English at home, French at school, Arabic everywhere else."

"Your Arabic's very good, it seems to me."

"Good enough to send unwanted men packing. Writing it is more of a challenge."

"And what about Latin?" asked Sam.

"Loved it. A group of us from my school in Carthage had lessons from a sensitive, poetic Italian. He was a Sicilian, in fact, escaping from his claustrophobic family in Taormina. He was a brilliant teacher."

Alison thought she would not be affected by her father's death in her third year at Oxford. She had seen several deaths in hospital. Her medical friends quite often exchanged stories about dying patients. Death was very much part of the syllabus. But her father's death was another matter altogether because so unexpected. His body was flown back from Tunis to Gatwick and he was buried, beside his parents, in Hampshire. Immediately after the funeral, her mother explained that there was a very large amount already for Alison in a trust fund which would now be hers. Her father's death changed everything. Her mother quickly disposed of the house in Tunisia and returned to Hampshire. Alison spent the best part of a year helping her mother find her feet again in England. Oxford, exceptionally, offered to give Alison a year off. But in the meantime she found that she had lost the desire to be a doctor. She was destabilised – and vulnerable.

She wondered whether the university authorities would allow her to switch to archaeology, an interest which absorbed more and more of her free time and was fuelled by her Latin. She wanted to stay in Oxford, the place as much as the university, for that is where her friends were. Then came one of those chance meetings with Edward, a friend of her father's, which led to something completely different. He said she would be foolish not to capitalise on her unique qualities. What he really meant was her good looks. He saw a glittering career for her in public relations or in the media. The business school was at first reluctant to accept her as she was not a graduate; but with Edward's discreet help an arrangement was reached. After all, as Edward said, what good was a business school if one couldn't do business with it? Alison was allowed to focus on the marketing elements of the MBA course.

Alison found the frequent journeying from Oxford to Sam's house in West Hampstead wasted time. She begrudged the two hours plus that it often took. She regretted buying a hybrid car because it simply didn't get her to Sam fast enough. She could have bought a very fast German saloon for cash. She even sat in several in a pillared, cream-painted show-room in Park Lane. But they were all too showy, with an overpowering smell of leather. Since some of her course work on marketing was better done with the practitioners of the art in London, Alison convinced herself that it was convenient to leave several changes of clothes, books and a laptop at Sam's house. From early autumn, weekends with Sam in London became longer and longer.

Though being in love was new to neither of them, this was profound. Their love gave their lives new meaning. It sharpened and heightened their senses. From mono to stereo. From pen and ink to the full palette of oils. Things mattered and thoughts were meaningful. There was an extraordinary degree of mutual understanding built on respect. Such oneness might have been expected in a couple who had been together for years, but they had been together for weeks only. Already Sam knew what Alison wanted to say before she had said it, what she wanted to do before the message had been formulated by her brain. It was eerie sometimes. Sam didn't realise he was stressed until Alison massaged his neck and shoulders.

Later that autumn, as Alison, fresh from bed, was washing her hair over the basin with a hand shower, the sky darkened and the morning light became battleship grey. Out of the bathroom window she saw large drops followed by squalling waves of rain, rain as heavy as fell on Gene Kelly in the film, dancing in it and singing. Sam appeared silently behind her. He had his raincoat on and was holding open another identical one for her. How did he know she had an urge to be in that rain, to feel it powerfully on her face? She moved backwards, smiling, into the trench coat and wrapped it round her shoulders. They ran downstairs barefoot, like children, into the decked back garden, so as to feel the rain on their heads, to rinse in the rain in Alison's case.

She was carried away with him by his enthusiasm for the working of the Roman city. He was obviously in his element at the Museum of London. But at the same time London was frustrating from the archaeologist's point of view. Virtually all the Roman city had been built over many times. No sooner was a site revealed and excavated than it had to be covered over again and handed back to the building contractors. Sam said he felt like an artist whose work was defaced as soon as it was finished. But he found outlets for his creative energy in museology, the organisation of the museum, bringing history to life. Here, too, there were frustrations. Sometimes it was budgets. But increasingly there were differences of opinion about strategy with Sam espousing more radical departures from the classical "show and tell" tradition than the old guard would allow. When one of his Edinburgh Festival friends, now an independent TV film producer, approached him, Sam took the opportunity to take a break from the museum. He had not much liked the theme "Sex and the Romans" but the research that had already been done was sensational and provocative. He was given plenty of liberty with the final production and as presenter. He knew it would upset the establishment but he felt strongly that if the programme encouraged more people to take an interest in the Roman world, it was worthwhile. It had given him a substantial financial boost, fan-mail and a media profile. Whilst it suited him to remain at the museum where he could access the institutions he preferred, his new-found independence was making him restless.

With Alison, it was not long before he pulled out his detailed maps of Bisuli. Since Alison knew the area, too, there was plenty to talk about in a general way. The difficulties the Tunisians were having with the restoration of the amphitheatre; the mystery as to why the town was abandoned and as to why successive generations stayed away. Although he always became animated when talk reverted to the place – it was clear it was constantly on his mind – he was holding something back. He seemed reluctant to show her two files of papers in particular.

It was an impulse purchase by Alison that broke the log-jam. They enjoyed present giving. It was rare that they didn't find an excuse to give each other little gifts. Sam knew that Alison thought fountain pens would soon become sought after, so bought an interesting looking Conway Stewart to start her collection. She responded with a book on Egyptian hieroglyphics. They were fascinated to learn that hieroglyphs were not used to write vowels, only consonants. Sam was intrigued that hieroglyphs should sometimes be read in bunches or squares, not in lines. He speculated that we were impoverishing ourselves by sticking to linear script. It led to linear thinking.

On this particular Friday evening at the end of November, once she had recovered from the journey from Oxford and he had poured her a glass of wine, Alison said,

"I've brought you something. I hope you like it."

She bent down and produced from her capacious week-end bag two rather heavy leather tubes, old but obviously well-cared for. Sam took one from her, genuinely mystified.

"I've no idea what this is, what they are."

"Go on, open one and let's see."

The tubes revealed two brand new camera lenses, one 24mm wide-angle, the other a 200mm telephoto, both nestling in blue velvet.

"The wide-angle will allow you to cram more into your site

pictures," Alison said. "But it also distorts. Parallel lines converge so that temple pillars come together at the top. The telephoto allows you to bring the background forward."

Sam kissed her on the cheek. "The leather tubes were my father's. He used to collect Leicas and these cases were spare."

"They're as lovely as the lenses. You're spoiling me."

He kissed her on the side of her neck, then leant back in his chair and turned to her.

"I'm going to come clean about Bisuli. I haven't wanted to confide in anybody here yet. Archaeologists tend to gossip."

"Their business is dirt, I suppose," Alison said. "Sorry. Do go on."

"Well, there's something I haven't told you. In fact, two completely different things."

CHAPTER 9

S am refilled Alison's glass as well as his own then turned to face her on the sofa.

"Celia's alive," he said explosively, as if he'd been waiting to say it for a long time. "But I don't know where she is. She's definitely alive."

"How do you know?" Alison asked.

"When I rang her parents' home, I spoke to her father. He bristled with hostility at the very sound of my voice and vice versa. For some reason he's always disliked me. His actual words were 'My daughter is better off without you.'"

"I see," said Alison.

"The next day Celia's mother rang me. She was calling from a neighbour's house, without her husband's knowledge. She had been upset to hear the words her husband had used with me. She didn't agree with everything he did. She said she quite understood that I was concerned about Celia. The fact was they had had two letters from Celia since September. They were couched in strange language which at first made them wonder if they really were from their daughter. But the handwriting was undoubtedly hers.

"Celia had apparently said in the first letter she had decided to rest the original project and pursue another. She said she did not want her parents to tell anyone what she was doing or that she was staying on in Tunisia. Celia's father believed it was because she didn't have a work permit or something like that. Celia's mother thought immediately that she had met someone else.

"In her second letter Celia said it had been a hard time but that she was over the worst. She said she was looking forward to returning to London when she would tell us what she had been up to. Celia's mother said she had thought a lot about the phrase that 'she was over the worst'. To her that indicated that something bad had happened to her. That's why she was really worried."

"No clues, I suppose, as to where she was writing these letters," Alison asked.

"No. They were both postmarked 'Tunis' though."

Sam drained his glass before continuing.

"Celia's mother is a born worrier. Especially where her daughter is concerned. She was torn between wanting reassurance that Celia was safe and at the same time respecting Celia's wishes not to tell anyone what she was doing."

"Well, I'd be worried as hell if I were her," said Alison. "All mothers worry about their daughters."

"Anyway, with her husband's grudging approval after the second letter she wrote to her MP who in turn wrote to the Foreign Office. The Foreign Office was clearly puzzled as to what Mrs Purchas wanted. They said that her daughter was not a minor and that unless she was in danger or had had an accident, there was little they could do. The Foreign Office letter was signed by Bill Wells."

Sam sounded relieved to have talked about it. But Alison could see from his eyes, from the strain in his voice, from the tension in his shoulders, that he was caught in a mesh of painful emotions. She put herself in Sam's shoes. If what Celia's mother had said was true and Sam had been deserted by Celia for someone else, she might have been seeing that someone else for a long time behind Sam's back. He would find that behaviour hard to forgive. Who could that someone be?

Sam said he was really surprised that Celia was not going ahead with the St Augustine film. She had found his life and thoughts – about society, good and evil, human destiny – of profound significance. She had been so enthusiastic about it. Celia did not quit a project that easily. Admittedly, she did not have the financing for the film tied up but the chances of her finding the money were quite good. For one thing, Sam still had not played his own ace: he had not yet mentioned the film finance problem to Abdelaziz Ayeb.

If Ayeb could be persuaded that the film would help his plans for Bisuli by arousing more public curiosity in Roman Africa, he might well come up with millions.

Why, Sam wondered, did Celia not mention to her mother what the other project was that she was working on? Presumably another film. But a film director didn't behave like that.

How was she supporting herself? Where was her money coming from? Someone was supporting her, surely. So Sam came back to thinking that Celia had been deceiving him. He had been duped. This went a long way, he said to himself, towards justifying his affair with Alison.

Later, Sam pulled a folder of drawings and plans from the bookcase immediately beside his computer.

"The other thing I haven't told you about is my dilemma at Bisuli. For me, archaeology has always been a means to an end," Sam said. "It's all very well studying antiquities. I am not decrying the discipline. But we can only learn how life was lived in the Roman Empire two thousand years ago if we see it in its context, see it in the round…"

"With a wide-angle lens…"

"Better still in three dimensions."

"So you're working on another TV film?"

"No. Good guess, but no. Nowhere in Africa, well in the world in fact, is there a working Roman city for visitors to see. To rebuild one in crowded Europe is impossible. We've done wonders recreating bits and pieces here and there – individual villas, public buildings, bridges and so on. But imagine if we could rebuild Bisuli as it was at the height of its importance, about 200 AD, during the reign of Septimus Severus. Think what an attraction that would be."

"But wait a minute. Isn't Pompeii even better than what you are proposing? I mean, we can see the actual inhabitants who were unable to escape the ash and lava. And so much was preserved more or less intact."

"Of course, Pompeii is magnificent. It's unique. In one sense, it is the most exciting site I know and it has taught us so much. But how much better if we have carts clattering down the streets, citizens buying and selling in the market, slaves cooking bread, scribes writing letters in the forum, people living their daily lives."

"I don't want to be a wet blanket, Sam, but there is not a lot standing above ground at Bisuli. You would have to start from scratch with most of the ordinary houses," Alison said.

"That is actually part of the attraction. There are places where we could have a free hand. Where we have foundations, we will build on them. Most of the amphitheatre has already been rebuilt, some parts of the small theatre, the capitol and four or five large villas. We need to recreate the baths and reconstruct the forum. I would like to rebuild with Roman-era materials but using today's equipment."

Sam took a sheaf of e-mail print-outs from a folder and flipped through them. "Most important of all, I have the backing of Abdelaziz Ayeb. A most interesting man. I have come to admire him."

Alison put her glass down slowly, looked first into the middle distance for a second or two, then into Sam's eyes, the eyes she loved.

"You really admire him? Don't you think…"

Sam stopped her short by putting his hand up, palm forward, in a 'stop' gesture.

"I won't hear a word against him."

"I see. So," she paused, "so you knew Mr Ayeb before the Foreign Office reception. Long before."

"Of course. We are in touch at least once a week one way and another. Although he is putting up most of the money himself, we agreed that it would be sensible to spread the risk. Indeed, the main reason that Ayeb came to London last month was for the day of private talks with my City friends after the official visit. This is a big project, Alison, and a very sensitive one from pretty well every point of view. We needed to dot the i's and cross the t's as regards the finance. Our business plan excited a lot of interest from the venture capitalists – and from funds from the Gulf, would you believe."

"But haven't you kept people like Bill Wells informed, so that they can put in a good word for you when the time comes?"

"Not yet. Ayeb is concerned about competition, nervous that the idea will be stolen. He has enemies who would be only too ready to put a spoke in his wheel. So knowledge is restricted to potential backers and each has agreed to keep the proposal confidential. Once you tell the British Government – besotted with 'transparency' – the cat is out of the bag. Secrets are much better kept in the City than in the Foreign Office these days. Ayeb and I agreed not to be seen sticking together at the Foreign Office party and he preferred not to mention the project when talking to our government people. Ayeb is nothing if not shrewd . And very discreet when investment is concerned."

"Can you expect a good financial return on this investment?" asked Alison.

"Naturally. The joy of the project is that we can start producing an income from visitors to the attraction before the whole of Bisuli is rebuilt. If we start in the north with the amphitheatre, the theatre and the Dolphin baths as well as the forum and if we have ten or twelve blocks of the grid built, we already have a sensational attraction. By putting the contracting resources into it that I have in mind, we could have our first visitors in three years from the word go. To make their experience special, I would like actors to live on the site for, say, four weeks at a time – maybe more – working, shopping, cooking, eating, playing with their children, sleeping in Bisuli. There's plenty of water. The baths would be fully functional."

"Sam, the baths will attract the wrong sort of interest, surely. They would have to work behind closed doors, wouldn't they?"

"It's funny you should mention that. It's one of the biggest areas of disagreement that I have with Ayeb. As a Muslim, he is concerned about immodesty, though, God knows, there's plenty of it at his resort hotels. The Romans, let's face it, were not over-concerned about modesty."

"Their toilets bear that out," said Alison.

"Indeed," said Sam. "And the importance of the baths for the Roman town-dweller cannot be over-emphasised. Our visitors to Bisuli should be fully involved. Visitors, especially parents with children, will have to be properly forewarned about the nakedness. We haven't agreed the detail of that yet but it will undoubtedly be a part of the attraction."

Alison moved from her chair to sit at Sam's feet. She was looking at the detailed plan of Bisuli that Sam had spread out on the floor. Sam ran his fingers through her hair whilst they talked. Responding to the head massage, every now and then Alison would lift her face to look at him. She hugged his knees. She put her finger inside his sock and slowly moved it around his ankle.

Supper had to be delayed and there was a compromise over who should prepare it. Alison prepared a spinach salad with mustard dressing to start with whilst Sam made *Wiener schnitzel* with buttered noodles and toasted sesame seeds. To accompany it, they drank a bottle of Beaujolais, a Fleurie in fact. Since her legacy, Alison enjoyed few indulgences. Abandoning budget airlines was one. And drinking good wine was another. Sam's wine-rack now bristled with black bottles promising years of exquisite pleasure – and no headaches.

Sam had arranged yellow roses into a sort of football as a centrepiece. A ceiling light picked out a model helicopter uncomfortably lying on its side at the other end of the table from the remains of supper. Alison was easing her way through a bowl of plump Tunisian dates when Sam leaned across the corner of the table.

"What do you think about the Bisuli project?"

"I'm flattered that you have confided in me."

"It's your project as well, now that you know about it."

"Yes. I want to help. It's an exciting idea."

Sam interrupted her.

"I had so much been hoping that you would say you would help." He kissed her forehead. "But I have a problem. A problem of conscience, I suppose."

Alison raised her eyebrows in surprise.

"I had always been intrigued as to why Bisuli was so suddenly abandoned – oh, around the year 220 I suppose. The coins and pottery finds allow us to be pretty sure of the date. Usually when places are abandoned by one set of people, they are quite quickly repopulated by another. But that wasn't the case at Bisuli. No one wanted to live there. I don't pretend to have conclusive proof yet but I think I will soon."

Sam took out another contour map of Bisuli and the area around it.

"This was an extraordinarily fertile place in Roman times. Wheat, fruit, vines, olives – but above all wheat. Bisuli owed its existence to wheat. The huge aqueduct from Zagouan to Carthage was not far away – here it is on the map – but the Bisuli wheat fields relied on rainfall, more abundant then than it is today. They irrigated, too. All these marks on my map represent ancient wells. Here, here and here. "*Bir*" is the Arabic for well and you can see how often it occurs around here. The wells also provided drinking water, of course.

"The water table was much higher two thousand years ago. My belief is that it became contaminated all around here at the same time as the towns were expanding dramatically. The sanitary infrastructure couldn't keep up with the growth of these places. My theory is that Bisuli was decimated and abandoned in 220 AD by a typhoid epidemic. Indeed, I suspect the locals were battling with typhoid for many years beforehand."

"What makes you so sure?" asked Alison,

"When towns are built on slopes like Bisuli is, there is an increased risk that sewage will end up at the bottom of the slope in the river. The irrigation systems everywhere dispersed infected water across the water table," Sam continued.

"But that's just supposition, isn't it?"

"True. But last summer I had a shock. Tahar Haddad allowed me to plot in more detail what everyone for decades had assumed were ordinary temple foundations next to the forum. I didn't tell him at the time what Ayeb and I were planning to do in Bisuli. Anyway from the start I was puzzled by the space. It was slightly hollowed out, like an enormous sand bunker on a golf course.

"On my first full day there was one of those thunderstorms that come out of nowhere in July in that part of the country. I sat in the car at the edge of the forum as the rain tipped down really heavily for ten minutes. Instead of collecting in the bottom of the hollow, the water was draining away almost as fast as it fell. I thought that was odd, so when the storm had passed over, I used one of my survey poles to test the ground there. I jumped back pretty damn quick because the pole went straight down. I didn't touch bottom."

Alison passed him a glass bowl of apricot halves in kirsch with vanilla ice-cream. A delayed dessert.

"Do go on," she said, leaning forward with her bowl so the sweet liquid did not spill.

"That afternoon I set up a resistance meter to begin to map the site again."

Alison looked puzzled.

"It's a gauge which measures electrical resistance in the soil. You put down probes every metre or so. Electrical resistance of soil decreases if it is damp. Soil above solid stone structures dries out more quickly. Using those results and an old aerial photograph which Tahar gave me, after three weeks I produced an intriguing diagram."

"Do you have it here?"

"Yes. Here it is. You can see the outlines of a large building, sixty metres by thirty, set into the slope with nothing by way of straight lines, that's to say walls, in the middle. The diagram perhaps doesn't indicate well enough how steep the hillside is here. It was really built into the hillside. There are tell-tale signs on the side furthest away from the forum of pillars and eleven steps. An uneven number of steps is an indicator that one is dealing with a temple."

"Why?"

"It was considered a good omen to put one's right foot on the first and last steps. An uneven number allowed one to do that more easily. But what made this building different is that it had a vaulted roof – at least that is what I suspected. And because it was built into the hill, the top of the roof was parallel with the forum. I kept on returning to the hole at the bottom of the hollow."

"But temples were obviously to be found around the forum, weren't they?" said Alison.

"Yes. But this one was more than just a temple. I don't know what led me to do it but later on I lay flat beside the hole and listened carefully. There was a gurgling noise: the sound of running water. Quite distinct. It had to be a spring."

"So. A temple, a vaulted roof and a spring…"

"I should have begun by saying that in Bisuli archaeologists had found an unusually high number of cult artefacts, religious rite artefacts."

"Such as?"

"Incense boxes, vessels for catching sacrificial blood, votive objects. It's as if the citizens of Bisuli were especially devout, especially fervent."

"Perhaps they had more need of the gods. Is that what you think?"

"Exactly. I think there was an epidemic or several epidemics of typhoid. So they built a special temple over a spring to which they could attribute healing powers. A healing temple."

"In Rome, I remember reading that malaria patients were quarantined on an island in the Tiber in a temple dedicated to Febris, goddess of fever."

"Yes, but no trace of the cult of Febris has been found outside Rome to my knowledge," said Sam. "On the other hand there are temples to Aesculapius all over the Empire. I suspect that some of them were more like sanctuaries or even hospitals. Certainly people slept in them, for they believed that cures for their sicknesses could be revealed in dreams and what better than to dream in the temple."

Sam paused to look up at the window being rattled by the winter wind. When he turned back, he looked squarely at Alison, in the eyes.

"Alison, if I'm right and this is a fever sanctuary of some sort, it would be unique in Africa. It would have to be properly excavated. That would take at least two seasons, probably three, depending on what was found. But it is right in the centre of Bisuli. It would mean holding up our project."

"Wouldn't Ayeb understand?"

"Absolutely not. He has to have the project approved and off the ground before the President leaves office next year."

"But I'd heard from someone that this President will never leave office, that he's appointed himself for life," said Alison.

"You're right. But Ayeb has very, very good relations with the security authorities in Tunisia and they have been picking up little signs here and there of trouble brewing for the President. Tunisians have become increasingly exasperated by the vote rigging at elections."

"Those ninety-five percent for the President scores?"

"Yes. And for his party at other elections. Time after time. No one believes it."

"Then why don't the voters blow the whistle?" said Alison.

"Because if they step out of line they lose their jobs, they are prosecuted on trumped up charges or held by the police without any charges at all. They know what awaits them in Tunisia's prisons. They are harassed. Their families are harassed. Their lives become a misery. One long nightmare."

Sam paused a moment.

"But it's the lack of free speech which the people find difficult to tolerate. They can see from their televisions now that other people can say what they feel, can criticise their leaders, can hold their governments to account. Satellite TV has been an eye-opener. They tried to stop satellite TV at first but it was like putting a finger in the dyke. They couldn't stop the tide of information from abroad from washing over the country."

"Ah, I see. At least, I suppose I see," said Alison.

"My archaeologist's heart is telling me that we owe it to the world to excavate the place. My historian's brain is telling me that this is a unique opportunity, an unrepeatable opportunity, to recreate a Roman town."

"And make some money?" said Alison.

"Well, yes. It goes without saying," said Sam.

"Sam, there's something that's been troubling me. I haven't wanted to bring it up because I didn't want to upset you. And anyway, I'm sure it's all much ado about nothing. But you know how little things prey on the mind the more you think of them."

Sam stiffened almost imperceptibly. Had he left a loose end? Was it about Celia?

"What were you photographing in the Foreign Office, in that Emergency Unit or whatever it was called, after the reception?"

"You noticed?"

"Well, I wasn't absolutely sure but now you're confirming it." Alison's heart raced; she felt sweaty and her mouth was dry. She could not, would not believe they were even having this conversation.

"Sam, are you, were you...spying?"

"Of course not, Alison. It was just that I could see that my friend Abdelaziz was clearly very interested in the exercise and wanted to have the scenario paper, or whatever it was. I could see that he was not going to be allowed to take it out of the building, so I did him a favour. It so happens that the camera in my mobile phone is good for close-ups; that's why I bought it actually."

"So you photographed the document and slipped the camera to Mrs Ayeb outside."

"Hmm. You are observant, you really are. Alison, what we were taken to see, don't you remember, was only an exercise, a practice, a dummy run. Bill Wells said so, to us all, didn't he? Didn't he?"

Not knowing what to believe, Alison nodded.

"Well, absolutely no harm is done, I can assure you. If I had thought for one moment that I was, I don't know, compromising national security or something, I wouldn't have taken the pictures. Relax, darling, relax."

Each partner in every loving couple compromises. Each hosts

an internal battle between head and heart. Little voices whisper subconsciously. Their messages are usually unwelcome. Why should she complicate the most beautiful relationship she had ever known or perhaps ever would have. She loved Sam.

She didn't listen to her voices.

CHAPTER 10

London. Three months later.

To coincide with Alison's Easter vacation, Sam had obtained an extended leave of absence from the museum. He had booked his usual accommodation in Tunisia for a month from mid-March. Alison was looking forward to seeing her friends there from her lycée days. Her inheritance meant she could easily have taken a suite in one of the new swanky hotels had she wanted to. Or she could have taken a fully-staffed luxury villa on the beach. She could have spoiled herself.

But keeping her friends was a priority. She wouldn't have felt comfortable receiving them in a suite. She remembered something her mentor at the bank had said. "Money insulates you but isolates you too." If she had behaved in Tunisia like a little rich girl, her friends would have fled. So staying with her boy-friend in his rented house was better.

For another thing, she did not want to be apart from Sam more than she could help. Over the winter she had spent almost as much time with him as she had in Oxford. He remained fascinating. Of course he was older. Of course he was on the rebound. Of course she had doubts about his friends – or at least one of them: Abdelaziz Ayeb. But Sam was a man in a million. Attractive, a polymath and kind. Certainly kind to her anyway. Staring at him for long minutes in bed, Alison thought his eyebrows were like the bumpy outlines of Scottish hills. Above them his forehead was a wide winter sky streaked with cirrus cloud. And below the straight nose, the ribbed lips of his firm mouth ended in kissable smile creases.

He was a man who dared think on a large scale. True, he was unashamedly ambitious but she admired that. He was willing to take risks and most of them seemed to come off. She hoped she wasn't dazzled by his media profile which was growing steadily. This tousled haired intellectual was in demand on TV in particular where archaeology and history were both having a renaissance. Perhaps British viewers thought that archaeology was better than the endless programmes on house-buying or cooking.

He could, she supposed, have given up his Museum of London job had he wanted to. But he didn't. The museum rather liked the fact that they unexpectedly had a potential star on their staff. With little gestures here and there – lunches with trustees, extending leave no questions asked, a better office – they made it clear they wanted to keep him.

Throughout the winter Sam had been exchanging long e-mails with Ayeb about the detail of turning Bisuli into a visitor attraction with a difference. Ayeb, as usual, was keeping his cards close to his chest and was urging Sam to restrict knowledge of the project as much as possible. Ayeb had set up two new companies within his group: one for re-constructing the Roman town and one for managing the enterprise once it was launched. Sam was to be a salaried director of both companies. In addition, he had been paid a special, one-off consultancy fee.

One of the attractions for Sam was that Ayeb had the resources within his own businesses to design and execute the project without needing outside contractors. This was of inestimable value in that part of the world. There would be none of the wheeling and dealing with third parties, none of the backhanders or premiums to pay, no argument over terms and conditions if Ayeb's own people were in charge. Technically, Bisuli belonged to the state so there were huge problems of ownership and heritage protection to be addressed. Whenever Sam raised the question of Bisuli's status, which he did on many occasions, Ayeb waved it aside. "I'll take care of the politics," he would say with a dismissive wave of the hand. But it worried Sam greatly. It was clear that the political deal on which the enterprise rested would not extend beyond that year's presidential election. The project had to be underway by then or not at all.

It irritated Sam that Ayeb never ceased to thank him for giving him all the exact details of that oil-spill off the Tunisian coast in the autumn. Ayeb Environmental Services was miraculously on the spot before competitors had even heard there was a spill. When it transpired that some of the oil had escaped the booms that Ayeb so rapidly supplied, it was inevitably his contractors who were selected to clean up the shore line.

Above all, it upset Sam that Ayeb was not prepared to make any provision for the proper study of the fever sanctuary, if that's what it was. His theory of one or more typhoid epidemics in Bisuli was still no more than a theory. If only he had time, he could have some dental pulp samples taken from teeth found at the site and tested, though it would be hugely expensive. If there were DNA sequences similar to those of the typhoid bacterium, he had the proof he needed. A quick descent into the sanctuary was in any case becoming daily more attractive to him. He had told no one except Alison that the roof had not completely collapsed. There was a substantial enclosed space. That was why he could hear the gurgling spring. And there was an echo when he had banged underneath the structure with his survey pole.

For a week before their departure, Sam had been meticulously planning how much kit he could fit into the Land Rover. It amused Alison that that he had marked out on his dining room carpet, the exact dimensions of the vehicle's luggage space. Alison then watched the space being filled with the tools of his trade – resistance meter, probes, laser measuring device, bundles of red and white survey poles and half a dozen well-filled plastic crates. He was re-positioning the crates for the third time that morning, four days before departure, when there was a rap on the front-door.

A middle-aged, distinguished-looking Tunisian in an inappropriate for the season off-white linen jacket, and noticeably new shoes, thrust out his hand.

"Good morning, Dr Glover. I wanted to telephone first but then thought it would be better to avoid it."

"Dr Haddad, my dear friend. Come in. What a surprise. I can assure you nobody listens to our phones in England," said Sam, smiling. He shouted upstairs.

"Alison. Tahar Haddad is here. Yes. Tahar from Bisuli."

Alison came downstairs with a box-file of papers, put them on the hall table and shook hands with the unexpected visitor. Having introduced Alison and after Alison and Tahar had exchanged small talk about Tunisia, coffee was produced.

Looking at the hardware on the carpet, Tahar said,

"I see you are preparing your equipment for Bisuli. That is what I have come to talk to you about."

"But I didn't even know you were in London, Tahar."

"*Une visite éclair.* Just a flying visit. If it was more than that, I would have contacted you."

"I'm sure it wasn't just to buy shoes," said Sam, gently probing.

"Oh, you noticed them," Tahar said.

"You never take holidays, Tahar, unless you have reformed, so I'm sure you aren't here as a tourist," joked Sam, still trying to draw him out.

Stroking what was left of his grey hair which had been ruffled by the wind outside, Tahar said nothing for a moment. He looked approvingly around the book-lined room. Sam had never known Tahar tell a lie. He was normally transparently honest. This time he clearly had something on his conscience.

"I came rather suddenly and without Mr Ayeb's knowledge. He thinks I am visiting relatives in the south of France. I went first to Paris to talk to someone from UNESCO and then, here in London, I met yesterday with the man from the World Bank who was in Tunisia last year. I wanted them to know what is happening. But I should not be telling you this because you are so close to Mr Ayeb."

"It's alright to tell me, Tahar. It's true that I work for Ayeb but that doesn't mean that I tell him everything that my good friends tell me. Our relationship is strictly on business terms. Anyway, what did you tell these people in Paris and London?"

"That Mr Ayeb has a plan, which he will announce next month, to commercialise Bisuli. I said that in my professional view it would be a travesty, 'un sacrilège', to invent constructions there when we still do not know where they all were or how they looked. What Mr Ayeb is planning would not allow people to see what is real and what is not. It would hide years of careful work by archaeologists from many countries. It would destroy the site. I asked if UNESCO could speak out to draw the world's attention to this disaster. I asked if the World Bank could speed up the loan it has promised for Bisuli. Such actions might make Ayeb think again."

Sam smiled. Tahar was naïve if he thought that.

"And what did you say?" asked Sam.

"Franchement, j'étais déçu. I was very disappointed. Very disappointed. The man from the World Bank even said that he thought in Washington the Bank would look favourably on what Mr Ayeb was doing because it made economic sense. Can you believe it! The lady at UNESCO said that Mr Ayeb was very good friends with the Secretary General of UNESCO, that Mr Ayeb would soon be Secretary General of the World Economic Forum and that these things had to be kept in mind."

Tahar drank his coffee and made a kind comment about Sam's photograph of the mosaic portrait of a famously unidentified woman – the Lady of Carthage – hanging by the doorway. He leant forward in his chair.

"Dr Glover. You are an archaeologist as I am. Your mission in your work must be the same as mine: to reveal the past by scientific study. We are scholars. We are not in the entertainment business, are we?"

Sam pursed his lips, hunched his shoulders and gestured with his hands palms upwards, as if he was feeling the weight of two ripening melons.

"Would you be able to live with yourself, would you be able to meet your professional colleagues, would you ever again be held in esteem if you sold your soul to Mr Ayeb?"

Sam showed no further outward signs of distress but Tahar's arrow had struck home alright. It was too late. He had taken Ayeb's money. But surely Tahar had accepted a sweetener from Ayeb too? It was the way Ayeb worked. He made offers too good to refuse.

"I have been in charge of the site at Bisuli for many years now. I am proud to say I know everything that goes on there. I know you have discovered something important beside the forum. I think it may be the key building in the whole site."

Sam looked in surprise first at Alison, then at Tahar. How did he know? Who told him? Had Tahar been watching after that rainstorm? Had someone been looking at his diary? It didn't matter. Tahar knew.

"You told Mr Ayeb last year that you believed there was more than just a temple there. He told me. He also told me, later, that you thought it might be a therapeutic centre, that Bisuli had probably been afflicted by typhoid fever. The more I looked at the site over the winter and thought about your theory, the more sense it made. It would explain the profusion of temples, the profusion of sacrifice and prayer objects. This was an affliction sent by the gods who needed to be propitiated. It would explain the abandonment of the town at the height of its prosperity. But as for the building, we need more evidence."

Sam couldn't believe what he was hearing. He suddenly realised they were both thinking along the same lines. His way forward became clearer.

Tahar continued. "Mr Ayeb thinks he can do as he likes, doesn't he? But there is something more powerful: international public opinion. As you know, the media will be present at Bisuli next month, in large numbers, at Mr Ayeb's request for the unveiling of his plans. If they could see that we had just discovered something of fundamental, historical importance which was about to be destroyed…"

The risk-taking side of Sam was immediately engaged. Alison could see that this tactic appealed to him. There was no point in her warning him that he was playing with fire. Tahar, too, knew they would be playing for high stakes.

"I would be pleased to help you in any way I can to find the evidence we need," said Tahar. "But Mr Ayeb is a ruthless man. I hear many rumours about him. If the local media cannot speak freely about those who have the power in my country, we depend on word of mouth, information from friends and rumour to tell us what is really happening. There is an expression for it, isn't there – '*le téléphone arabe*'. And the foreign media is so important to us too, of course."

Alison spoke for the first time. "I lived there. I know what you are saying very well."

"What sort of rumours?" asked Sam.

"They say he disposes of people he finds obstructing him. They say he did just that even with a journalist from the BBC last year."

"A female journalist?"

"Yes. I believe so."

"Tell me more. Please tell me more," said Sam.

"I know no more than that," said Tahar. "My wife said she heard it at the hairdressers from the wife of a policeman in La Marsa."

CHAPTER 11

Lovers are always curious about their predecessors. The convention is that one does not ask questions. But Alison found herself increasingly thinking about Celia.

What aroused her particular curiosity was the manner of Celia's disappearance. There had been an argument, a bad one, but Sam had been vague as to what it was about. Alison couldn't understand why, let alone how, a woman could vanish when accompanied by two professional colleagues. Nor did she understand why and how Celia had returned to Sam's rented villa the next day, picking up just some of her things and leaving a coin on the bed. Was it a joke? Payment for services rendered? It surely wasn't something that just fell out of her pocket as she packed a bag.

Sam's behaviour had been equally strange, Alison thought. Why had he not devoted every breath in his body to finding out what had happened to her? Having lived in Tunisia for many years, Alison understood Sam's unwillingness to invoke the help of the local police. But he seemed extraordinarily unconcerned about her fate. At first Alison assumed there must have been an emotional reason for Celia's disappearance. Sam was a complicated man with huge energy. He was difficult to keep up with. He was obsessed with his project in Bisuli. He neglected people's feelings. Was this why Celia had left him?

On the other hand, why didn't she leave a note? Or phone Sam later? After a row, lovers usually want to know how the other has been hurt. To disappear as she had done was bizarre. Even less normal was that she had not tried to contact Sam.

Or so she thought.

The letters to her parents at least showed she was alive. But their language was odd and they were unnaturally vague. Alison decided to do a bit of detective work since others didn't seem interested in doing any. In the week before they left for Tunisia, when Sam was in Manchester, at the invitation of the British Council to talk about curating a travelling exhibition on Roman Britain, she began searching Sam's papers. She knew she shouldn't, yet she felt she had to. Suppose there were other girlfriends who had "disappeared"? Suppose Sam was not quite the man he seemed?

Alison did not find any love letters as such. Anything of that sort would probably have been in e-mails. Or shredded. Men were not sentimental. She had already checked his computer as best she could. There were plenty of messages to and from Celia, with loving beginnings and tender endings, but they were otherwise boring – invitations to film screenings, meeting arrangements, could he join her at the weekend – that sort of thing. There were also long messages about Aurelius Augustinus and the lives of Christians in Roman Africa.

But Alison eventually found what she was looking for, in one of the drawers of Sam's desk, underneath his printer. It was one of Celia's business cards on which Sam had scribbled "Depart 18.22. Arrive 21.15." On the back was printed what was presumably Celia's private address in London NW6 . Alison made a copy of it.

The address was within easy walking distance of Sam's flat. It was a typical Victorian end-of-terrace house with six steps up to the front door. Rubbish had accumulated in the small front garden including the brown skeleton of a Christmas tree still attached to its stand. Steps also led down to a semi-basement entrance. White wooden plantation shutters prevented a full view into the front room. But when she craned her neck and stood on tip-toe, Alison made out an elaborate gilt framed mirror over the fireplace reflecting an expensive crystal and stainless steel light-fitting. A large full-length portrait of an African couple hung on the wall beyond that. On a bookshelf was a bronze statuette, a red Venetian glass chalice and three leather-bound books.

It was quite possible, Alison persuaded herself, that Celia had returned from Tunisia on her own and was living perfectly normally here. She could even now be at the back of her house making tea or working. Or she could be at a film studio and would be back any minute after a dawn start to her day. Perhaps she had been working at night and was asleep.

Alison was carrying a clipboard and pen. She would say that she was canvassing; that she had Celia's name from the electoral roll; was wondering about her voting intentions; and what her most pressing local concerns were.

There was no reply when she rang the doorbell so she used the knocker. Too late, she realised she had knocked far too hard.

"Here's a knocking indeed! Who's there, i'the name of Beelzebub?" someone declaimed from the opening basement door. A stubbly, square face under a pudding-basin haircut looked up with distinctly bloodshot eyes.

"Oh, sorry to disturb you. I was looking for a Miss, er…" consulting the clip-board, "Miss Celia Purchas."

"Hasn't been here for *yonks,* darling" resumed the camp voice, from a red shirt, sheepskin waistcoat and tight green trousers. "Weeks and weeks and weeks. Is it something I can sign for? She said I could sign for her whenever she was out, so I've collected quite a little treasure trove."

Alison was disarmed.

"I know I shouldn't have signed for so long. But delivery people are always in *such* a rush, aren't they? And not without good reason round here, you know. The traffic wardens are *vicious.* I think, personally, they've got bets with *all* the other traffic wardens about who can stick on the most number of penalty notices in a day. I mean, have you *seen* them, on the *dot* of nine thirty they're writing out their first ticket. We're in a nine thirty to ten thirty no parking zone, you see. And now that they've got their little digital cameras, there's *no* stopping them, is there?"

"So she's still living here, is she?"

"Look, *do* come in from the cold, darling. I can't *possibly* discuss my poor dear Celia in this *glacial* wind or we'll all catch our *death*, won't we?"

Alison couldn't help but accept the offer.

"Mind the steps, love, they're *frightful*. They get no sun and a sort of primeval slime has built up which is probably why my rent is so low."

Photographs of graffiti in various European languages filled matching brown frames in flying duck pattern and took up a good part of one wall. On the other hung an interesting looking collection of tassels. In two hops, the tenant was tugging up the duvet and plumping the pillow on the un-made bed. With a sweeping gesture, he invited Alison to sit on the better of the two armchairs beside the ash-full hearth.

"*Terrible* thought. Are you from the Council? After all I've said about traffic wardens. And if you are from the Council, I can see you're wondering whether I use smokeless fuel for my fire. Well, let me reassure you. I *do* buy smokeless fuel from the *lovely* Bangladeshi in the shop at the end of the road. We're *terribly* lucky to have him. But even *he* ran out during that cold spell. So I'll confess. I've been collecting twigs from Hampstead Heath."

Alison must have raised her eyebrows.

"Well, small logs I suppose. Just lying around."

The loneliness of the unmarried actor was frightening. Until he'd talked his fill, there was little hope of Alison making progress.

However, she made another attempt.

"It's just that I have Celia Purchas' name from the electoral roll and am canvassing. But your name doesn't seem to be registered at this address."

"Oh no, dearie, no, no. Well it wouldn't would it? I mean I'm not ashamed of my name or anything. Indeed, I have two. The stage name is the one you'll have heard of – Jocelyn Charles. No? Shame! *Nobody* goes to the theatre anymore. The fact is I'm a strolling player, you might say. Though I've been here for a *year* which is a record. Two bits of *wonderful* luck in the past year. Did that awful commercial with the wide-eyed Labrador for the pet-food people

'Fiedog'. It's so ironic. I loathe dogs. So self-centred. Then would you believe it, Friar Tuck in panto for eight *whole* weeks. Just getting my voice back. God *knows* if there will be any more work, though, from the way things are looking."

Unbelievably, he paused to draw breath.

"When was Celia Purchas last living here?" Alison thought it a good moment to stop the unsolicited life history before it relaunched.

"It would be, let me think, just before the first 'Fiedog' audition. Mid-September?"

"And she hasn't been back since?"

"No, but I don't enquire too closely about the private lives of attractive young women, do you know what I mean?"

Joe Charles leant forward, conspiratorially.

"There was a man in her life, that much I know, because he was often here. Mind you, she was often at his place, too, no doubt. They were a couple alright. But I remember him – blonde, muscular, curly-haired. He used to come with *enormous* bunches of flowers. He loved flowers. He always brought them. But on one occasion she wasn't in. I heard him at the door just as I heard you. He brought the flowers down here to leave with me till Celia got back. Beautiful yellow Peace roses they were. Lovely scent. He asked if I had a bit of paper and I was frightfully impressed because he wrote something in Latin – *'rus in urbe'* – I think. Means 'a bit of country in the town' or something like that, doesn't it? And he signed it 'Sam'.

Although she had mentally prepared for this, it still came as a shock. She felt hot in the airless flat. She got up to go.

"As far as I know, she was working up a film idea for Alfred Feldstein from, what's it called: Malwood films in Soho, that's right," said Joe.

"Twice someone from Malwood Films has been round here, looking for her. I do hope she's not been snatched by that Sam because he's only after money, that man. Trust me, I can tell it a mile off."

"No, I'm sure not. I mean, I think that's unlikely. I'm sure she'll be back soon. Thanks for your help. I'm going to mark her down as temporarily absent."

He saw Alison to the door. She climbed up to street level and strode down the pavement, not stopping, Jocelyn noticed, as a genuine canvasser would, at the next house.

Walking down Berwick Street in Soho the next day, Alison's eye was taken by a shop selling 'wholesale clubwear'. She smiled as a completely frivolous thought occurred to her. It would be totally out of character but something Goth might take Sam's mind off the ancient Romans, might bring him up to date. Fortunately for Sam, it was 'closed due to flu'. Three doors further on, Malwood Films occupied the two top floors above a coffee lounge.

"The last time we talked to Celia was, let me see, towards the middle of September last year," said Alfred Feldstein. "She was ringing from her friend's rented house just outside Tunis so said she had to be brief. She had had various new ideas for the film. Apparently, St Augustine had an extraordinary, deep friendship with a young man of his own age in the town of his birth. Then, when they were both about twenty, the friend tragically died, of a fever. She was intrigued by this and wanted to explore it. She also thought a good half of the movie could be shot in Tunisia."

"It's just I would dearly like to get in touch with her. And I have a message to her from a friend as well," Alison said.

"Well, we'd like to hear from her as much as you would," Mr Feldstein said, reaching for his coffee, bought, Alison noticed, from the shop on the ground floor.

"She said she had found some good Tunisian production people with whom she was working. The good news is that Celia is not locked into a schedule with us yet. We're still at the ideas stage. We have an informal understanding so far. If she decides not to pursue it, I won't start crying. Money is going to be tight this year and next. Anyway for the next five years the public is going to want 'feel good' movies. Now I'm not sure whether there's enough of the feel good factor in the story of a talented young man from the fifth century who sowed his wild oats in Carthage and became a saint!"

"She said she was working with local production people in Tunisia?" Alison asked.

"Yes. Actually we had to pay them in euros to an account in Paris and that puzzled me."

"Do you have their names, by any chance?"

"Yes. I suppose we must, because of the payment we made for their services. Let me ask someone to dig out their details. One was called Ferid, I remember."

"You're very kind," said Alison, who felt that at last she had a straw to clutch.

CHAPTER 12

When Sam and Alison arrived in Tunisia, almond trees were in full bloom. Orchards of blossoming apricot and orange meant the bees were spoiled for choice. Millions of wild flowers, mauve, white and especially yellow, were responding simultaneously to the warmth of the short spring. Fluffy mimosa and blue plumbago powdered the parks and gardens. Sam bought bunches of sweet, white jasmine for the bedroom.

Before leaving London, Alison had fixed a meeting with Rafiq and Ferid at one of the new hotels at Raoued, north of Carthage and not far from Sam's villa. Ferid's e-mails showed they were greatly concerned about Celia and wanted to talk. The two men were already in the lounge bar with its view of the pools, palms and sea when Alison arrived. Her signal of recognition, a dark-blue straw hat, worked perfectly. They had found a quiet corner where they would not be overheard. The young men nevertheless seemed nervous and uncomfortable.

Alison could understand why. They were the last people to have seen Celia. They were supposed to have been looking after her or at least assisting her. Yet they returned alone. They knew all too well that if the police were to become involved, they would be presumed guilty. But of what? No body had been found. No ransom demanded. The two men had good reputations as far as Alison knew. They had good jobs. They had no motive to kidnap or worse, kill, a visiting film maker. For one thing, this was someone who most probably would be giving them significant contracts. But at the same time, Celia was an attractive woman and the two men had been alone with her the whole day.

For ten minutes the conversation was predictably cautious. They talked about America, about the film industry in Tunisia and the plans for Celia's film. Then Alison said what she should have said at the beginning, that Sam Glover had no knowledge at all that she was meeting them. She did not want to upset him.

There was a distinct change in their attitude: they started to open up. Rafiq wanted to know why Alison was making these enquiries. She said she was concerned in case something bad had happened to her. It was unusual for someone to disappear. She hadn't returned home. She hadn't been in touch with the film company in London. She hadn't contacted Sam with whom she had been on the best of terms.

"What do you really think happened to her?" Celia asked. "Have you any ideas at all?"

Leaning forward, Rafiq's body language indicated he had something significant to impart.

"I can tell you more. I haven't been able to tell anybody the whole story. But you must assure me you will not tell Mr Sam," Rafiq said.

"Or the police," Ferid added.

"Alright. I agree."

"At the place where Celia disappeared, I saw what happened," Rafiq said.

"At the ruined basilica?"

"Yes. That's right. I left the car with Ferid inside it to have a cigarette. I am supposed to have stopped smoking but just occasionally I give in and have one. I walked round the side of the ruins. I had never been there before but there's a track which leads onto a small road. I was surprised by a car leaving from behind the ruins and coming towards me. I stood behind the bushes so I think I was invisible but the car was just two metres from me. It was a white Renault. There were two similar looking men inside. And Celia was in the back. I'm sure it was her. I'd been with her all day, so I could not be mistaken."

"Was she smiling? Was she struggling? Did she see you?"

"She didn't see me. All I saw was her hair; the top of her head.

But it was enough. The car was past me in no time." Rafiq made a speed gesture brushing his two hands one past the other. "Vroom. Like that and gone. It was a new car. I saw two other things. There was a doctor's sign in the windscreen of the car. And on the back window I clearly saw a sticker saying 'Garages Renault, La Marsa'."

"Why did you not tell Dr Glover about this? It's very important."

"For two reasons. I don't know why but I supposed Celia knew these men. I supposed she did not want to be seen. And that she did not want Dr Glover to know. But more important, we know Dr Glover is a close friend of Abdelaziz Ayeb. He is a very, very strong man in our country."

"What do you mean exactly?" asked Alison, naïvely.

"His influence is everywhere. For example, his bank is financing our production company."

"Look, I must find out more," said Alison. "I know how resourceful you are in the film production business. You regularly do the impossible, don't you?"

The two men smiled. Few people understood what production people did.

"If a director called for twenty camels by dawn tomorrow, you would have them ready, wouldn't you? For a fee of course," she said, touching her handbag.

She went on: "It shouldn't be too difficult, should it, to discover whether a doctor has recently bought a white Renault from that garage in La Marsa? I mean La Marsa is a fair size but it is not really huge, is it? And then to let me know. Only me. No one else."

She saw them hesitating.

"Or we could go to the police for help."

"We can do it for you," Rafiq said.

As Alison drove back to their villa, she decided not to say anything to Sam.

Ever since her fall on an icy pavement in Oxford in January, Alison had had a pain in her right shoulder. At first she thought it was just a strain which would quickly disappear. She prided herself on her fitness. If she did not do her floor exercises every day, she did not feel right. Exercise was part of her life and as important to her as her seven hours of sleep or her muesli. Alison knew from her years of living in Tunisia that doctors there were good and that some of the specialists were outstanding.

So within two days of arriving, she was in the office of Dr Zarrouk, the shoulder specialist friend of her father when he was alive. Both were obsessive collectors. In Dr Zarrouk's case it was decorative glass, 'art glass' as he liked to call it. How Dr Zarrouk had amassed a small fortune was never clear to Alison because the doctor preferred chatting, partying or playing the piano to diagnosing and treating his patients' shoulders. However, when he became serious and got down to work, he was brilliant. He said that he preferred an oblique approach, whatever that meant. Alison suspected he was good at chess.

"Have you seen Suzanne?" was the first thing Zarrouk asked having given Alison an almost painful bear-hug embrace. He was shorter than Alison, completely bald and immensely strong. She remembered his party trick, hoisting her into the air by the elbows. This he was able to do until she was twelve. And he would beat all-comers at arm-wrestling after the Sunday barbecues at his house in Carthage.

"Suzanne? Who is Suzanne?" she said, falling into the trap.

"My latest Lalique." He strode over to a two-drawer, walnut bureau opposite the door and folded down the panel to reveal his latest piece of glass.

"Do you like it?" he said, picking up the heavy bronze base on which rested a perfectly produced dancing figure in frosted crystal, with a frosted drape. "It is said to be René Lalique's daughter, Suzanne. The horizontal hold of her arms with one palm facing up and the other palm facing down, is an exercise I use to test my patients' shoulders. Did you know that those pieces signed 'R. Lalique' were made while he was alive and those just signed 'Lalique' were made after his death?"

Alison looked just below Suzanne's feet and saw the signature. It was 'R. Lalique', of course.

"My friend from London is a collector like you. I must bring you together. Do you know the Collector's Club in Chelsea?"

"Of course. I have the dubious distinction of having been able to tell them that a French cameo glass vase they had behind the bar was a fake."

"What is cameo glass, if I may ask?"

"It's glass made up of two layers of different colours. The top layer is usually etched or carved to create a picture in relief. Art Nouveau. Beautiful. But there are fakes."

As he moved the ultrasound device round her shoulder, he said "Women curiously enough have more shoulder problems than men. But what you have is relatively straightforward: calcific tendonitis."

"Straightforward it might be but it's extremely painful," said Alison.

"I know, I know," replied Dr Zarrouk.

"You can either do nothing, live with the pain and wait three years for it to get better. Or I can perform keyhole surgery under a general anaesthetic. The calcium comes out of the muscle like toothpaste out of a tube. If all goes well, the problem is solved. Until the other shoulder plays up."

Alison decided to think about it. She was always suspicious of surgeons' advice. Of course they wanted to operate. That was their bread and butter. The question was, could one believe what they said about their success rates?

As she was about to leave it occurred to her to ask if he knew of any of the doctors in La Marsa. He said he knew a couple there.

"We doctors are a bit of a mafia, you know. We do mostly know one another, especially in a small country like this. The one that first comes to my mind there is young Omar Ansari. A brilliant man. He had no need to go into general practice. He could have earned twice as much as a consultant. But he always had a high sense of moral duty, did Omar. Wanted to be a physician to the poor."

Alison was listening intently. Once the doctor started, he was difficult to stop.

"We knew each other in medical school in Lyon. The third

musketeer was Farhat Chebbi. I still see him once a week, I suppose. He's director of the pathology lab a kilometre away from here. Strangely enough, he frightened me to death six months ago when he told me he had just analysed several cases of typhoid. We don't usually get that in Tunisia. Our sanitation is good on the whole. The cases were somewhere not far from Tunis – just to the south, I think. And it was Omar Ansari, of all people, who sent him the swabs for analysis."

CHAPTER 13

Six and a half months earlier, when Celia first heard from Major Mifsoud that none of them would be able to leave Bir Assaya, she was not so much afraid as despondent. What in her thirty-six years had she done to deserve this? How was it that she, Celia Purchas, eight years with the BBC, now an independent film maker, could be so naïve as to have been caught in this way? What on earth made her come here?

The question must have been asked by every investigative journalist on the planet, Celia supposed. And the answers would have been the same – exposing evil and wrong-doing. It sounded so banal, so altruistic.

The unpleasantness of her situation was undeniable. She was stuck in an overcrowded, unsanitary, unfit-for-purpose camp which was rife with typhoid fever. It was imprisonment in all but name. The rolls of barbed-wire, the guards and the guns endorsed the feeling.

The only redeeming feature was that she found herself living cheek by jowl with two exceptional Tunisian men – Omar and Khaled Ansari. The three of them had made their living quarters as comfortable as they could. It was a better built hut than the others with a living space which Celia had decorated with patchwork made by Hope Kakwani. The table was the natural, indeed the only place where they could sit and talk. Khaled was usually the first home after his day's work patching up the buildings, dealing with pests or supervising the plumbing project. He'd wash as best he could then join Celia at the table. He was undeniably an attractive man with his curly black hair, koala-bear eyes and gentle smile.

"Why did you choose me, pick on me at the Antonine Baths,

Khaled?" Celia said one sun-baked evening as she finished wiping the day's dust off the make-shift wooden worktop.

"It seems so long ago," Khaled replied, running one hand through his still-damp hair. "I'd like to say it was because I fancied you."

Celia stopped fussing with cloth and duster and looked Khaled in the eye. Until now both brothers had behaved impeccably towards her. By frequently talking about their wives, at least at first, they were making it clear there would be no impropriety. But the wives had featured less in their conversation of late. They seemed to be fading into the pre-Bir Assaya, pre-typhoid past.

It wouldn't have been unwelcome to Celia if either man had shown interest in her, interest in her as a woman. She had gone beyond just missing Sam. It occurred to her that she might never see him again. She had become so involved with the migrants' lives that she had neglected her own. She felt lonely and undervalued.

"Did you fancy me?" she felt bold enough to ask.

"It wasn't that. I'm still not sure why I went up to you. I'd been boiling with anger about what I'd discovered about the treatment of migrants and I was desperate to tell the outside world."

Celia knew he wouldn't rise to her bait. She'd been silly. Too direct. She tried another approach.

"Do you regret bringing me here, Khaled?"

"Of course I do. I had no idea we would be stuck here."

She wanted to break his resistance.

"It's so difficult here, for a woman," she said. "Look at my hair. Weeks without seeing shampoo or scissors."

Khaled stood up, looked towards the door and window, then with one stride was standing behind Celia.

"Your hair is lovely," he breathed. "Lovely." He put his steady hands on her shoulders, still standing behind her. He was slightly taller than her and he had to bend a fraction so that his mouth was level with her ear.

"You must know how tempted I am," he whispered. "Very tempted."

Their bodies were touching and Celia could feel his broad chest on her back, his knees on the back of her thighs. She bent her arms at the elbow, without turning round, to hold his arms in place where he was squeezing quite hard. She knew that if she turned, he would kiss her. This was a moment she had been longing for. Not that she hadn't had similar thoughts about Omar. She had. But there was something more intense, raw, fervent about Khaled that drew her to him now.

To make the moment last, Celia did not turn but stroked his strong hands.

"Were you happy before, Khaled?"

"What do you mean?" He paused. "Until a year or so ago I was happy. A privileged life, I suppose with a lawyer father and an ambitious mother. You saw the family house. Big for Tunisia. Comfortable. Omar and I were spoiled now I come to think about it. I married my first girl-friend – well almost my first – a distant cousin. It is very common here. We were so young. We agreed to delay having children until we were more established. The training for a civil engineer goes on for ever. Then came my delayed military service when for the first time I met young Tunisians from all over the country. I found we had been told lie after lie by the regime, that a whole generation outside the capital had been neglected or worse – discriminated against."

Celia held onto his wrists and tilted her head backwards. He had always been reluctant to talk about himself until now.

"It's good to touch you, to hold you," he said. Neither moved for some seconds.

"I was scared for the first few days here because I thought they would inevitably come looking for me, the army that is. Eventually I told the major why I was so nervous. To my surprise he said he was happy to keep me here and would not hand me back even if he could. We've become good friends, the major and I.

"With you I'm frightened for another reason."

"What's that?" she said.

"That I'll lose my self-control, probably lose my heart."

136

"Well, that wouldn't be the end of the world, would it?"

"I don't know, Celia. I don't know. I've told you often about my wife. I'm sure she is being faithful so how could I not be the same?"

As Celia turned round to face Khaled, the door opened and Omar walked in, his white coat unbuttoned, carrying his stethoscope. Celia and Khaled disengaged fast but could not tell whether Omar had seen them holding each other. He certainly made as if he'd seen nothing.

Celia realised that if she was to make a half-decent film report, it would have to be with the major's tacit agreement. This she obtained from him early on, but on the understanding that he would deny he had given his consent if asked. Celia had other practical concerns as well. She wasn't sure how long her batteries would last. And she had no idea as to when or how she could get the story out of the place.

She settled into the camp routine and learned new survival skills. How to live with flies. What could be eaten safely and what not. How to think positively.

She got into the habit of washing economically. The water was in a yellowish plastic tank resting on two poles above a cubicle made of brushwood. It was well-water, slightly insipid to the taste. She wondered where it came from. She remembered Sam telling her about the importance of water to the residents of Bisuli and for the wheat. It was probably water from the same source as Bisuli which wasn't far away. Major Mifsoud said it had a high sulphur content. Each camp inmate was rationed to the equivalent of a lavatory flush. She quickly learned to capture the precious water and use it several times over. She had a debate with herself about the best time for her ablutions. On the one hand, the insects were less of a problem at dawn. But on the other, it was easier to dry off once the sun was up.

It was absurd that such an inhuman camp should be in such a beautiful location. She would sometimes stare for minutes on end at the rising sun when it glowed behind the distant hills edging them with orange thread. As soon as the sun appeared, so did the shadows of the trees surrounding and hiding the camp. On one side, she now saw, there was a deep gulley, a sort of ravine. Major Mifsoud said he had found a scorpion there, six centimetres long. Scorpions, he said, could survive nuclear radiation. Perhaps, he said gloomily, they would inherit the earth.

The black trees were silent witnesses to the suffering of a thousand men and women. When they saw the Mediterranean, after travelling for weeks, the migrants thought their suffering was over. They had left their hungry families and their feuding tribes for a better life in the north. Their flight was across deserts and through mountains, hiding in trucks, living by their wits. They only had the haziest of ideas about Europe. When Celia was able to communicate with them, they told her Europe was the place to go because it was safe. People in Europe, they said, wore shoes all day long. Houses had running water which you could drink and it was free. You could learn to read and write. There was medicine if you were sick. Everyone had work. When Celia asked the men about their fears, they said firstly that the Europeans would be stronger than they were; secondly, that there would be no African women and third, that the food would not be good.

All had paid at least five hundred dollars upfront to come this far. Most knew they had to pay the same again to the people traffickers to cross the Mediterranean. One in eight would die in the attempt. Few understood the dangers – drowning above all. But anything was better than the life they were leaving behind – war, no work, starvation and disease.

The migrants were easy for the Tunisians to spot at the coast or in the towns because they did not speak Arabic. Black skin colours stood out amongst the Mediterranean and Berber faces and complexions. Tunisians prided themselves on their dress. But the migrants arrived with only the clothes on their backs. When there were just a few at the beginning, they were not a problem. They were ignored or given alms. They fended for themselves. They congregated close to where the traffickers operated. Every migrant knew that every other migrant was carrying cash. Sometimes there were fights. Sometimes they succumbed to temptation and stole from market stalls or bakeries or orchards.

At first the public turned a blind eye. But when the crimes became more frequent, when the trickle of humanity became a river, the locals showed their displeasure in no uncertain way. There were traffic accidents. Several were attacked by guard dogs. Suspected thieves were beaten by stall-holders. Citizens in some places were taking the law into their own hands. Even children shouted racist taunts at them.

But it was when tourism was threatened that panic set in. Abdelaziz Ayeb knew he would have support when he insisted the army be used to deal with the problem. Nothing, he said, should put the tourists off. So the migrants were rounded up and sent, in buses and lorries, to Bir Assaya. It was called a temporary holding camp. Celia was prepared to believe it started that way. But once the quarantine order was lifted, what plans had been made for the migrants? Surely someone was planning something?

After the shock had sunk in that she was a virtual prisoner, Celia's first thought was to let Sam know that she was alive. She discussed it with Khaled and Omar who wanted to inform their families, too. To her surprise, they strongly advised against using their mobile phones. They were sure their calls would be monitored. Their suggestion was to persuade the daily food truck driver to take messages out. Khaled was quick to befriend a driver the day after the quarantine was declared. The driver's army pay was miserable and Khaled's cash, in tightly folded new notes conveyed in a handshake, was to ensure a regular courier service to the outside world.

It worked well for Khaled and Omar who soon heard via the driver that their families had received their letters. They were reassured and understood they were not to worry.

Celia however did not have the same quick response. Her first letter to Sam was an apology for her bad behaviour.

139

Darling Sam,

You must be wondering where on earth I am and what I am doing. I hope you haven't been too worried. I can't tell you the detail but by chance I stumbled across a big story when I was in Carthage. Something of a scoop. It desperately needs to be exposed. But there is a delicate complication.

Temporarily (inshallah) I'm stuck with my story for reasons beyond my control. Sorry to be so ambiguous but I'm anxious not to make life more difficult.

I am so sorry for having lost my cool with you the other night and for having said cruel things and for behaving like a child. I only ever wanted to protect you from yourself. Don't you find that it sometimes takes someone else to tell you what you know deep down to be true but don't want to admit? I just couldn't help saying it out loud: you trust too much in your business partner, you really do.

Please, please forgive me. It's none of my business. I want to forget all I said that night. I was a bit stressed out and fretting about finding studio space and the right locations.

I will always love you. As soon as I'm able, I'll join you at the villa.

I hope you found the Febris coin I left for you. At least I think the inscription says Febris? I must have had a premonition when I bought it from a roadside stall because there's a horrible outbreak of typhoid fever where I am.

Do, I beg you, let me know you received this by replying to the PO Box number on the back of the envelope. Letters sent to that address will be brought to me, I'm assured.

With all my fondest, dearest love,
Celia.

When the truck driver had still brought no response, Celia wrote again.

Darling Sam,

A week has gone by and I've still heard nothing. I am so concerned about you. I checked that my first letter was indeed put into the post and that you should have had it two days later at the latest. Other letters posted at the same time arrived safely, so I'm mystified. I hope you haven't left Tunisia on my account. I'm still counting on returning to London with you as planned.

You'll be surprised when eventually I'm able to tell you where I am and why I have to stay! My instinct tells me that it's better that I should keep quiet about it all for the moment.

What worries me more than anything else is us. Have you forgiven me, Sam? I miss you terribly after just a few days. We go so well together, you and I. When I said you should join me making films, I wasn't joking. I know we could work together, live together, love together brilliantly. But the decision is yours, of course, my sweetheart.

If I have no reply to this second letter, I'll stop using this channel though I don't know how to reach you safely by any other.

Please, please reply to the PO Box number. Take care. Take great care.

I love you,

Celia.

Neither letter reached Sam. Ayeb had them on his desk within hours of Khaled handing them to the truck driver.

Celia spent the first three days mostly with the sick. She was, after all, masquerading as a doctor. Omar insisted she take every possible precaution. She tried. She wore a mask, gloves, cap and coat every time she was in the sick huts. But the washing facilities were primitive, the resources non-existent for improvement. How could she perform adequate hand-washing when there was no hot water and when the quality of the cold water was dubious?

She quickly recognised the pattern of typhoid fever. The temperature slowly rising to forty degrees; profuse sweating; gastroenteritis and, strangely, nosebleeds. Sometimes the fever was accompanied by delirium and the patient thrashed around not knowing where he or she was or what they were saying. Celia knew that when the symptoms appeared of internal bleeding there was nothing they could do to prolong life. But she was told over and over again that the migrants wanted her there. She held their hands. She cooled their faces. She wet their lips.

For the first few days she did not visit the rest of the camp unless she was accompanied. When she did start to move around it, she was shocked. She thought she was inured to scenes of hardship and poverty after her many visits to Africa as a journalist. But nothing prepared her for Bir Assaya. One hundred men and women were supposed to sleep in each of the ten flat-roofed huts. As they fell ill they were moved to the cabins reserved for the sick.

Some of the migrants tried to look busy – sweeping, tending fires, creating shade. But their boredom was pervasive and pernicious. Most sat doing nothing, looking resigned, vacant and depressed. These were people brought up in open spaces – herders who walked dozens of miles each day with their cattle; farmers whose plots were scattered as far as the eye could see; hunters who could be gone for days at a time. Forced to seek safety, food and work elsewhere, they now found themselves surrounded by armed guards and barbed wire. These were people on the point of mental and physical breakdown.

The migrants were from different ethnic groups, different tribes and different religions. They could not forget their tribal quarrels even here. Celia found Hope, the lonely Nigerian girl, particularly morose one morning. She waited till she was alone on the bench outside her hut.

"What's wrong, Hope? You're not sick are you?" she asked.

Hope shook her head.

"I am not sick, but someone wants me dead," she said.

She pointed to her precious rag-doll which was under the bench. Sharpened sticks had been pushed into each of its eyes and another through its belly.

Celia embraced the long-legged girl. Hope clung to her and said "I'm not afraid."

Celia found herself alone with Omar after lunch that day. He was resting on his back on the three straw-filled cushions – more like stuffed sacks – on the floor beside the table whilst Celia was drawing giant sized everyday objects for her language class. She had been talking about Hope.

"Why would someone do that to a young girl?" Celia asked him.

"Jealousy," Omar answered. He put his arms behind his head so that he could see Celia better and as he did so, Celia couldn't help noticing that his shirt had pulled out of his trousers exposing a taught stomach with a fluffy nap of dark hair.

"Hope is a marriageable young woman for a man from the same tribe – Yoruba, I think. Perfectly marriageable. She must have been courted – or worse – by many men since arriving here. I expect she's shown her feelings, even if it's only a smile, to one man and told others to keep away. And it's one of those spurned suitors who wants to cast a spell on Hope, through her doll."

"Voodoo?" asked Celia.

"Vodun is what it's called in Nigeria. Spells, though, are usually the business of sorcerers, so perhaps there's one in the camp."

"But Hope told me she was a Christian."

"Christian or not, she would understand she was targeted."

"She's brave. She said she wasn't afraid."

Celia stopped drawing and turned round in her chair to face Omar, then crossed her legs. With one hand she involuntarily ticked her hair behind her ear, a gesture usually foreshadowing something new. Omar held her gaze and, still on the cushions, moved onto his side with his arm bent, one hand supporting his head. When he smiled, the creases on his face made him look older than his years. She started to laugh.

"What's funny?" smiled Omar.

"It's your hair. I can't believe I cut it so badly yesterday. The sides look like the eaves of a roof; there's an overhang."

She uncrossed her legs and knelt in front of Omar, touching the uppermost side of his head, then running her fingers through his hair. Omar lifted his hand and placed it on hers.

"Be careful," he said. "We might regret it if we do anything foolish. And anyway, what about my brother?"

Celia withdrew her hand and returned to the table. Omar, too, got up and put on his white coat. Picking up his stethoscope he said, very quietly, "I'm sorry. Another time."

In her third week at Bir Assaya, as she was helping Omar to nail up old, nylon bread sacks in the glassless windows, Celia thought she had a migraine coming on. A throbbing pain started up behind her forehead. She knew what would come next: nausea. But curiously, this time she noticed pains in her knees and elbows as well. She sat on the end of a patient's bed and rubbed her forehead hard with the tips of her gloved fingers for a minute or so. She felt increasingly queasy and hot. Her ear started to throb. She pulled her mask down to her neck for more air.

"Celia, are you alright?" Omar said, thinking she was just a bit tired.

"I need to go to my room for a moment," she said. She stood up, swayed forwards as if bowing to an unseen dignitary, rocked back to vertical, then crumpled to the floor like a marionette.

Omar lifted her back into a sitting position on the bed, before pushing her head forward between her knees. But her body would not hold the position and she fell sideways first onto the end of the bed, then in a heap on the floor, unconscious. Omar ran to fetch Khaled from just outside the hut. The two of them, for the second time, found themselves carrying Celia by the arms and legs. This time, they were watched by dozens of pairs of eyes. From the sick bay to Celia's hut was about a hundred metres. By the time the distance had been covered, half the inmates of Bir Assaya knew the new lady doctor was ill.

With Omar's expert attention, Celia regained consciousness quite quickly on her own bed. He pressed her to drink some water with sugar dissolved in it. Her pulse was low and her temperature high. Then came the abdominal pains, something he had seen in that camp all too often.

Khaled soaked a tee-shirt in water, wrung it out and gave it to her. Omar motioned Khaled to the door with a nod of his head. There they were out of earshot.

"With the high temperature and the abdominal pain, that's no migraine," he whispered. He looked back at Celia, then at his brother again.

"It's in her favour that she started off a hundred percent

healthier than any of the migrants. On the other hand, it's unlikely that she has any of their antibodies. I'm convinced some of the people here have developed protection against the *salmonella typhi*. Otherwise our casualties would be far greater."

"Are you sure it's typhoid?" murmured Khaled, hopefully.

"Quite sure. Let's put her on ciprofloxacin straight away." Omar's voice dropped a bit more. "I feel guilty that I allowed her to stay so long with the sick. She didn't need to. She's not a doctor. Same goes for you, Khaled. You need not have come back."

"What was that phrase by Pascal that we learnt at school? *'The heart has its reasons which reason does not understand.'* Doing nothing about this was not an option. You know that, too, don't you?" On the other side of the room, Celia shivered audibly. Omar pulled a brown army blanket over her.

Celia responded well to the drug. After five days she was up and about though weak as a baby, as she put it. What puzzled Omar was that Celia had been meticulously careful about her food and drink. She drank only bottled water as the migrants did. The one area she and the others didn't think carefully about was washing. Everyone used the same well after which the camp was named. Major Mifsoud was adamant the water was pure and Omar's primitive tests showed that as far as he was concerned it was safe for washing. He wasn't to know that the well drew its water from the same water table as Bisuli. Or that *salmonella typhi* could lie dormant for two thousand years.

The camp atmosphere changed when that fateful instruction was given to isolate it from the rest of the world. The complex of antagonisms diminished in the face of a common predicament. The hostility that Celia had felt at first from Major Mifsoud and the soldiers faded as they realised the awfulness of their situation. Mifsoud was deeply impressed by Celia's determination to survive. He observed her talking sometimes for hours at a time to groups of migrants, he presumed to boost their morale. He saw her making notes about individual cases or so he thought. As for her filming, which she did regularly until her batteries ran down, he turned a blind eye as promised.

Even before Celia had fully recovered her strength, she was discussing with Omar and Khaled how the fly population could be controlled. Whether flies were the culprits as regards typhus or not, they certainly carried other unpleasant bacteria.

With Mifsoud's blessing and under Khaled's direction, the healthy migrants were organised to rebuild the camp's sanitation system. Cess pits were dug at the lowest point, which was fortunately at the camp perimeter. Ten sets of covered latrines were constructed, one set for each hut, and they were then linked underground to the cess pits. Next to the latrines, the washing facilities were up-graded. Extra wash-basins were made out of oil-drums. The waste water was used in the latrines. All dirty and fresh water was properly covered for the first time.

The camp kitchen was the next to receive Khaled and Celia's attention, always with the aim of stopping flies from settling on food. The female domestic house fly produces between one hundred and two hundred eggs in her fifteen day life. In the propitious conditions at Bir Assaya, the fly population was increasing exponentially. The building was in no way hermetically sealed, so fly screens were out of the question. Celia advocated more smoke in the kitchen to deter the insects. One of the migrants came up with a better idea. He suspended a sort of horse's tail, made of straw, above the food preparation area. He somehow attached string to the tail via a pulley so that the contraption could swish back and forth, not only deterring the insects but also providing ventilation. Khaled, who was often surprisingly impractical considering he was a civil engineer, said he had heard that farmers in France mixed the mushroom "amenita muscaria" – red with small white spots – with milk and left the mixture in the kitchen for unwitting insects. It contained a dangerous alkaloid, lethal to flies.

"Interesting, Khaled, but how do you suggest we find mushrooms if we can't leave the camp?" Celia said.

"I don't know why," she added, "but I've never been enthusiastic about mushroom hunting. But today I'd willingly hunt for them if it meant we could get out of this festering hole."

"I was forgetting how nice mushrooms can be," replied Khaled. "I remember in France we used to find yellow chanterelles. Now, fried with a little garlic and salt…"

Fantasising about food was a pleasant amusement at first, but after two months was not so funny. The others quickly told him to stop.

Khaled was in favour of rebuilding the huts and enlarging them with stone from the abandoned quarry outside Bisuli, where Celia said there was no shortage. But without cement or any of its ingredients, the project was impossible. Mifsoud was not prepared, in any case, to allow working parties to leave the camp for any reason. He was a loyal, professional soldier and had his orders. It is true he had suspected his subordinates at first of trying to undermine his authority but that was all finished. The dangers now facing them all – officers, soldiers, civilians and migrants – were the same. No-one was to leave the camp and no-one would.

Obedience, for Major Mifsoud, was what the army was all about. He would go further when he was in a talkative mood and say that it was what life was all about. His family was proudly middle-class and had been involved in the olive-oil business for generations. Their bottling and wholesale trading company in Sfax was obstinately old-fashioned. Tradition was everything, down to the printed labels which had not changed for years. Innovation was unwelcome *chez "Mifsoud Frères."* His two elder brothers were always destined to take over the family business. The Mifsouds were unquestioning supporters of all authorities – the mosque, the mayor, the governor – because the authorities, in the Mifsoud view, held the world together.

There was no room in the family firm for Ali, so with his father's encouragement he joined the army. The hierarchy was reassuring to someone who lacked initiative. Promotion had been slow. Ali reached his ceiling at the rank of major and it was clear to all save him that he would go no further. It rankled that younger men were being promoted from below him in the army list. It upset him that they were nearly always university graduates from more privileged backgrounds. What is more, they tended to be the very officers who went around questioning authority. There was something wrong with the system, Ali Mifsoud was beginning to believe.

He had been told that his selection to command the holding camp for migrants was a sign 'that he was held in high esteem'. He had been told that he had 'the special qualities they were looking for'. His administrative and support role experience coupled with stamina and 'unfailing achievement of annual objectives' marked him out – so they said.

But as the weeks rolled by, Ali Mifsoud began to have doubts about his commanders' intentions. After his weekly report in mid-November, he tentatively asked to be put more in the picture about developments in HQ thinking. Nothing happened. A fortnight later, as he realised he was being left to rot and as typhoid continued to take its toll despite flies being controlled, he found the courage to raise the question of what would happen next, once again. The edge in Mifsoud's voice this time obliged the junior officer at HQ to transfer him to the Minister of Defence's *chef de cabinet*. Mifsoud hated taking orders from civilians but this man spoke for the minister himself and who knows who else above him. The conversation, which the major started with such high hopes, was not a success.

"Major Mifsoud, apparently you have a problem."

"Well Sir, now that we have been operating this temporary camp for over six months, I wondered…"

"What did you wonder, Major," interjected the superior voice down the line.

"I am, Sir, as I am sure you know, holding just under a thousand African migrants in a temporary camp. The conditions, Sir, are not ideal."

"In what way could they be ideal, Major? Tell me that. We are not in the leisure business now, are we?"

"No, Sir. Of course not. But total isolation was imposed because of the sickness that broke out and this has imposed some stress on my men who are wondering about their families, about leave and so on."

"We've been pleased with the way you have carried out your task, Major."

"I was wondering, that's to say my officers were wondering as well…about the time-table."

"Time-table, Major?" the *chef de cabinet* asked sardonically.

"Well, Sir, what the plans are for moving the migrants either back to where they came from or to better accommodation. We've improved sanitation here but the typhoid outbreak continues unchecked. The sick really need to be looked after in hospitals, in my opinion."

"I am surprised at you, Major. You are not paid to have opinions and you know that. Policy and strategy are determined here, with the most senior authorities in the country. The most senior people, you understand?"

"Yes, Sir. But it would be useful for me to have a rough idea of for how long we will all be in quarantine, as it were."

"Until the problem sorts itself out, Major. Continue to report weekly."

Ali Mifsoud replayed that conversation to himself over and over again. It was interesting that the *chef de cabinet* had talked of "the most senior people." Perhaps the young doctor and his brother were right when they kept referring to Abdelaziz Ayeb. Perhaps it was the mega-rich, in practice, who ran the country. Or at least the country was run for them.

It was simple. Either the authorities, Mifsoud said to himself, genuinely did not understand the gravity of the situation in the camp. Or they did – and were cynically ignoring it. Mifsoud had made it quite clear in his weekly reports, that the situation at Bir Assaya was untenable; that there could well be large scale loss of life because of the epidemic. All to no avail. He sometimes had the impression that his superiors were happy at what was happening. Even for a loyal, long-serving military officer with an unblemished record, it was difficult to believe this. Yet the facts spoke for themselves. He had, to all intents and purposes, been abandoned. Bir Assaya had been closed as a barracks for years and years. It was not even marked on the maps. He had totally inadequate buildings and supplies. His men were not being rotated. He also had civilians, non-migrants, incarcerated at the camp. His communications were ridiculously restricted, as if there was a war on. He had sympathised at first with the official attitude towards the migrants. They were upsetting, it could not be denied. And it was disturbing to be brought face to face with the results of man's inhumanity to man. Something had to be done.

But this was not the way to solve the problem. Deep down, Ali Mifsoud had a clear set of values. He considered himself a good Muslim despite failing too often with his religious obligations. Although the migrants had entered the country illegally, they meant no harm. He had eventually been able to communicate with some of them. The conflicts from which they were fleeing were horrific, even for a soldier like him.

"Great pain urges all animals and has urged them during countless generations, to make the most violent and diversified efforts to escape from the cause of their sufferings." So wrote Darwin.

The same was true for human beings. It applied to Major Mifsoud's migrants. But it also applied to Major Mifsoud.

CHAPTER 14

To relieve the boredom of the migrants and to improve morale, Celia and Khaled, with Major Mifsoud's support, began organising classes. Originally the idea had been to teach just English and French but it soon became apparent that there was a huge demand for reading, writing and other life skills, too. The classes were extraordinarily successful. Celia and Khaled learnt that it was impractical to teach more than fifty people at a time. Even with that number, many of them were too remote from the teacher. The ones at the back couldn't hear. Fortunately, not all could attend. Some were sick. Some women were too shy to participate. Some felt it would be beyond them. One or two had problems of pride. They would not admit that they could benefit from classes. So they did not come.

From the time they had arrived at Bir Assaya, Khaled, Omar and Celia had been frustrated by the difficulty of communicating with the migrants. Cumbersome combinations of English, French, Arabic and sign language were developed. This led to some welcome moments of relief when Khaled, for example, tapped the side of his nose – a typical Mediterranean gesture – to indicate how clever one of his pupils was. The student concerned, a trader from Chad who took himself very seriously, thought that it meant that he smelt bad and took umbrage. He spent the day in a sulk and sat at the back of the class.

On another occasion, Celia tried to explain that month and moon had two different meanings in English. For her Swahili speakers, however, they meant the same thing. Time was an approximate notion for them. It was somehow more infinite, less dimensional and less controllable. For some of the West Africans the moon represented Mawu, the daughter of the Creator. This was, she admitted to her eager students, all very confusing. She urged them not to give up trying to understand English. They needed to be patient. It rang a bell when she said patience was a virtue. One of the students, Petrus Nalumeno, was a Swahili-speaking tribesman. Curiously, he was entirely unselfconscious. *The lion who walks slowly eats meat*, he said. Celia was puzzled by the proverb. Undaunted, Petrus explained it by getting on all fours and imitating a stalking cat giving rise to long applause from the happy class.

Determination to make the classes worthwhile increased with each depressing communication between Major Mifsoud and his H.Q. For as long as there was a suspicion of typhoid, the camp remained in quarantine. The major, like Omar and Khaled, was convinced that this was to protect Abdelaziz Ayeb's tourism investments more than anything else.

The soldiers delivering food to the camp each day were conscripts from the Manouba barracks just outside Tunis and worked in pairs. The major had already gained their confidence long before Celia arrived. This was easier than he expected. For one thing, he knew their barracks very well. The preceding five years of his army career had been spent there. He knew the sergeant-major and his battered wife. He knew many of the junior officers, their nick-names and their stories. He knew every inch of the parade ground. He even knew the name of the regimental cat with white boots – Katoushka.

The conscripts assigned the Bir Assaya task were from all over the country but had several things in common. Shortage of cash, boredom and a depressing lack of jobs led the list. None of them wanted to be where they were. None of them thought National Service was necessary. With each brief meeting, Major Mifsoud learnt that morale at the barracks was poor and getting worse. Interestingly, this had happened with the arrival of a new colonel who had a relaxed, 'modern' attitude to discipline. He thought the army ought to be in step with society. He wanted all ranks to stop saluting him and the other officers outside barracks. There was less emphasis on punishment and more on reward. The Commanding Officer's daily parade of miscreants was suspended. Justice was dispensed by the sergeant-major instead. Decisions, not surprisingly, were arbitrary and often unfair. Nobody listened to the soldiers' complaints. Nobody seemed to mind that the men were unhappy.

On the administrative side, army regulations were being ignored to a shocking degree, the major thought. Orders were being carried out only when soldiers agreed with them, or so it seemed. Bureaucracy had always been bad but now the backlog of paperwork was measured in months. Inventories were not being checked. Leave wasn't being certified by superior officers. Staff cars were being used by officers' wives. Items went missing. Nobody cared.

Celia, Omar and Khaled had been increasingly concerned about obtaining a change of clothes. It was a shock for Celia, who thought she was a seasoned traveller, to see how white cotton turned grey with primitive washing facilities. The change of trousers she had picked up at Sam's villa had become torn, stained and above all too big. Celia reckoned she had lost several kilos. Because she had so few clothes, Celia was condemned to washing them before going to bed and wearing them straightaway in the morning. Her clothes never had the chance to dry properly. The result after a few weeks was that everything smelt musty or, as Omar tactlessly put it, like wet horses.

The major was surprisingly sympathetic about the clothes problem when Celia raised it. He knew there was a military clothing store at the Manouba barracks and, by exactly what means Celia never discovered, he had the conscript food-truck drivers bring him three complete sets of kit. Celia was delighted with her good quality underwear, all made in Tunisia she noticed, and her crisp, green uniform. Omar and Khaled were less delighted about wearing uniform but acknowledged that they both smelt much better.

It had been the major's abiding concern in recent years that the army was going soft. In Bir Assaya, he had plenty of time to think about it.

When he had first joined, the politicians had left the army alone, had valued its special status, seeing it as a sort of ultimate guarantor of the State. But in recent years the President and his all-powerful ruling party had been putting more and more pressure on the armed forces – the Army in particular – to become yet another cog in the repressive political machine. Major Mifsoud was sure that the President had kept the Army under-resourced on purpose with out-dated, second-hand US Army surplus equipment. Whenever the President saw the remotest threat to his position, he stamped on it hard and at once. Any minister who made the mistake of being popular was shuffled out of the cabinet in double-quick time. Any newspaper editor who ventured an opinion at variance with the President's, mysteriously lost his job. Any Army officer who was not conspicuous in his support of the party was never promoted.

There were, the major consoled himself, a couple of very senior officers who had managed to keep low profiles outside the Army, who had escaped the President's notice. They never allowed him the chance to find fault with them. They kept up the old tradition of being one step removed from the propaganda machine and the political mafia. They were keeping their powder dry.

But they were the exceptions. The rest of the Army seemed to be losing its sense of values. Major Mifsoud no longer minded about promotion, no longer minded much what his fellow officers thought of him, indeed no longer minded much about the Army. He was disillusioned. And the longer he found himself incarcerated at Bir Assaya, the more determined he became to free the migrants and to expose what was being done. With the others, he had devised Plan Exodus, which was well-thought out, sophisticated and bold.

The first step was to write false 'orders' to the colonel at Manouba barracks concerning a fleet of buses. The 'orders' were to be from the Minister's *chef de cabinet* at the Ministry of Defence and after being so badly treated by him on the phone, the major took a particular delight in writing them. He told Celia that it was the act that had given him the most pleasure in six months. The 'orders' were classified 'Secret'. The tone and terminology were exactly what the colonel in Manouba would expect: peremptory, precise and not to be queried.

The problem was getting the orders, (there were two separate messages), onto the military intranet or Milnet when he had no computer at the camp. He had been hoping that he could entrust the task to the conscripts that he had been cultivating. It was risky. A couple of them, the major reckoned, would have been willing to put the messages onto the system at the right times in exchange for a modest reward and promotion recommendations. But the job was simply too important. One slip, one last minute change of heart would prove fatal to the whole of Plan Exodus.

The idea for the abandonment of the camp had been taking shape at meetings after dinner every night in Major Mifsoud's office. The crucial meeting however was in the last week of March. Omar and Celia were disagreeing about when to tell the migrants that they were working to liberate them.

"It isn't so important," Khaled said. "They will be overjoyed whenever they hear the news whether it's a week before or the night before. The question I worry about is where they can be taken."

"I'll tell you in a minute," said Celia. "A lot of work has been done on this thanks to Major Mifsoud."

"It will be no mean feat convincing the migrants that we are not repatriating them," said Khaled. "And getting them onto the buses might not be as easy as you think."

"I don't see that as a problem," the major said. "They will accept any way we offer of getting out of this camp. For them it's a prison where they have seen friends die. Anything would be better."

"Are you sure we will be sent twenty buses?" asked Celia. "Won't they be suspicious at Mandouba?"

"The orders to the colonel are absolutely clear and the colonel will execute them," said the major. "Of that I have no doubt. The buses are to be ready, fully fuelled by midday on 9 April with twenty trained drivers. He has been told it is for a realistic exercise: an evacuation in aid of the civil power. Side arms are to be worn by the drivers but not loaded. Each bus is to carry twenty litres of drinking water. The second message I have devised, to be issued on 8 April, will contain precise movement orders for the drivers. The drivers and buses will return to barracks eight hours later." The major sounded confident.

"So not one, but two order messages have to be sent on two different dates," said Celia.

"Exactly," the major said. "But I'm not yet sure how to do this. I have not wanted to bother you with this before but for the past ten days the entrance on the road to our camp has been under constant surveillance by what I assume are police – they're never in uniform – in a series of different cars. In someone's eyes I'm obviously not to be trusted."

"Correct me if I'm wrong," said Omar, "but isn't it rather odd that one branch of our security forces should be watching another?"

"We've never had much time for the police, particularly the secret police. They're a law unto themselves. Difficult to explain."

"I'm an outsider – and I don't speak Arabic," said Celia. " But before I became a virtual prisoner here, I could feel there was a lot of tension in the air. The police were everywhere. People seemed so nervous of speaking, even about hiring a film studio. Perhaps they were nervous of speaking to a foreigner, especially when there was a large portrait of the President staring at them, like a challenge. The mere fact that they feel it is necessary to have portraits of the President everywhere is actually a sign of insecurity, isn't it?"

"I have not thought before about the President's portraits," said the major. "I suppose we have become so accustomed to them that they are part of the scenery. What I am sure about is that our internal security forces have been *"crispé"* for many months now."

"On edge?" said Celia.

"Yes. On edge." He paused. "I'm still left with the problem of getting these messages onto the Milnet."

"I have an idea," said Omar. "We ask the supply truck driver – it doesn't matter which one – to deliver another body to the morgue for an autopsy. It has become a routine, sadly. But this time the coffin will contain a live body. Neither driver nor escort will want to open

156

it or even be near it. They know we have an epidemic of some sort here. Breathing inside the coffin can be arranged by some simple carpentry. Basically, holes in the side."

"Who will be in the coffin?" said Celia.

"Me," said Omar. "For the good reason that I know Hedi Soukni, the director of the morgue. There might be a difficult moment on arrival at the morgue, especially if Hedi is not there. But when I find him, I know he will help. We'll go to the barracks in Manouba together. Once inside, we'll need guidance from you, Ali, about the best computer terminal to use, the passwords and so on."

The others were momentarily lost for words. The idea was clearly dangerous – but good.

"Will you stay in Manouba or return to us? If so, how?" said Celia.

"In a coffin. The same way I went."

"Desperate times, desperate measures," said Celia. "What do you all think?"

No-one dissented. The major came back to the relocation problem. It was one thing to take the migrants out of the camp but quite another to relocate them.

"I have responsibility for these people," the major said. "I must be sure in my mind that we are not condemning them to an even worse fate; that they will have some sort of future; some sort of decent life."

"Of course I have been thinking about that," said Celia. "It's been my preoccupation for months. I suppose I became a journalist in the first place because I had a conscience. Same goes for my film making. For all the long days that I was so ill that I couldn't lift my head from the pillow, I thought of nothing else. I have a special attachment to these people now. Having lived with them, having filmed them, having taught them, having heard for myself what they have been through, I am determined to do something. When Khaled first approached me – Major Mifsoud, I have already told you this, so it is no longer a secret between us – when Khaled first approached

157

me six months' ago, it was to ask for my help in publicising the plight of the migrants to the world at large."

Khaled turned towards Major Mifsoud who returned the look with a shrug of his shoulders and a sort of a smile.

Celia continued. "It just so happens there's an unusual way we can do this. I know the area outside the camp because I have an archaeologist friend who has been working at a Roman site near here. With Major Mifsoud's help, I have been in contact with him."

Omar and Khaled raised their eyebrows, looking first at each other then at Celia and the major. Khaled broke the silence.

"Good," he said. "Very good."

Celia then outlined what would happen with helpful interjections from the major.

Khaled had wanted to discuss things with the migrants or at least their representatives. The trouble was, there were no recognised representatives. Even if individuals had been selected, they wouldn't have been able to speak with authority for others. On an issue as fundamental as this, the migrants would have been highly suspicious of each other. Tribal and ethnic hostilities were never far beneath the surface.

Khaled also made the point that if the plan was for the migrants to enter Europe illegally, those that helped them would be accessories to a criminal offence. And the people traffickers, he said, should be exposed and punished, not encouraged.

Omar was worried about the migrants' vulnerability. Morally and physically, they were poorly equipped to survive, even in a benign environment like Tunisia. And if they carried some of their sickness to hitherto unaffected populations, he would never forgive himself.

Slowly, a solution emerged from the late night discussions in the poorly-lit, stuffy office. It was high risk but worth it. It depended for success on individuals rising to the challenges of their lives, on estimates of how some key players like Hedi Soukni, the director of the morgue, would react and, on luck. But what was there to lose? Anything would be better than staying prisoner in Bir Assaya.

There were innumerable practical problems to solve. Celia was not surprised to find that Omar and Khaled's phone batteries had been completely dead for months. Both men had managed to send brief messages to their families via the food truck drivers to say that they were safe and well. The only communication which Celia was sure had reached Sam, was a text message sent from a truck driver's phone, thanks to Major Mifsoud. It had to be succinct.

'sam, am alive but trapped with cohort migrants and typhoid. forced quarantine but exodus 10/4 in 20 buses. eta your site hora quinta. tell auntie, thunderer, grauniad etc. lol c.'

Sam had explained Roman time-telling one Sunday afternoon in London. They divided daylight into twelve equal parts. The parts were obviously longer in the summer than the winter. She felt fairly sure that *hora quinta* would cover the mid-morning period. Celia was less sure about the size of a cohort; but it certainly wasn't more than a thousand and it might be a bit less.

Sam's text message reply had to be equally brief:

'celia, thank god you're ok. Was so worried. Can guarantee you all best reception. Sam.'

As predicted, neither the young driver nor his escort wanted much to do with the coffin on the second of April when told that it was a disease victim to be taken straight to Dr Hedi Soukni at the morgue. Khaled and Major Mifsoud loaded it carefully into the otherwise empty truck. The two over-dressed young men in the unmarked car outside the camp gates peered closely at the army truck as it turned into the road. One of them looked at his watch and made a note. The same truck came and left at about the same time every day so there was nothing suspicious as far as the men in the car were concerned.

Inside the coffin, Omar felt he was more comfortable than the conscripts in the front. The worst bump he felt, of many, was on arrival at the morgue when the two soldiers couldn't be rid of the coffin quickly enough. It was dropped unceremoniously onto the marble slab in reception.

He worried that the soldiers would stay whilst Hedi opened the coffin. In case of trouble, Omar had borrowed Major Mifsoud's revolver. Using both hands, he now slid back the safety catch whilst holding the gun under his leg to muffle any click. With any luck, the mere sight of him suddenly sitting up in the box with a loaded pistol pointed towards them, would give him a few seconds' advantage.

Insulated by rolls of old towel and grey but clean bed sheets, Omar could hear little of what was passing outside. He heard some steps, some voices, then nothing. He judged the soldiers had left. He could feel his heart racing as he gripped the gun in two perspiring hands. He had to react as swiftly as humanly possible. His life would depend on one scissor-like movement. He tried to control his breathing but he could now feel the effects of the lack of oxygen: headache, dizziness, and dry-mouth. The seconds seemed like minutes. The noises stopped.

It crossed his mind that he could easily be put into cold storage. On the other hand he reckoned Hedi would want to find out quickly whether this was another typhus case. Omar took a calculated risk. He knocked upwards on the wooden coffin lid three times. Then three times more, but harder.

Hedi was in the adjoining room making final adjustments to his green surgical gown and mask when, stupefied, he heard noises from the coffin. He jumped an inch off the ground as if he'd been given an electric shock. He looked left and right round the ante-room in case he was mistaken. He stared wide-eyed at the clothes hanging in a small cupboard by the open window. As they swayed on the rail, for a split second he wondered if there was a person concealed behind the jacket and beige trousers. He pulled his surgical mask down so hard that somehow the elastic caught one branch of his spectacles which now sat skew-whiff on his nose, distorting his vision.

"Hedi?" The voice was muffled as if through a tube of rolled-up paper.

"Hedi?"

He cautiously walked to the door and the coffin on the slab beyond it. He then quickly turned round and locked the door behind him. He was not in the habit of talking to the dead.

"Is there someone in there?" Feeling foolish, Hedi adjusted his glasses and moved a step closer to the closed wooden box.

"Yes, there is. Me."

Hedi again looked over both shoulders.

"Who is 'me'?" he said to the coffin, more softly this time.

"Who do you say you are?"

"Omar. Omar from La Marsa. For pity's sake, let me out of this thing. I'm boiled alive in here."

By force of habit and without thinking, Hedi laboriously pulled on a pair of surgical gloves from a box at the end of the slab.

"Please Hedi."

"Right. Here you are." He undid the clips at the side of the coffin and stood back as Omar sat up, blinking, with the pistol in his right hand.

"*El hamdou lillah!* Praise be to God!" Hedi said, raising both his arms slightly. "For an awful moment I thought I was hallucinating."

Omar was still waving the pistol in the air.

"Put that thing down. Don't be ridiculous. Omar, what the hell are you doing here?" Hedi helped him up. Omar was stiff. Climbing out of the coffin was awkward and needed a chair, held steady on the shiny tile floor by Hedi. Finally the two stood facing each other.

"I'm pleased to see you, Hedi, you can't imagine. It's a long story."

Omar had feared he might have difficulty securing Hedi's cooperation. He was, after all, hoping to involve him in the commission of several different crimes at once. He was being asked to put his career on the line. But Omar's prediction of his fellow doctor's reaction was absolutely right. Hedi did not hesitate to cooperate. Opportunities for a humble provincial morgue director to do something of real humanitarian value, on the wider stage, came, Hedi thought, but once a lifetime. This was his moment.

Accessing the barracks at seven-thirty in the evening as two doctors was easy. They did not even need to switch on the blue light that they had fixed onto the roof of Hedi's car. Omar wore a white coat. Hedi carried a folder of papers with a blank death certificate on top. The duty guard waved them through with scarcely a second glance and returned to his TV. The major's directions were completely accurate. The computer in the adjutant's office responded immediately to the password which had not been changed in a year. Whilst Hedi kept watch, Omar typed up the imaginary orders from the Ministry of Defence. He was almost ready when Hedi said,

"Hide. Quick. Someone's coming." As he spoke he switched off the light at the door. Omar just had time to log off the Milnet but not to shut the computer down.

Seconds later, the adjutant came striding down the corridor, humming. He opened the door noisily, switched on the light and flung a newspaper into the waste-paper basket not two metres from where Omar was hiding the other side of a tall metal filing cabinet. Omar could not see Hedi, who was behind the curtains. Omar put his finger round the trigger of the revolver in the pocket of his white coat. Once again he felt his pulse rate rise and the perspiration stand out on his forehead. He was not good at this sort of thing. He hadn't fired a gun since his military service ten years ago. He hadn't even shot a rabbit. But this mission was too important to fail. A military officer's clerical assistant was not to be allowed to get in the way. All Omar could see of the man was his lower half.

"Oh no! I don't believe it. I forgot to switch off my terminal when I left," the adjutant said out loud in Arabic.

He sat in front of the screen. Omar was convinced he would click onto Milnet out of habit. But he didn't. He exited all programmes and closed his terminal down, tapping on the keys loudly.

"How could I be so stupid! It will be my third security breach in a month!"

He yawned and lay back in his chair for a moment.

"I'll lose a day's pay. What the hell," he mumbled.

He opened a drawer beside the computer, fished out a key and unlocked a cupboard behind his swivel chair. Omar heard the cork slurp out of the bottle, heard the liquid poured into the glass and caught the unmistakeable smell of whisky.

"To our new colonel," the adjutant toasted.

Must be lonely, thought Omar, to speak so much to himself.

There was a long "ahh" noise as the spirit was swallowed. The adjutant put the bottle back, locked the cupboard, switched out the light and closed the door.

Ten minutes later, the message sent, Omar and Hedi were able to note down from the adjutant's notice board the phone numbers (direct lines) for the Head of the Gendarmerie and the provincial Governor. Might well come in useful, Omar said to himself.

Omar passed the night with Hedi and his family. He found dinner extremely awkward. He was under scrutiny from an understandably curious wife and son. He had not eaten so well in six months and could not resist taking second helpings of everything. Hedi explained that his old friend had just completed a long trip and was exhausted. Omar apologised and said he hoped they didn't mind if he went straight to bed after dinner. Before sinking into the most comfortable bed of his life, Omar used Hedi's mobile phone to send another cryptic text from Celia to Sam. He finally sent 'coming home soon' messages to his own wife and Khaled's.

At eight o'clock the next morning, the coffin was on its way back to Bir Assaya. Hedi loaded it empty into the covered truck where Omar was waiting to climb into it.

Dr Hedi Soukni felt rumpled and bristly. He returned to his disordered office in the morgue and sighed as he sat on the couch in front of his desk. The mandatory portrait of the President, looking smug with his grin and dyed hair, stared down at him. As he stared back at the baneful image a fat blow-fly flew onto the electric blue bars of the insect grill on the filing cabinet and sizzled.

Hedi hadn't been able to sleep more than a few hours the previous night after returning from the barracks. He was probably now up to his ears in trouble. But he had no regrets. What was happening to those hundreds of migrants cooped up in huts in what Omar said were appalling conditions was scandalous but not entirely surprising. There was scant respect for the human rights of Tunisians these days let alone defenceless African migrants.

He twisted on the couch as he remembered the autopsy he had carried out on the female lawyer, a well-known dissident, who had been brought to him a week earlier in some secrecy by her family. After his examination he had no doubt in concluding that she had died from torture, deliberate neglect and denial of medical care in prison.

Since his facility was the closest to the Mornaguia prison in Tunis, Dr Soukni received most of those who died there. He had of course noticed how the numbers of political prisoners or suspected terrorist detainees dying in mysterious circumstances had increased in recent months. He had noticed the lengths to which the prison authorities went to disguise real causes of death. It made his job increasingly hard. One political prisoner was presented to him as a suicide. Yet there were clear signs that he had been manacled at the time of death. He had learned to be particularly suspicious of heart failures in otherwise healthy young political prisoners. Electric shocks left no bruises. Nor did suspension from cell doors. Or near drowning. Or being left naked.

Torture was bad enough. But much, much more was now rotten with the regime. The mould was spreading insidiously but exponentially in the neglected fruit bowl that was Tunisia. It's strange that disease can lie dormant for years then unexpectedly flare up and be lethal.

He leant forward and put his head in his hands. Now that he thought about it, it was the increasing sense of repression that angered him most; that he couldn't say what he wanted; that no one felt able to talk freely. He bitterly resented the fact that the newspaper from France that he most enjoyed reading was not on sale when it contained a news item or article that the regime didn't approve of. And he was furious that one internet site after another was blocked. What right had they to do this? It was no way to live.

What Omar had said the night before about the malevolent influence of Abdelaziz Ayeb was so true. But he was not the only sinister figure in Tunisia. He was part of a mafia, a gang of ruthless individuals often related to the ruling family and using bribery and corruption to enrich themselves. Fear was the means they achieved their ends.

The country had always lived with patronage. But what Hedi Soukni saw now went way beyond that. The rotting regime mirrored the infected camp he'd just learnt about from Omar. He had had enough.

He sat up and looked at the portrait on the wall again. He walked up to it, raised his arms – and lifted it off the wall. Carrying it over to the other side of the room, he leant it against a cupboard, upside down. He suddenly felt liberated.

Much later that morning, when Hedi was starting on his backlog of paperwork, he heard the unmistakeable clack-clack of female footsteps on the concrete path outside. He opened the door to an attractive, European woman.

"Dr Hedi Soukni? I'm so pleased to meet you. My name is Alison Grainger. I wonder if you can help me."

"Do come in. Please."

After the routine exchange of pleasantries, Alison said,

"I am looking for a missing person. A white Englishwoman in her mid-thirties. A film director called Celia Purchas."

"You are welcome to inspect the bodies here, Madame, but to my certain knowledge I have no Englishwoman in my cold store. Or in my records."

"That's a relief. But let me explain what brings me to see you in particular. How I have your name."

Hedi did not recognise the first name Alison mentioned – Dr Zarrouk. The second name however – Dr Farhat Chebbi, director of the pathology lab in Tunis – brought instant recognition. Then when she pronounced Omar Ansari's name, Hedi could scarcely believe it.

But he was more than slightly suspicious about this graceful, good-looking foreigner unexpectedly seeking him out. Was she really acting of her own accord? Or had she been put up to this by State Security or Abdelaziz Ayeb or who knows what other organisation?

"You say that the person you are looking for – what did you say her name was?"

"Celia. Celia Purchas."

"You say she was a friend of a friend?"

"Yes. A man, an archaeologist actually."

"Why is he not doing the searching?"

"He's incredibly busy preparing for a big media event at Bisuli."

"Ah," said Hedi, still somewhat puzzled. This was not surprising. The links between Celia last being seen in a doctor's car with a La Marsa Renault Garage sign on it, via a shoulder surgeon, his friend Omar, a pathology lab director and now himself were extraordinary. But they were credible to Hedi who was anyway in the mood to speak out, to unburden himself. He felt able to be honest with the lady.

"Omar left here in a coffin several hours ago. But he was very much alive!"

It took Hedi another half hour to describe what he suspected the situation to be at Bir Assaya; that up to a thousand migrants were being held there illegally in appalling conditions; that typhoid had broken out. He said Omar had several times mentioned there was an English journalist, a woman, stuck with them. He said that the order for the migrants to be rounded up, then to be put in an abandoned camp and left there in isolation, came from Abdelaziz Ayeb. Hedi described his sinister influence, especially with the police, with whom Hedi dealt a lot professionally.

Alison had her first convincing evidence that Celia was alive. She took out her mobile phone to ring Sam.

"Please don't use the phone. They are all monitored. Any important information you send by phone will be in Ayeb's hands within hours. It is imperative that no word at all about what we are doing should reach him. Nothing at all."

"Of course. How silly of me. I keep forgetting. You have been incredibly helpful. I have so much to tell Dr. Glover that I am becoming lightheaded. Of course, I'll keep quiet until I see him. I must drive straight back to Bisuli now. They have to prepare for visitors!" Alison said.

"You will be shocked by my ignorance but even though I have lived in this country all my life, I don't know where Bisuli is."

"You soon will," said Alison, smiling.

CHAPTER 15

S ince her meeting with the director of the morgue, Alison had been thinking about what she had learnt. Not for a moment had she thought that what started out as feminine curiosity about a woman called Celia, would lead to her coming across a humanitarian scandal that would affect her for the rest of her life.

She felt a need to clear her head as she drove in a loop round the south of the city of Tunis, passing the Bardo Museum where she had been forced to spend many hours as a girl looking at the mosaics. She had revisited the extraordinary building with Sam as a guide and realised how much she simply hadn't understood as a teenager because it had not been properly explained. She thought Sam would still be at Bisuli even though it was getting late.

Bisuli was a hive of activity when she drove in. Awnings were being installed to shade the media's seats and the various camera positions. A stage had been built at the far end of the amphitheatre. A booming sound system was already in place and was being tested. Marquees were going up one by one and signposts had sprouted all over the site. To protect the mosaics and to prevent visitors from falling down steps or over remains, barriers had been hastily erected.

Alison was mesmerised by an operation high up at the amphitheatre which she thought Sam might also be watching. A crane was slowly positioning the last large blocks forming the rim of the magnificent building. Sam had told her in admiration that Ayeb had promised the workers bonuses if they finished within the week. The amphitheatre had been in relatively good condition but excavation and restoration had yielded quantities of information which Tahar, the site superintendent, rightly insisted on cataloguing. Excavating the vaults and trap doors under the arena had also taken much longer than foreseen by Ayeb. Again Tahar needed to record the detail. He discovered rare graffiti which confirmed the vast numbers of wild animals brought here to be killed for the amusement of the public two millennia ago. Ayeb protested about the time it took. But Tahar insisted there were no half measures. It had to be properly recorded.

Sam had in fact left to go home to his villa in Gammarth and there was a message for Alison in Tahar's office to that effect. The car journey back to Gammarth gave her more time to think. Obviously, it would be wonderful news for Sam that this Celia, whom she had never met but who must have meant a lot to him, was alive. But it was harder to understand how she had come to find herself in the first place with hundreds of illegal migrants in an abandoned army barracks. It was equally puzzling why she had been there so long. It was shocking, if true, that the rounding up of the migrants and the creation of the camp was at the behest of Abdelaziz Ayeb. Did Sam know what type of man he was? How could he possibly be in partnership with someone like that? And what was Celia's text message really saying? Alison realised she didn't understand most of it – the references to "auntie," "thunderer" and "grauniad" for example. Presumably Sam knew what it meant.

She arrived in Gammarth as the evening sun illuminated the painted facades of the villas on either side of Sam's as though they were on a film set. From the back of the house they looked out over an empty, windless sea. From one side came sounds of nasal Egyptian pop music. On the other side, a woman was taking down a long line of washing. She was testing the dryness of baby-clothes against her cheek.

After Alison had described as best she could all that she had learnt at the morgue and how her trail led there, Sam said,

"You've missed your vocation, Alison. You should have been a private eye. You put me to shame. I don't know why I didn't probe Rafiq and Ferid harder to get the truth out of them. They are crazy not to have come clean with me."

"They were scared. Scared for themselves and scared of you."

"I suppose I see why they didn't want to embarrass me. But I still don't know why Celia didn't come home later that night."

"No. I don't know either," said Alison truthfully. "But it's none of my business."

She waited whilst Sam stared out at the setting sun. Then she asked,

"Did you understand her text message?"

"Of course. I've been acting on it all week. I'll tell you later. But what more did this Dr Soukni tell you about the camp? I find it hard to believe."

She told him all she had heard. "My information is third hand but there's no reason why it would have been made up, is there? It must be accurate. It's just incredible that such things could be happening without anyone discovering or asking themselves where all the migrants were disappearing to."

"Perhaps," said Sam, "it was taken for granted that they would never fail to find boats to take them to Europe."

"When people have problems they don't like, they don't talk about them. Debts, affairs, embarrassing diseases. Migration is a taboo subject. It's being swept under the carpet. Nobody likes to talk about it."

"Yes. And there's a feeling that talking about it makes the problem worse?" said Sam.

"It couldn't be any worse, could it? We must confront our own demons," Alison said.

"That is what Celia is making us do on Good Friday."

After the sun had sunk, the air chilled and they went indoors. Sam talked about the event that Abdelaziz Ayeb had planned for the launch. The media had been invited in force and in style. Knowing how much a holiday in the sun at this time of year was appreciated by the northern Europeans, Ayeb was flying out camera crews and journalists on his own planes and putting them up in his own hotels. Local T.V. had been very helpful and was making facilities available to British, French, German and Italian counterparts. Ayeb was offering himself for individual interviews to virtually all comers.

The tourism sector had stirred itself and journalists had offers of hire cars, guides, extra nights and even free massages.

"Ayeb really wants to make a splash. He is setting up a state-of-the-art media centre with all the facilities you could ask for. The press will be offered two good meals on the site, one hot, one cold. A catering firm has already started moving equipment in for its field kitchen. Of course there will be loos galore, a medical tent, a mobile police post not to mention sumptuous goody bags and brochures."

"Will the government be there too?" asked Alison.

"Three ministers – Tourism, Culture and Foreign Affairs. But Ayeb wants to keep them at arm's length. He's a control-freak. If the government is involved, he'll lose some control. He's right in a way. If the media see rows and rows of state officials, ministers and what have you, they'll think it's the usual propaganda."

"What about the diplomatic corps?"

"All the ambassadors in Tunis are invited. All but a handful have accepted. Friday prayers will prevent some ambassadors from the Islamic countries from attending. And it is impossible for the Vatican representative to attend on Good Friday."

Sam drew the curtains and then brought cold chicken and salad from the kitchen. As they ate at the round table in the living room, Sam started to unburden himself.

"Celia's texto was a bombshell, as you can guess. She managed to tell me a hell of a lot in just thirty words. The references to auntie, thunderer and so on were asking me to alert the BBC, The Times and The Guardian. In fact, I've done rather more than that."

He paused again.

"You might be surprised by this, but I've told Ayeb that I want to reconsider my position, to reconsider my presence here altogether."

"Wow!"

"He thinks I'm renegotiating our financial arrangement. He'll take it badly when he realises the truth. Very badly."

"And the truth is?"

"That he and I are through. I've finally listened to what people keep telling me. I've been shocked by what I have learnt. And what you are telling me just confirms my decision.

"At first I admired him as someone who got things done. I sympathised with him because he had had to fight his way to the top. I admired his negotiating skills."

Sam looked uneasy but took a deep breath before continuing.

"I'll admit I was attracted by his wealth. Here was someone, at last, who was ready to invest in my ideas. He has so much money – and a bank – that anything, anything is possible."

Alison closed her eyes. She wished Sam hadn't said that. Of course she had wondered, almost from the moment she had met him, whether it was her money that interested him. She had convinced herself that it wasn't. That their relationship was different, special.

Sam stood up and talked as he walked.

"Ayeb liked the best. Meetings with him were glimpses into another world. The world of the super-rich. He isn't afraid to be unconventional. He likes bling. And exercising power. He's been very clever. His international reputation makes him fireproof as regards his own government."

Leaning on the back of a chair, Sam looked Alison in the eye.

"You know, most businessmen would not have had the courage to invest in the Bisuli Project. Most would have had to spend years consulting all the local worthies, the heritage bodies, planning committees, government agencies, ministries and so on. Not Ayeb. He just did it. Bang! Like that."

He showed the bottle of Tunisian red wine to Alison, who nodded. He poured two glasses and put the bottle onto a mat so that it would not mark the polished table.

"But there's another side to the man and I don't like it. It is Tunisians who are hinting to me that I have to be careful. They keep telling me about the sinister influence he has over the whole security apparatus. It is so powerful and Ayeb uses it at will. On the business side, it's unnatural that he has the details of all the big projects before they are announced and wins every tender. Is it just chance that the new airport directly benefits his resorts, his hotels? How is it that he has appropriated the best beaches and owns the best golf course? Opposition is silenced with cash."

"But, Sam, that's the way they all work, isn't it? Cash is king! Money buys them everything. Everyone has a price."

"Maybe."

There was another pause as he looked at Alison, kindly.

"But your discoveries – or rather Celia's – about the migrants is the last straw.

"Incidentally, Alison, I've found out that Ayeb now meets Bill Wells every time he goes to London. Ayeb told me they have 'common interests', whatever that means. You will not be surprised that Mr Wells will be here for the festivities next week, during the parliamentary recess."

CHAPTER 16

For Omar, the ride back in the coffin was less comfortable because Hedi had taken out the soft padding and the spare space was filled with one thousand index cards, fifty pencils, and dozens of batteries. At the camp, it was all Khaled and the major could do to lift the coffin off the truck without arousing suspicion.

Celia could not help but smile at the solemnity with which the migrants collected their blank index cards. They were the size of small postcards ruled with thin blue lines on both sides. Major Mifsoud had asked them to put their names, ages and countries of origin on them. For the rest of the week, groups were to be seen huddling together over their cards which became progressively more grubby and dog-eared. There were arguments over the pencils inevitably. Khaled eventually cut each pencil into three. As a means of keeping bored people busy, Major Mifsoud had hit upon a successful ploy.

Walking through the camp in the late afternoon when the shadows of the trees moved over the huts like ink stains, Celia saw Hope sitting on a stone bench. She had covered her whole card in writing.

"Can you show me?" asked Celia.

Hope looked up from her piece of card with her round, even writing. She put the pencil in her mouth and Celia was thrilled to see a faint but genuine smile on her face.

"My name. Here's my name," said Hope, pointing to the top of the card. "Hope Kakwani. And my country, Nigeria."

"And what's the rest you've written?"

Another flicker of a smile crossed Hope's face, which, like everyone else, had its daily powdering of fine dust. Embarrassed, she put the card and both her hands between her knees.

"Come on," said Celia, leaning against her, lightly. "Please show me. I'll tell no-one."

"It's a song, no, not a song, but a poem." Hope brought the card up and read her poem.

"I dreamed today, when night was gone
And morning brought the light,
I dreamed today, when sun began
And birds resumed their flight

Of mother waking sleepy me,
Then feeding my new brother,
Of mother weeping silently
And knowing that I love her.

I dreamed my village now was safe,
That wells were full of water,
That fields were growing with new life,
And echoed with our laughter.

I dreamed I would do all I could,
To work and send them money,
To save my village, save my world,
And save my lovely Mummy."

Hope dropped her hands into her lap. Celia could not speak for a second or two. Then she said,

"Hope, that's the most lovely poem I've ever heard."

Still sitting on the bench, Celia turned and hugged the Nigerian girl. Hope's smile had widened even more. She could not see Celia's tears.

The way was now clear for the countdown to the exodus. Twenty four hours before the operation was to begin, the second fake message was sent to the colonel – by Dr Hedi Soukni – with precise instructions for the buses and their drivers.

That same day, Major Mifsoud addressed the whole camp in the afternoon. It was a tricky speech. He did not want to reveal the final destination because he feared it would anger many of the migrants. But he told them it was no more than a very short journey. He said no-one would be taken back the next day to where they had come from unless they asked for that; and that anyone who was sick would be taken to hospital. He told them that they would be free to choose between various options once at their destination. It was important that they all remained calm and stayed together. They were to be ready to leave at nine-thirty the next morning. There would be food at the place they were going to, so there was no need to take it with them.

Pandemonium broke out slowly. Many of the audience didn't understand what Major Mifsoud was saying at first. Some of those that did were suspicious and worried. But a majority, the great majority, literally jumped up and down with joy. *"Uhuru kesho"* (freedom tomorrow) shouted the Swahili speakers. When others got the message, the dancing and shouting broke out in earnest. Mostly dancing. The late afternoon sun was obscured by the pink dust from hundreds of shuffling feet. In Africa there are times when dancing is more important than talking. Some men just ran round the huts with their faces up to the sky, whooping. A bunch of happy herdsmen rolled on their sides, over and over, with their arms akimbo. Khaled, Omar and Celia embraced one another.

Then Omar visited the sick huts to give the news to those inside, a dozen or so. There could be no singing or dancing but there were courageous smiles. He spent much of the evening with the weaker ones on their mattresses or beds, reassuring them individually as best he could. He had found a ball of string at the morgue. He used it to attach his medical notes to each sick man so that doctors at the hospital were not completely in the dark.

As darkness fell, the air of expectation in the camp was tangible. The migrants had eaten early. In the kitchen, the utensils had been cleaned and left neatly hanging up to dry. The chief cook, a fearsome Touareg from Niger, carefully dismantled the mare's tail fly-deterrent. Behind the kitchen, a group of Baggara from Chad were cutting up pieces of cooked goat for the next day. They were cautious people; they always carried food when on the move. Around the huts, flames fluttered from fires burning for the last time. The supper-time smells of couscous and beans gave way to the tang of wood-smoke.

In the huts, people had long since gathered together their precious bundles of personal possessions. Knives, flip-flops and tee-shirts were common components. Thin metal coffee pots and billy-cans clinked in some bundles. Richer migrants had blankets or shawls. One optimist was packing a porcelain piggy-bank. Another was packing a home-made football. Copies of the Koran were in evidence, too. As Major Mifsoud walked round for the last time he noticed more Muslims than usual holding prayer beads.

Every group produces its clown and Bir Assaya was no exception. It was Mohammed, the Malian cattle-herder with the earphones. Randomly, he would say in impeccable French, *"Voici les nouvelles de huit heures"* ("Here is the eight o'clock news") and raise his eyebrows as if listening to important news headlines. Sometimes he wore the headpiece under his chin, sometimes on the back of his neck. On this very special last night he was wearing the earphones on his temples – and chewing the jack. But the audience this time was only half laughing. All thoughts were on the camp gates.

In Major Mifsoud's office, lit by two oil-lamps, Celia betrayed her nerves by jiggling her knees up and down. Her eyes hurt and her legs ached. She blamed it on tiredness. Khaled, playing with the keys to his Toyota, was pacing to and fro like an expectant father. The major was carefully unscrewing the aerial of his military radio and fiddling with the back of the receiver. His office had never looked so tidy. Throughout the day he had been burning official papers, securing the ammunition store, emptying his drawers. He thought it ninety-nine per cent certain that he would be given a long sentence at his court martial for desertion, insubordination and counterfeiting. But he had never left behind an untidy office and he didn't intend to start now.

Like the others, he had his doubts too. Serious doubts. Had the two messages been safely received by the colonel? Had the colonel suspected something? Would the buses contain armed troops with a warrant for his arrest?

"I hope I'm not making the biggest mistake of my life," Celia said, looking through the window at the moon. "I'm increasingly conscious that we're about to change the lives of all these people. They haven't asked to be taken out of here. We've simply decided for them. Do we have the right to do that?"

"This is no time to have doubts like that," said Khaled. "Doing something is better than doing nothing."

"Only if that something is going to help them," she said.

"But look how happy they all were this afternoon when they learnt they were leaving," said Omar. "My brother is right. Left here, they would only continue to suffer, mentally and physically. So would we."

Celia turned her back to the window. Lines of tension surrounded her mouth and eyes. Her head turned from one brother to the other. "If this plan doesn't work, if their lives don't improve, we will have betrayed them. We will be no better than criminals..."

"We must not start worrying like this or blaming ourselves," said Omar. "We're all anxious. It's only natural."

Major Mifsoud had said very little that evening. But he concealed his nervousness no better than the others. He kept re-ordering the same little pile of papers on his desk. For the twentieth time he repositioned the pens, pencils and ruler around his blotter, as if meticulously setting a dinner table in the regimental mess.

"We all need some sleep. Let's conserve our strength for tomorrow," he said turning down the wicks on the oil lamps. Black wisps of paraffin scented smoke hung in the still air like question marks.

But other, darker emotions prevented the major from moving to sleep mode. In the early moonlight outside his hut, his memory was backing up months of accumulated bitterness and regret. He blamed himself for not having realised from Day One what the authorities' intentions were. He blamed himself for the deaths of so many innocent migrants. He blamed himself for having taken so long to put an end to the suffering of a thousand men and women.

He had not been feeling well for months. Ever since setting foot in this pestilential prison, he'd been living with stomach cramps and heaving bowels. Codeine stabilised him and dulled the pain. But his stocks of it had been finished for a week and he missed the drug desperately.

He dropped his right hand to the leather holster of the service revolver hanging heavily from his belt. He knew how shameful it would be if he was arrested for disobeying orders. This might be the last day he would wear a side arm like this. He ran his thumb backwards and forwards over the smooth leather flap. A jumble of black thoughts came into his head. But beside his hand, above his belt, his guts scrunched up and twisted and brought him back to earth.

He took a deep breath of the suggestive, soft air. Tomorrow he would be in Tunis. He imagined he could already smell jasmine, fruit blossom and the spicy odour of joss sticks in the souk.

Something glinted on the wall of the hut to interrupt his reverie. He froze on the spot.

Not out of fear. But so as not to disturb one of nature's minor miracles. Moonlight was reflected in the wide open eye of a gecko targeting a tired fly with its elastic tongue. A nanosecond later, the fly had been swallowed. The lizard moved on.

The major smiled and went to bed.

Next morning, at nine o'clock, a guard reported excitedly to Major Mifsoud who was standing outside his office door, on the step.

"Sir, the buses have arrived."

"Let them in." He was in command now. This was his last operation and his most dangerous by far. Turning to Khaled, he said,

"We must impress on the migrants that they should remain calm and keep the blinds down. Lieutenant Khaled, take this radio. You know how to adjust it, don't you? Right. If you travel in the Toyota in front, you can keep in touch with me. If our messages are intercepted, it will be too late for anyone to do anything about it. You Doctor, and Celia, you know what to do if the police try to stop us. We drive on. We don't stop. We are military. It's unlikely that even Mr Ayeb will try that. Twenty army buses with uniformed drivers: we are not easily stopped. Let's load up!"

The second-hand, sandy-coloured military buses ground through the tubular metal and wire gates in first gear. They turned round inside and lined up facing the fence with a precision which pleased the major. The rhythmic, clunky noise of their diesel engines was soon drowned out by the nervous chatter of the jostling migrants. It reminded Celia of the countless bus-station scenes on her assignments. One day she would do a film based on bus-stations in Africa. That was for the future. First she had to get through today. She'd had an uncomfortable night and was feeling no better. But she was too busy to worry about it.

Major Mifsoud and his officers used a light touch trying to bring order to chaos. They divided up the boisterous passengers, with their pathetic bundles of hand-luggage, into groups of forty to fifty. Once inside the buses, the migrants couldn't decide where to sit. They jumped between the green plastic seat benches like so many shrimps. Each person must have sat in three different places before settling into a fourth. There was no point or possibility of stopping this. It was a chemical reaction. When the fizzing stopped, the mixture would clarify.

Dealing with the bus drivers could have been tricky. They had not been given their destination – for reasons of secrecy, they were told at the barracks – so it was up to the major to give them the order that they were going to Bisuli, ten kilometres away. Few of the young drivers had heard of Bisuli and none knew where it was. This made the major's task easier. He told them and explained that for the purposes of this exercise they were going to take minor roads, sometimes unmade ones, for reasons which he was not allowed to explain further.

The major was not sure whether the policemen in plain-clothes outside the gate realised what was happening or not. When they saw the buses, they were immediately on their radio, that was clear. But because the blinds were drawn, they couldn't see who the passengers were or indeed whether there were any passengers.

The buses were elderly. It was a slow and noisy procession. The drivers wisely kept in low gear along the track from the camp until they hit the paved road to Mohammedia. At that point the bus with the sick migrants turned towards Tunis and the hospital that Omar had chosen and Dr Soukni had alerted in advance.

The other buses took the road following the old aqueduct before turning onto a piste which was scarcely wide enough. Taking this route, there was less likelihood of road blocks or being stopped by the police. As the buses jolted in the pot-holes, the migrants shrieked with a mixture of fear and delight, mostly delight. There was no way the blinds would stay down in any of the windows. The passengers wanted to see the outside world and nobody would stop them.

Celia in the Toyota with Khaled, leading the convoy, knew the piste, only because Sam had taken her there the day before her fateful trip, months earlier, to the Antonine Baths in Carthage. What she had forgotten, though, was that the piste crossed a dual-track railway line. The crossing was not even remotely passable for the buses. The rails stood well proud of the track. They were a four part steel barrier to further progress. Celia and Khaled got out of their car to see what could be done. As the convoy came to a halt, Major Mifsoud was not best pleased and muttered something about lack of reconnaissance and maps.

He could see that at least one of the bus drivers was tempted to question what was going on. The major went up to him, in full view of several of the others, and said,

"The route we are taking is the correct one according to my orders. The orders cannot, repeat cannot, be questioned. If there are obstacles we must overcome them as best we can. Is that understood?" It was.

Khaled, the engineer, said earth ramps to cross the rails would do the trick but without tools it would take some time.

"We have the manpower," said Khaled. "If, say, fifty men could build a ramp on this side up to the level of the top of the rails, put small rocks and stones between the rails and then a ramp on the other side, we are in business."

"It will have to be cleared away after the buses have gone across," said the major, "otherwise we risk derailing a train."

"Of course," said Khaled.

It was predictable that there would be further chaos on the buses. The rumour spread amongst the migrants that they were going to be put onto a train. None had ever been in a train and none wanted to go in one now. As Major Mifsoud went from bus to bus to calm people down – and to ask for volunteers for the manual labour – half a dozen migrants took the opportunity to go their own way, to escape. The drivers saw what was happening all too clearly but mindful of the major's presence and the fact that he did nothing about it, kept silent. No-one gave chase.

With both the major and Khaled giving instructions, the ramps were constructed in twenty minutes. The danger was that a train would come before the job was done or the buses had crossed over. Luck was with them – just. The ramps were built. The convoy crossed the tracks and then stopped on the other side whilst more volunteers restored the scene to what it was before. As they were finishing, the rails started to vibrate and hum and they could clearly hear a train approaching. Khaled, Omar, Celia and the major all shouted to the men to run back to the buses – fast. They were unused to trains, to their speed, size, power and noise. Some were more curious than frightened. They wanted to see the train close-to. They had to be pushed back towards the buses, several lost their balance and fell, but Celia in particular screamed at them to get out of the way. It was a goods train pulled by a panting engine. Whether the driver applied his brakes or not, the train didn't seem to slow down. The major was the last to leave the tracks: he wanted to be sure that no migrants had lingered on them undetected. Even Major Mifsoud hadn't reckoned on the speed of the diesel engine. It missed him by centimetres.

From the first bus, and once all were re-embarked, he radioed Khaled and Celia to lead on.

"I was nearly killed by that wretched train," he said.

"Suffering does not go unnoticed by God," said Khaled, quoting from the Koran.

"And he shall reward those who endure," added Omar.

The caravan moved on. The military vehicles made an unusual sight as they gained speed on the sandy track winding between gleaming fields of spring grass.

A flock of sheep did not bother to look up at the rumbling buses. The curly-haired shepherd wondered what so many black faces were doing in them. It was none of his business. But by the time he mentioned it to his best friend, the policeman's son, in the market, it was too late.

CHAPTER 17

For days, the amphitheatre had been resounding to the hammering of carpenters and the hum of engines. Lorries had been arriving with scaffolding, stages, marquees, screens and speakers. Tahar was concerned that Abdelaziz Ayeb should not interfere with Sam's excavation and successfully kept him in and around the amphitheatre on his afternoon visits. Unless Ayeb climbed to the very top of the building, he would not see what Sam and Alison were doing. They could work undisturbed.

Tahar himself was much occupied with synchronising the last minute arrangements for the opening extravaganza. With three days to go, he was still worrying that the power supply would not be sufficient. Ayeb had had to intervene with the electricity people to insist on a reliable temporary supply, enough to power the lights, the sound stage, the hydraulic camera arms, the media centre and the small army of services needed outside the amphitheatre itself. But the engineers still hadn't done their final tests and tempers were fraying on all sides.

Security was a further aggravation. This was the first time the amphitheatre had been used for a public event. Tahar knew the structure was completely solid. But it was built by first century Roman engineers who did not have twenty-first century obsessions with safety. There were no safety rails, balustrades or handrails and it was up to the individual spectator not to slip or trip in an upper tier. There were places, it was true, where a step in the wrong direction would mean a fatal fall. A young bureaucrat from Tunis had tried to insist that there should be large numbers of portable toilets since thousands of people were to be on the site for several hours. The tiresome man was placated with a free ticket. Tahar's nightmare was not with adequate sanitary provision but with souvenir hunters and the sheer numbers of people tramping all over his precious excavations. He had spent every day since returning from London working all the hours God gave for a project with which he fundamentally disagreed. Nothing could be more stressful. He would have preferred to have been with Sam rather than, as he put it, producing a variety show.

For his part, Sam was keeping a low profile with Ayeb. He answered his calls, of course, but found excuses not to be at Ayeb's every meeting about Bisuli. As things stood now, Sam had three days to focus on the fever sanctuary. This building had to be accessed, opened and explored in the little time remaining before the opening ceremony when Sam planned to part company with Ayeb. It would be exciting, too, if something was discovered worthy of showing to the eminent archaeologists invited to the opening. And if Sam's discovery caught the media's attention, it would do his reputation no harm. The problem was how to go about the excavation and where to start. Normally, he would have dug several exploratory trenches, but that was out of the question now.

The danger with working fast, Sam knew all too well, was that critical archaeological evidence would not be recorded, small items would be missed or more likely be destroyed. If this was a fever sanctuary, Sam would expect to find votive tablets describing patients' complaints and the manner of their cure. There might also be thank-offerings – jewellery or precious household objects, for example. A statue representing Sleep or Dreaming would be a key indicator and snake images would be a clincher. The snake, the Romans thought, rejuvenated itself by shedding its skin.

Sam and Alison were unloading equipment brought from Tahar's workshop and placing it at the edge of the sanctuary site. The atmosphere was strange. Sam was in a state of great anticipation whilst Alison was unusually quiet, almost distant. Sam was fairly sure he knew why. The thought of Celia returning in three days' time was haunting her. Hopefully, working with him on the fever sanctuary would be an antidote and would take her mind off Celia.

"Knowing our bad luck," said Sam, "the place will be flooded. And we haven't brought a pump."

"I don't think it will be flooded, but the photographs will tell us, won't they?" said Alison. "And you would have heard a different sort of echo," she added.

Unloading finished, they stood looking once more at the whole plot like golfers considering their next shots.

"I had thought we should measure from the centre of the vault and, with the results from the resistance meter, make an informed guess as to where the entrance might have been. But we don't have time. We just have to be bold. I now think we must drill through the roof – a small hole but big enough to pass a telescopic rod through. We put a lamp on the end of the rod and my camera. We set the timer, lower the rod…"

"Isn't there a danger from gas – methane or nitrogen or something?" said Alison

"No, I don't think so," said Sam. "After all, if water drained into the building via the roof, then logically any gases could escape by that route."

"What I will be looking for in the photographs is a configuration of stone or brick which might point to an entrance. If we can pinpoint a safe gap at ground level, then we can dig from the outside at the right spot and gain access."

Sam had spent the early morning measuring and marking. The trouble was that there was no model on which to base measurements. As he walked round what he guessed was the edge of the buried building, he detected a long line of darker spring grass which was suspiciously straight. He felt sure it marked the edge of the street. The entrance would possibly be half way along it. He placed white pegs to mark the spot just in case it might be useful later on.

The power source for the drill was a diesel generator in a bright yellow tubular steel frame which was supposed to be portable. Sam and Alison had found it brutally heavy. But they had managed, somehow, to bring it to the edge of their site. They had tested it first thing in the morning. Apart from making a smoky start, it worked perfectly. Even better, it was fitted with a silencer.

Sam had selected a spot to drill which was high up the vault but not the precise centre. First he had to remove half a metre of topsoil. He found it stony and more difficult to shift than he had thought. His spade continually struck pebbles and stones which slowed him down. Perhaps he should have started with a mechanical digger. It hurt him to be discarding the topsoil with scarcely a glance. At any other time in his professional life he would have been using a much smaller spade and sieving the soil, sorting the broken brick and tile into layer order, brushing and washing anything of interest.

Alison busied herself with fixing the powerful German-made light to the telescopic pole. The pole was something that Sam had made by attaching two extendable gardener's pruning tools together, giving a six metre reach. She had already attached the digital camera, checked its battery strength and ensured that the timer was working.

After fifteen minutes of digging, Sam's spade struck accumulated broken tile and below that, brick. He scraped along the brick as far as he could in all directions until he came to an edge. He then widened his excavation by a couple of spades' widths to ensure that topsoil did not tumble as he drilled and to give himself space to cool the drill-bit with water at intervals.

Alison was going through the motions of being helpful, but no more than that. She felt the very opposite of energetic. For minutes at a time she had been staring at Sam whilst he was digging. What did she have to go back to, emotionally, if she lost Sam? Would she lose him? Or was Celia in the past? For good. Alison felt a stifling cloud descending on her. She turned away and took a deep breath.

"We're ready to start, Alison. The drill is linked up. Could you start the generator? Is the water handy, too? Great."

She shook her head as if to clear it and refocused.

The drilling was relatively straightforward. Sam's biggest fear was that the noise would attract unwelcome attention. But plenty of noise was coming from the builders around the amphitheatre and also the breeze was in his favour, carrying the noise away from the

187

site entrance. He withdrew the drill twice to check that he was going straight. After twenty-five minutes, the drill lurched downwards, almost pulling him with it. He looked up at Alison, whose blank face registered nothing.

"We're through."

The picture flashed across his mind from the nineteen-twenties of Howard Carter turning his head back to Lord Carnarvon with an expression of heart-stopping wonderment having just looked inside the hole he had pierced in the sealed door of Tutankhamen's tomb.

"We're through, Alison! Aren't you pleased? More quickly than I expected," said Sam, impatiently.

"That's great. Is it big enough, at least for the photography?" asked Alison.

"Yes, I think so. Let's try."

Sensing that he would do it faster than her, Sam screwed the aluminium rods together. He switched the light on, set the camera timer to its maximum and looked at the second-hand on his watch. He lowered the rods down the hole as fast as he could, lying flat on his stomach with both hands in front of him. They slipped down their full length easily. As the minute approached, he held his breath to keep the rods absolutely steady. He could see the flash working. He pulled the camera up. Kneeling in the mess of topsoil he had made, he hurried to see the digital image. His hands were trembling with excitement. He peered at the bright screen on the back of the camera.

"Brilliant. We have a pretty good picture. It's of the floor. No flooding as far as I can tell. See, that's a bit of broken column, isn't it? To the side, it's not clear. Then on the other side, there's a heck of a lot of rubble. There must be some moisture there because the dust doesn't look dry."

It took Sam ten minutes to reposition the light and camera, reset the timer, lower the rod into the hole and pull it up again. It took two hours to photograph the whole floor area and another two hours to capture the walls. These later pictures were less distinct and more confusing. But there were two spaces in the mass of broken masonry, rocks and earth which gave Sam hope that there might be unfilled spaces, or bubbles within the rubble where artefacts – inscriptions, stone furniture, mosaics or statuary – might be unbroken or less contaminated by moisture. He had asked Alison to record the position the camera was facing with each of the forty-eight pictures. That night he printed A4 paper copies so that he could piece together a view of what lay beneath the dome.

Apart from the two spaces or avenues, exciting though they were, there were two other sensational features. One picture showed what was possibly the edge of a stone pool. It was difficult to be sure because of the overlying mass of rubble. The other was what looked like a statue of a goddess still in its wall niche. There was an inscription underneath it which was slightly obscured by debris. He magnified the picture as much as his printer would allow. After a long look with a magnifying glass, Sam thought he could read "QUOD AVERTAT FEBRIS" – "which may Febris avert." He could scarcely believe his eyes.

No representation of Febris, the goddess of fever, had ever been found, even in Rome. If Febris was worshipped at Bisuli, fever must have been prevalent. It was unlikely in this non-swampy spot to have been malaria. It must have been another fever, probably a lethal one, perhaps typhoid. What a coincidence, then, that Celia should be battling typhoid as well? Or was it?

He was dismayed that Alison did not share his excitement. She remained distant, withdrawn, in a world of her own. He tried to connect with her several times with little gestures but he couldn't get through the barrier she had thrown up around herself. He tried to touch her but she deflected each such attempt. When she spoke, it was in a matter-of-fact way; polite but cold.

Sam's mind was in a maelstrom of conflicting moods that night. He swung from jubilation, confirmation, satisfaction at one moment, to depression and anxiety the next. It was not especially hot for April but he was perspiring in bed. He opened the window wide and noticed how clear the night sky was.

For the first time for months, Alison had decided to sleep on the couch. She said she'd been feeling queasy and more than usually tired. Wearing only his boxer shorts, Sam tiptoed along the corridor and into the sitting room. Alison's clothes were in their usual wild heap with her bra suspended on the arm-rest of the chair. She was lying with her legs curled up and her face towards the window. Her blanket had slipped and was mostly on the floor. Her wavy hair was arranged on a blue velvet cushion as if in a pre-Raphaelite painting. One breast was perfectly outlined where her nightdress pulled tightly over it. She had one hand between her face and the cushion whilst the other lay on her thigh.

How could he have allowed himself to fall for Alison without knowing what had happened to Celia? When she had finished her film on St Augustine, Celia had said she had wanted to have a baby. So did he. So why had he been such a fool with Alison? He was ashamed of himself. Ashamed of himself for cheating on Celia. Ashamed he hadn't had more faith.

The net curtain ballooned inwards, moved by the draught between the window and the door where Sam stood. He could not stop thinking about Celia's reaction when she saw that Alison had taken her place. He could not stop thinking about Celia. He realised that all along she had been in his mind; that he had missed her but had tried to deny it. Would she love him ever again? He couldn't wait to see her soon, to touch her, to stroke her cheek, to tell her he loved her after all. He longed to hold her tight, tight, tight.

He was confused, unsettled, angry with himself. He was in turmoil about whom he really loved. He looked, transfixed, at Alison's closed eyes, the moonlight on her nose and her half-open lips. He stood stock-still. The only sound was his own breathing. The light of the night-sky caught the water in his eyes and the tear-drops rolling down his cheeks. One drop fell on his bare foot. He looked down at it, then at the scarf, her scarf, that he was twisting in his hands.

He was interrupted by the first words of the muezzin's pre-dawn call to prayer – *Allahu Akbar*'. It was a timely reminder, repeated again and again as other mosques made their calls to prayer, that there was a world outside this room, a world beyond his insignificant personal problems.

Back in bed, he was evermore sure of his night-time decision to get inside the sunken building himself, the next day, by the roof. The photographs were tantalising but did not give him the proof he needed to be able to identify the building once and for all. Nor did the pictures show where the spring was. Getting inside, in person, was the only way he could show that he was right.

Early mornings in April in Tunisia are magical. The land comes alive. Grass and flowers are touched with dew which sparkles as the sun comes up. There is the promise of quick growth and warmth. Sam could see the fragile flowers of purple bougainvillea framing the windows of the neighbouring villa. The spring light heightened the sense that this was an important day. It was marred for Alison by a churning tummy, a touch of nausea. It was soon over and as she nursed her breakfast mug of coffee in the kitchen, he outlined his plan.

"I know it's risky, Alison, but it's the only way. I'll either enlarge the drill hole or take out a whole brick section so that it's big enough for me to slip through. We know exactly how deep a drop it is – four metres to the broken pillar in the first photo. Then I'll need, what, another twelve metres of rope so that I can attach it to the huge fallen drum column at the top of the site? So sixteen metres in all. I've seen where Tahar keeps the ropes. It's not locked, which is a blessing."

"How will you come up?" Alison asked in a monotone.

"Either like a monkey, hand over hand. Or I am pulled up."

"Pity we don't have a winch," she said.

"You could, I suppose, tie one end to the tow point on the car, put it into four wheel drive, first gear, and pull me out that way. We'd have to protect the side of the hole with plastic sheeting to prevent the rope from chafing or getting snagged. But I'm sure I can climb up the rope alright. I've done it at the gym. Let's also take some baskets for hauling stuff to the surface if we need to. Come to think of it, maybe we should use two ropes – one for goods, one for humans."

"Let's hope Tahar has enough rope," Alison said.

"I'm sure he has. But first I have to drill a large hole. We've a beautiful day for it."

The drilling proved harder than expected. It was two hours before Sam had something sufficiently wide for his liking. Frequently, he had to push on the drill with all his weight. Indeed, he was concerned about damaging the tip of the bit, so hot did it become. He had to rest more and more frequently because the vibrations were beginning to hurt his shoulders. But by midday the drilling was done. His excitement was really beginning to mount now.

In a few minutes, he had fixed a headlamp onto his helmet and put it on. He tied both the ropes round the huge pillar drum stone and threw the free ends down the hole. One rope had a large straw basket attached to it. Inside, he had put another smaller basket with a trowel, a collapsible spade, another torch, a brush, some soft foam-rubber, the digital camera, a measuring rod, some self-seal plastic bags and a bottle of water.

"Wish me luck," he implored.

She gave a faint smile and nodded. She stood looking down the hole at the top of his hard hat as he descended. She could see the beam from his headlamp waving from side to side as he let himself down. She could see how taut the rope was. She soon heard his voice quite clearly from below giving a running commentary.

"I'm down. I'm standing on a mound of rubble and large pieces of limestone. There's a foul smell, really foul. Like cat's pee but with more ammonia. I think I can see the second avenue from the photos, so I'll climb over these pieces of stone towards it. There's a big gap here after the rock. Ahah! I can see the pool."

There was a scuffling and scraping noise as he cleared away the dirt.

"I think, yes, it is. It's lined with marble, Alison. And the dirt is very moist just beyond it!" He was almost shouting.

"This is stupendous, incredible. It's a spring, alright. I must take some photos now before I move anything. I'll go over to the other rope and get the camera and measuring rod. Then I'll load up the spare basket with something I've found that will amaze you. An amulet, no two amulets stuck together. I'll be five minutes doing all this."

"Alright," said Alison. She stayed by the hole.

It happened quickly and she could have shouted a warning. But she didn't. A crack opened up in the earth over the vault like a fig pulled apart. It ran from the hole to the drum stone and the car. Within a second, another jagged slash appeared in the earth as she turned her head. There was a rumble like thunder from inside the building. With a crumping, vibrating roar, stones from the vault were striking rock and marble four metres below. Then the lip of the hole disintegrated as did the ground where she was standing. Alison felt herself falling headfirst. There was an air-rush, then blurred light flashes. Then all was black. Sam didn't have a chance either. Both his legs were trapped by a marble slab with part of an inscription from Horace. *"AEGRI SOMNIA"*, it read – a sick man's dreams.

CHAPTER 18

In case of a power failure in the press centre, Tahar Haddad wanted to have his diesel generator ready. He hadn't had a moment to fetch it from its usual place beside the workshop. When he did go to look for it, he was surprised to find it wasn't there. He doubted that it had been stolen. It was much more likely that someone was using it on a remote part of the site. It was only then that he realised that it must have been taken by Sam and Alison.

When he saw their car and his yellow generator beside it, something made him break into a trot. Neither of them was to be seen. The back of the car was open. Beyond it, dust was rising in little spirals. Something had happened, of that he was sure, and happened just moments ago. He called out "Dr Glover. Dr Glover", still running towards the spot. There was a deep, wide crater where a couple of days ago there had been a grassy, vacant lot. He stopped still as if frozen. He turned his head from side to side to take it all in.

"Dr Glover. Are you there?" he shouted.

The only reply was the squawking from a couple of curious crows, hopping heavily beside the rubble. Tahar scrambled down into the pit. He saw the ropes but at first couldn't think what they were for. He gingerly moved towards the centre, climbing over the chaotic ruins. Trying to negotiate a jagged jumble of rubble, he lost his footing and stumbled forward. He was glad to take hold of one of the ropes and he followed it, with difficulty, to its lower end. Two steps further towards the centre and he saw Alison. Had she descended on the rope? She was not moving but her eyes were open.

"Are you alright? Are you hurt? Don't move."

"Tahar. Thank God. Yes, I'm alright, I think. Bang on the head.

194

I must have lost consciousness. How long ... Where's Sam? Where's Sam?" she called out.

"I'm here. Behind you. Over here. Can't move."

The marble lying across his legs was the size of a tomb-stone. His hard-hat was still in place, though crooked and dented, the torch attached to it still on.

"Allah be praised that you are alive!" said Tahar. "Let me get over there to move that stone."

It was easier to move than he feared. The inscription on it was as clear as if it had been carved that day. Sam's trousers were ripped but Tahar looked to see if his legs were alright, half-hidden as they were.

"Can you move your legs?"

"Yes. No problem except for bruises, I think. And dirt. Thank goodness I had the hat! Alison, be careful when you stand. You were concussed for a couple of minutes."

"When did this happen?" asked Tahar.

"I'm not sure," said Sam. "I've lost track of time."

Tahar was conscious of his own heart beating hard and fast. For a second or two he thought he might himself have a heart attack. But it was just shock. He was not good with emergencies, or thought he wasn't. It was difficult to take it all in.

He looked from side to side, amazed. He had never for one moment suspected there was a building of this size, this splendour, buried beside the forum. It was spectacular. He could hear trickling water and saw the corner of the sacred pool.

With great care Tahar helped first Alison then Sam to their feet. Alison carefully brushed away the thick dust from her body, her hand pausing to feel her middle.

"I now believe in miracles, Alison. By any normal reckoning, we shouldn't be alive."

"It was so fast. The ground just split under my feet. I didn't have time to jump back. Anyway that wouldn't have been any good."

She wiped the dirt off her face with the sleeve of her shirt which was itself covered in mud and dust.

"We are so lucky," said Sam.

He was not only referring to being alive. The roof collapse had revealed to the April light a sight few archaeologists are privileged to see even in their wildest dreams: a unique, untouched Roman fever sanctuary. It was confirmation at a stroke of Sam's hypothesis. Even the shock of his precipitous fall couldn't detract from the pleasure of seeing that he was right.

He moved gingerly across the shattered stone towards the spring trickling out of a crack in the rock which was at the core of the sanctuary. He was oblivious to the pain from his left leg. He thought it couldn't be broken because he could put weight on it and could move his foot. Surely just a mega bruise – he hoped. It was safer to proceed in ape-like fashion, using all four limbs as he negotiated the broken tile, topsoil and the blocks of brick. He stopped an instant to hold in his hand a piece of cement. If only he hadn't been in such a rush, he would not have drilled like an idiot and the structure wouldn't have collapsed. On the other hand, if the roof was unsafe it probably would have fallen in anyway.

He was just able to make out the shapes of three pools below the spring. The lowest was filled with what looked at first glance like yellow bricks. He realised that patients, possibly at their last stop before death, would have drunk from the spring and washed in the pools. He had an urge to sip the water as it came out of the rock. His mouth was parched and dusty and his face was hot. The water twinkled where the sunlight caught it. He stretched out his hand, already cupped, to catch the healing liquid when Tahar shouted,

"Don't drink it, please! Whatever you do, don't drink it!"

"Why?"

"It's only a guess and perhaps I'm completely wrong. But I think this was the cause of the fever all those years ago. The spring is just recycling infected water."

Sam withdrew his arm, disappointed, and turned towards Tahar who was clambering over the ruins as fast as he could.

"That's nonsense, Tahar, surely?"

"Well, last summer all six members of the archaeological team from Aix fell ill when working fifty metres further down the hill from where we are standing."

"The house with the cistern?"

"Yes. We all thought it was food poisoning and recommended the usual cures, plus the local yoghurt which usually has a miraculous effect. But when that did not work and they became even more ill, we made a proper diagnosis."

"What was it?"

"A sort of typhoid fever."

Alison had by now joined them. She was nursing an egg-sized lump on her cheek. Dust rose like talcum powder from her tangled hair every time she moved.

"What are those things in the bottom pool?" she asked.

Tahar moved around an ornate capital from a toppled pillar to reach the lower pool. He picked out something which at first looked like a sea-shell or a fossil. He turned it over twice before holding it the right way up. It was a life-sized, carved, stone nose: the nostrils were unmistakeable.

Alison retrieved another stone object from the pool with the clear shape of a kidney. There were, she found, several of them.

"I think," said Sam, "these were votive offerings. These were the organs with which patients had problems."

"Incredible. I agree," said Tahar. "Let's put them all back in the water quickly."

"Where's the amulet you said you saw?" asked Alison.

"True. Where is it? Over there, I think," said Sam, pointing to the spot where his legs had been trapped. He struggled back through what must have been a vast, rectangular, covered space supported at the edge by thirty pillars.

Between and behind the pillars were wall niches, inaccessible to Sam or anybody without lifting equipment or at least some iron levers. The niche he could see more clearly than others still had a statue in it. It was the one he had photographed. He moved as close as he could. His helmet torch light was still switched on so he was able to illuminate the niche just enough to make out the form of a goddess – the contours of the body and the robes left no doubt – with wild hair. He couldn't be sure but with one hand she seemed to be leading a goat or a dog. In her other hand she was carrying what looked like pine cones. Roman deities, Sam knew as well as anyone, were highly stylised. But this was completely new. It would have to wait.

"Enough for one day," said Sam. "We have our evidence. Let's get out of here."

He took another look at the pools and spring, and at the amulet which he had now picked up. He looked again at the statue and smiled.

Fortunately, the structure had fallen in such a way that it was possible to climb out without difficulty. Tahar drove them to his office where they washed and cleaned themselves up. He then returned to the forum to enclose the ruins with red and white warning tape affixed to posts he hammered into the ground himself.

As he was collecting the remaining tape together in a neat roll, Ayeb's Mercedes approached and stopped right beside him. Ayeb rolled out of the back seat, like a slug. He was wearing a blue suit made of some slightly shiny material, which looked like silk, a cream-coloured shirt and yellow tie. Tahar guessed, correctly, that he had just come from lunch. Tahar also guessed, correctly, that he had been drinking.

"What do you think you are doing here, Mr Haddad? You should be at the amphitheatre. I was looking for you. Are you excavating again? What's going on?"

"This is the location Dr Glover and I have mentioned to you, Mr Ayeb. As you can see it is rather substantial. Unfortunately, whilst Dr Glover was working in it, the vault collapsed; about an hour ago, I would say."

"I had not been informed, either by Dr Glover or by you, that this place, whatever it is, was going to be excavated. I should be consulted about everything that is going on at Bisuli."

"I thought it right that we should know what was really here before it was too late…"

"You thought it right! *You* thought it right! Why didn't you consult *me*?" shouted Ayeb.

Tahar's patience snapped. He could control his anger no longer.

"Because it's *my* site, that's why," he half shouted.

"I have been in charge of this site for twelve years and I'm still in charge of it. When I took over here, there was nothing. Mosaics had been lifted, artefacts stolen, nothing was being managed. Goats were pulling down the few walls that were still standing. Everything was a mess. I have devoted the best part of my life to Bisuli. I have brought order to the place. I have coordinated the archaeology here. We now know there is something special here. Dr Glover has suspected it for some time and the proof is there, down there. Can't you see?"

If Ayeb was shocked at being talked to like that, he didn't show it. It was unheard of for anyone to answer him back.

"Mr Haddad, am I, or am I not, paying you to develop this place to be the major tourist attraction in North Africa? Am I or am I not paying you to execute my orders? I told you that nothing was to hold up our project. Nothing."

Ayeb turned his head slightly on his neck so that his chin was pointing to his shoulder. He moved closer to Tahar.

"If you don't want to work with me, Mr Haddad," he whispered, "just say so."

Tahar looked him in the eyes, his mouth opened as if to reply – but no sound emerged.

"Now, what do we do with this pit?" asked Ayeb, waving his arm at it. "The best thing would be to cover it over quickly with a couple of my bulldozers, don't you think, Mr Haddad. We don't want people falling in it on Friday do we? And we don't want it to hold up the project, do we?"

Tahar remained speechless.

"My concern now is to move on. We haven't got long. Once you have dealt with this, Mr Haddad, please concentrate on the amphitheatre arrangements."

That was the precise moment that Tahar, too, decided that he had had enough of Abdelaziz Ayeb. He walked quickly back to his office, shut the door and told Sam he would leave Ayeb's employ and quit Bisuli that night.

"Tahar, I beg you, don't do that yet. We think alike. I know exactly how you feel. This is a time for cool heads. There is a way that we can turn Ayeb's extravaganza to our advantage. Strange though it may seem, he is creating the perfect setting for something rather different from the launch of his doomed project. I have been preparing a little surprise."

CHAPTER 19

The day of the ceremony was blessed with glorious spring weather. The morning sky was cobalt blue and a light breeze fluttered the red and white Tunisian flags at the entrance to Bisuli and at strategic intervals around the amphitheatre.

At one stage, Sam had persuaded Ayeb that a guided tour of the whole site in electric golf carts would give the media the best idea of the Bisuli experience. Ayeb rejected this because it would be too difficult to control. Television crews would likely film the golf carts rather than the buildings.

An evening ceremony was considered with a laser show, *son et lumière* and fireworks. This too was rejected: Bisuli was not, after all, a night-time attraction.

They finally agreed on making the newly-restored amphitheatre the venue for entertainment and a speech, all before lunch. Visitors would be encouraged to walk round the rest of the site with escorts afterwards. Ayeb had gone to great lengths to recruit actors and actresses from different countries, including China, as guides. Money was no object. Ayeb's instinct was that the performance of the guides was more important than what they actually said. The most boring ruin would come alive if there was a knock-down handsome young actor explaining it. Life sized canvases showed how restored buildings would look. They were stretched across scaffolding at various locations – villas, shops, baths, temples – and left visitors in no doubt as to what would appear there in due course.

At a squeeze, in 200 A.D. the amphitheatre would have held twenty thousand people. Spectators today having 'fuller figures', to use mail-order catalogue language, the amphitheatre would only hold fifteen thousand. By nine-thirty a continuous stream of cars wound up to the Bisuli entrance gate. There was a brisk trade in snacks at the catering points. The huge car-park beside the entrance was a rich hunting ground for students of human behaviour. Couples argued endlessly about where to park in the empty space. They disagreed about whether to turn the car round now or later; about what to leave in the car and what to take with them; what to wear and whether to leave a window open.

It was not, after all, every day that one was invited to a Roman spectacle by Abdelaziz Ayeb. Speculation ran riot as to why he was doing this now, before the attraction was built. Some said it was to widen his international profile. Some said that it was to rattle the local political cage. And others said that the self-made multi-millionaire just couldn't help showing off. Whichever was correct, the fact was that after this event, there could be no going back without great loss of face.

Charming hostesses in nearly diaphanous beige linen dresses, fastened in Roman style with brooches on the shoulder, escorted visitors to their seats. There was a distinct sense of occasion. Soothing harp and flute music floated on the pleasantly warm morning air. As the seats slowly filled, so the hum of conversation swelled. The media had pride of place surrounding the purple decked tribune. Elsewhere in the lower tiers sat the ambassadors and their wives with large numbers of business people. Local dignitaries and their spouses, tour operators, hoteliers, leisure and entertainment representatives filled the front rows. Behind them sat representatives of the schools, colleges and universities, the schools of architecture and archaeology, historians, classicists, writers – the intelligentsia – not just local but with several American and European invitees. The upper tiers were reserved for Tunisians of every sort from the capital and all the surrounding towns and villages.

Sam and Alison took up position from early on at the site entrance. Ayeb made a small effort to locate Sam as the day's proceedings started but he didn't succeed. Sam and Alison had another agenda, a programme of their own. They had arranged a special reception centre at the far end of the car park with important props.

In the amphitheatre, the programme was audacious. At ten-thirty the VIP's, led by Ayeb, took their place in the shaded tribune whilst Bill Wells, in a cream suit and wearing the latest sunglasses, took a seat immediately behind it. A fanfare of trumpets heralded their arrival. The brass notes echoed regally round the stone circle. A lone youth in a loin cloth played pan pipes before a boys' choir recited a short poem and sang an ode in Latin.

Cymbals and horns then announced something quite different – demonstrations of Roman martial arts by the Tunisian body-building fraternity. Assorted athletes and actors, covered in oil, wrestled and threw javelins at targets from one end of the arena to the other. Following this, trap doors opened in the middle of the arena and a phalanx of gymnasts emerged to give a ten-minute synchronised display. This brought the first standing ovation of the morning.

Attention then switched to the mobile stage which had been brought to the centre of the amphitheatre. An orchestra materialised from below and the audience was treated to a ballet on the Dido and Aeneas theme, specially written for this occasion. The choreography was based on dance patterns from all over the Mediterranean, the costumes were vaguely classical and the music was unashamedly twenty-first century and melodramatically romantic. The result was bizarre. A mixture of Zorba the Greek, the Three Graces and Balanchine to the accompaniment of sugary violins. Whilst the front rows thought it pretentious, the top tiers loved it.

When the dancing finished, the orchestra played on and the fashion show began. This was indulgent fantasy on an imperial scale. For those far from the catwalk, it was easier to follow the proceedings on two giant TV screens erected at either end of the arena. Absurdly statuesque models paraded beautiful tunics, some white, some coloured, in wool, linen and silk. The accessories were clearly important – jewelled brooches, tasselled belts of twisted leather, intricate sandals, large earrings and necklaces of coral, amber or pearl. The countless girls competed for prettiness, classiness and chic. When the music reached a crescendo for the finale, four strong men wheeled an enormous jewel box to the centre of the stage. Crystals flashed in the sunlight from the lid that they slowly opened. Anachronism was heaped on anachronism as the orchestra played Sibelius and a pedestal rose from the box bearing aloft an exquisitely naked, golden blonde standing in a huge conch shell. It was Botticelli's 'Birth of Venus' brought to life. With one hand she held her waist-length hair to cover her modesty, whilst with the other she pointed to the tribune, the signal for Abdelaziz Ayeb to come to the stage to launch 'The Living Roman Town of Bisuli'.

It would be, said Ayeb, looking at the cameras, a unique cultural experience for thousands of visitors from around the globe. They would mingle with the inhabitants of Bisuli as they might have been, in the streets, in the market, doing their shopping. They would see citizens in their houses. They could eat what they ate, drink what they drank. See them at the baths, watch them working out, socialising, and debating the issues of the day. It would all be as authentic as possible. Children would be scolded, wives would quarrel with their husbands, and husbands would ill-treat their slaves. Visitors would watch workmen in their workshops and artists laying mosaics. Soldiers would get drunk. Gods would be worshipped in their temples.

Some journalists were baffled. The serious press didn't know what to make of it. Would tourists really be interested? Was it as fun as riding a camel or visiting an oasis? Did holidaymakers care? Tickets, Ayeb boldly declared, would cost less than a round of golf in Hammamet. Wouldn't the English at least, prefer the golf? Representatives of the serious papers looked at each other, puzzled. Could anyone be this vulgar and get away with it? Or was he sitting on a gold mine? Was this the future for all of us? Was nothing going to be left to the imagination?

The British tabloids loved it. This had popular appeal and more. Package tourists would remember the Roman communal lavatories, the nudes in the baths, the gladiators and the brothels. They would like the buskers and the wandering minstrels. Their readers would indeed drink the wine, eat the food and play dice. They would enjoy the blood-thirsty sports in the amphitheatre.

The TV teams were less happy. Poetry, dancing and the Birth of Venus weren't going to make the news, however they edited it. As for Ayeb's speech, it had zero visual impact. But something else soon did.

Tunisians at first thought it was a local wedding. Foreigners thought it was drunks. It started with a large scale hooting of horns – *beep-beep, beep-beep, beep-beep* – accompanied by the grinding of many combustion engines outside the amphitheatre. It grew louder as it approached the entrance. Then the noise stopped. Dozens of cameras swung round, as did every spectator.

The red Toyota looked tiny coming through the high-arched tunnel. Khaled was driving, Alison was in the passenger seat to guide him and Omar and Celia were in the back. Celia was actually standing on her seat, holding a large U.N. flag. She looked thin, pale and tired. Close behind, walking, shuffling, sometimes dancing came the rag-tag army of migrants creating a mist of red dust. They had gathered, more or less, behind their national flags like an Olympic parade. It had not been easy for Sam and Tahar to obtain the flags of Mali, Mauretania, Niger, Nigeria, Chad, Sudan and Uganda and others too. But they had and the effect was amazing. In carnival mode, cheering and waving their arms, one part of Africa was saying hello to another. The migrants were not at all fazed by the tiers of spectators because it was clear the happiness was infectious: the spectators were joining in. As many of the motley crowd of migrants as could, clambered onto the stage. Eight hundred or so of the others sat down cross-legged around it.

Abdelaziz Ayeb had returned to his seat, thinking perhaps that this was a part of the programme which he had somehow forgotten. It took a while for the reality to sink in. His show had been hijacked. He was at first struck dumb. He looked desperately on either side of him for Tahar who wasn't there. A look of total disbelief crossed his face. Then fury. But by then it was too late.

When Khaled started speaking in Arabic, he was too close to the microphone. But the sudden loudness of his greeting *"sbah el khir"* (good morning) had the useful effect of silencing the crowd. He moved a pace back like a dance instructor. To his surprise, he wasn't nervous. He had been imagining this moment for days. He and his brother, not to mention Major Mifsoud and Hedi Soukni were already in deep trouble. He knew he would be arrested and end up in Mornaguia prison with the other dissidents. But he was committed now. He'd burnt his bridges. He'd nothing to lose.

"I'm Khaled Ansari, an ordinary Tunisian. We Tunisians are famous for our hospitality and justly proud of it. But the poor people in front of me here, migrants from beyond the Sahara, have seen none of our hospitality, none at all. They have been locked up in a camp just ten kilometres from here at Bir Assaya in appalling conditions."

As Khaled outlined how long this had been going on and how the camp's very existence had been kept secret, he looked straight at the VIP box. It was in the shade and he was in the sun so that even narrowing his eyes he couldn't make out the individuals there. But he knew they could see him quite clearly and above all, hear him. He wanted them to squirm.

"We know who is responsible. We know who is protecting him. We know how it has all been kept secret."

He paused. Sounds in an amphitheatre resonate and echo. 'Protecting him' and 'All been kept secret' bounced round the tiers of murmuring spectators, swept across the heads of the seated migrants, curled round the Roman pillars at either end of the gracious building and faded into the bright blue sky.

"What you are about to hear will make you uncomfortable. Perhaps what you see already makes you uneasy. So it should, especially the Tunisians who are here. Inhuman and shameful treatment has been given to these migrants in our name. We have to put things right.

"It's easy to dismiss the problem as not being ours but someone else's. It is not an answer to ignore it in the hope that it will go away.

206

And it is certainly not an answer to hide people away because they are unwelcome."

He stopped again as 'unwelcome' echoed round the amphitheatre like an accusation.

"I want you to listen now to a film-maker, a foreigner from Europe and a very brave woman. She will tell you better than I, in English, why we are here to disturb you."

Celia moved slowly to the microphone leaving Omar, Khaled and Major Mifsoud behind her. She summoned Sam and Alison to the platform. She was shivering yet trickles of perspiration ran down her cheeks from her forehead. As she started to speak, fifteen thousand people fell silent. The Africans could not understand everything she was about to say. But they had a fair idea. The media had a story. They were about to record one of the most moving speeches most of them had ever heard.

CHAPTER 20

"**M**y name is Celia. I am British although it doesn't really matter where I come from. I am a film maker and a journalist. I am also very nervous.

"I have been living for the past six months with the one thousand brave men and women that you see in front of you. I have heard their stories. I have shared a little bit of their lives. I have seen their suffering. Indeed, I have suffered with them.

"I want you to take a good look at them please. Take a good, long look. They will not stare back at you because they are understandably shy.

"I ask you to look because some people with power and influence don't want you to see them, don't want you to know about them. They have been hidden away.

"The people sitting in the sand in front of you and on this stage with me, are men and women from every part of what is called sub-Saharan Africa. They are real. They are mothers and fathers, husbands and wives just like you. And they cannot be hidden away any longer.

"Do you see their flags? It was their idea to have their flags here. They said it made them feel proud. They are proud of their flags. They are proud of their countries. One day they want to go back to them. They love their countries, just as you love yours.

"They are leaving their cities, their towns and their villages in order to survive. It is hard for us to imagine in our comfortable homes, where we have clean water, security, good health, where no one is starving, what is happening in the rest of the continent to the south of us. These people can tell you if you take the trouble to talk to them. The people over there," Celia lifted her arm, which was shaking, to point to a group, "and over there, and there, holding the flags of Chad will tell you of the murder, the killing, the mass rape, the looting, the burning and the torture of their families in Darfur. The people over there holding the Sudanese flag, and the people from the Horn of Africa over there are also fleeing from murderous wars, from the destruction of their villages, from drought and starvation. Vicious, cruel, unimaginably brutal civil wars have forced people to flee from West Africa too. Look at the flags of Sierra Leone, Liberia, Ivory Coast, Cameroon, Niger, and Nigeria."

The tense, oval amphitheatre was totally silent. The only noise came from birds overhead. The crowd sensed that something unique was happening collectively and they were a living part of it.

"It is not just war – far from it – that has forced many of them to flee. It is economic hardship, economic crisis, collapsed economies – hundreds of times worse than any economic crisis we are experiencing. In fact, many of the people sitting in the sand are well-educated. They are traders, mechanics, farm-owners, teachers, leather-workers, skilled artisans. A teacher over there taught me a simple new equation: -

No Work + No Food = Starvation + Death

"Rather than starve, they run away, they flee. Wouldn't you do the same? But many of my friends here are fleeing their homes because they are being persecuted. Persecuted because of their tribe, their ethnic origin or their religion.

"Eighteen hundred years ago, in amphitheatres just like this, perhaps in this very one, Christians were tied to stakes driven into the ground to be torn to death and eaten by lions just as the twenty-two year old Vibia Perpetua and her servant Felicitas were, on the seventh of March 203 in nearby Carthage. African slaves were also killed here by gladiators for the amusement of the crowd. Persecution was an amusement for them. You might think that we had put all that behind us. Alas, sickening persecution is still an everyday occurrence in sub-Saharan Africa. These people, surely, surely, should be persecuted no longer.

"These people are fleeing because they have no choice, no other option if they are to survive. They flee because they are desperate. They flee to find safety. They have risked their lives to come this far. They are prepared to take further, enormous risks crossing the Mediterranean in hopelessly overloaded, leaking boats which leave these coasts every night. We don't know how many die, how many drown trying to get to Europe. We do know that they pay small fortunes in U.S. dollars to smugglers or traffickers.

"To arrive in Tunisia and in Libya, can you imagine the hardships they have endured crossing the Sahara desert? Many take a year to make the journey from Cameroon to Agadez in Niger, then to the Sebha oasis and then the Libyan or Tunisian coast. Even longer journey times are taken by those following the trails north from Mogadishu, across Somalia, Sudan and Libya. These are huge distances that would be daunting for even the best equipped safari drivers with satellite navigation and powerful vehicles.

"Imagine what it is like if you are in the hands of an unscrupulous people smuggler who will take hundreds of dollars of your money and will abandon you at the first sign of trouble with bandits, border guards or breakdowns. Imagine what it is like hiding in the back of a stinking truck in forty degrees of heat whilst border guards search it. On foot, imagine what it is like trying to survive a sandstorm when there is no shelter. Or what it is like when you fall sick."

Celia stopped and bent to one side as a stabbing pain began in her abdomen. She put one hand on her knee for a moment and then straightened up.

"I'm sorry. The authorities said that they had had complaints about these people. The authorities said they were upsetting you. Well, yes, migrants are upsetting. They are a problem, a huge problem which is going to be with us for generations unless we help them. Nobody knows how many tens of thousands are coming each year but we do know the numbers are rising.

"When I was told that these people were being rounded up like cattle and taken to a detention centre – more like a prison – just a few kilometres from here, at Bir Assaya, I asked to see it for myself.

Because an epidemic broke out and because I became ill myself, I had to stay there for six months.

"I could not believe what I saw there. I saw misery, sadness, depression and much tragedy. But I lived with people who could also be optimistic if given a glimmer of hope; who were determined, courageous, willing to learn languages and new skills. I saw good men and women desperate for security, desperate to retain their dignity and eventually to find happiness.

"Hopefully, for my friends here, the worst is over now. We all escaped from the camp this morning with the help of several brave people whom I will not embarrass by naming. We are all free again.

"My friends and I will make a film. These people will be the actors. They will show how they came to be here. They will tell their true stories. Their stories will shock you. They will shock the world. Perhaps this is the only way we can make ourselves face up to what is happening and then to do something about it."

Again, Celia stopped, this time to catch her breath. She knew she had one more effort to make: the appeal. Her body was crying out for her to stop, to be still. Her fever made her eyes shine.

"The people here will work at anything you give them – and that, I know, is a real problem for this country, all our countries. Because already there are too few jobs. But maybe, just maybe, there are some jobs they could do without local people suffering. Are we being inventive enough? How can this manpower be put to good use – farming, building, driving, making the economy grow? Some of you here, as spectators or watching on TV, will be employers. Please ask yourselves, could you help? Do you have work of any sort that these men or women could do?

"Others of you in the audience could perhaps offer food and shelter temporarily to just one of these people. If you have a spare room, unused servants' quarters, a spare bed somewhere, do you have it in your heart to offer hospitality until that lucky person finds a job? Of course, there will be formalities to be gone through, paperwork to be done, but these hurdles will be overcome, *insha Allah*. The Holy Koran says it is a duty to assist those who have

211

embraced the Faith and have left their homes. The Holy Bible says 'Thou shalt neither vex a stranger nor oppress him'. These people need help. Not more persecution. So I appeal to you all, wherever you hear me – help if you can. In the name of our common humanity."

Those closest to her noticed she was perspiring freely. Celia knew she had a high fever. It had come on so suddenly. Her head was now throbbing. She put her hand to her temple and closed her eyes. She could hear people applauding. The clapping seemed unnaturally loud. Was it her head or was it the acoustics? When she opened her eyes again she saw patches of black. She looked up to the top tier as if searching for more light. The applause continued. Everything started to turn as she became dizzy and lost her balance. She swayed from side to side, then crumpled at the foot of the microphone. The clapping stopped. There was a collective gasp.

Because she was sitting on the stage, almost under the microphone stand, Hope was the first person to comfort her.

"Your eyes are closed. You are very sick. But do not die. God will look after you. Take this." And she put her doll in Celia's hand.

Feeling it, Celia held it closer to her eyes as she tipped in and out of consciousness.

"I won't die, Hope. And you mustn't die either." Her eyes closed for a couple of seconds then opened again.

"Hope, there was a great man who once lived in this country who we now call St Augustine. When you are older, read about him. He said words find their way to the heart better when they are sung than when they are said. You must put your poem to music. Sing your poem. Then millions of people can hear it."

"I will," said Hope, smiling. "I will."

When Omar and Khaled, not for the first time, picked her up to move her out of the sun, they could immediately see how high her fever was. Beside the stage, in the shade, Omar laid her on the first material that came to hand – the U.N. flag.

As Sam approached, Omar said,

"It's typhoid fever again. Abdominal pain and nosebleeds are sure signs for me. We must get her some ciprofloxacin as fast as possible."

Hearing Sam's voice, Celia turned her head and opened her eyes. She could just see Sam, hazily, and she managed the slightest of smiles.

"Febris is angry, isn't she," she said.

"Yes, my love, Febris is angry." He took the coin out of his shirt pocket but she couldn't see it. Her eyes were closed again but her pulse was strong.

Omar and Khaled placed her gently onto a stretcher. Sam and Major Mifsoud took the other two handles. The refugees parted to make way for the sad procession like courtiers making way for a king. The stretcher crossed the eerily silent arena and left through the tunnel into the outside world.

As if an unseen hand was pressing the volume button on a remote control, the sound in the amphitheatre went up as soon as the stretcher party was out of sight. What Celia had said, and Khaled before her, had struck home. No-one moved to leave. The migrants stayed where they were. Tunisians and foreigners alike were stunned by Celia's collapse. They were horrified by the description of the camp, by the mention of typhoid, by the cruelty, by the sight and plight of the migrants. Members of the audience, often complete strangers to each other, started to talk to their neighbours. There were invocations to Allah, shaking of heads and gesticulation.

It was not only what had been said that was deeply shocking but the fact that these people had dared to speak out at all like that. Such action was suicidal in Tunisia. This is what now made the amphitheatre hum. How had these brothers, this Army officer and this Englishwoman been so incredibly bold? Didn't they realise the inevitable fate that awaited them? Did they have a death wish?

Thoughtful Tunisians realised that arrests wouldn't be made in front of the media and foreign ambassadors. Arrests would rather be made, as was the custom, at night and out of sight.

The three Tunisian ministers present had anyway sensed the mood of the public and realised that if the Ansaris or Celia were taken in for questioning, they would most likely become martyrs which was the last thing that was needed. Ministers were all too well aware of the reports of anger in the universities and of the increasingly outspoken human rights lobby. Workers in the south of the country were beginning to make critical remarks in public, too. Of course, such agitation was being snuffed out by state security as soon as it arose. But Tunisians were learning about what was happening miles away within minutes thanks to the internet. Many, many Tunisians would have filmed that day's extraordinary events in the amphitheatre. Clips would be on social websites in no time.

The knee-jerk reaction of the dozen or so members of the ruling elite present was to look for a scapegoat. They had been publicly embarrassed, humiliated even. This had not happened on such a scale before. It must not happen again, the President's press secretary muttered through clenched teeth. The obvious person to blame was Abdelaziz Ayeb.

In Tahar's office, Celia came round slowly and took some water. Sitting straight, she wiped her face with a towel and took the tablets that Omar handed to her. She gave him Hope's rag-doll and insisted it be given back to her. She walked a few paces but was clearly more comfortable sitting down. She asked to be alone for a while with Alison.

The office was a sea of rolled-up plans, overflowing files and artefacts. A large photocopier occupied one wall. An outdated computer screen and dust-covered keyboard monopolised Tahar's desk. On one wall was pinned a black and white aerial photo of Bisuli and on another was a large scale relief map, much marked with coloured pens. Lying on a small table in the middle of the room was an open box filled with what looked like wet tissue paper on which lay two exquisite amulets, corroded and partially fused together. But the twisted gold filaments and the blue, black and yellow stones embedded within them were intact. At last she felt well enough to talk again. She moved to Tahar's chair. Alison sat facing her, carefully folding up the crumpled, dusty UN flag.

CHAPTER 21

What is it that makes individuals behave out of character when they are *en masse*? Small numbers of tourists abroad behave well. But large numbers are embarrassing to behold. What sends a rioter out of his mind? Or a fan? The lover of football is perfectly normal watching his match at home on TV. But put him with his fellow spectators and he becomes unhinged, demented. The Italians use the same word *"un tifoso"* for a fan and a typhoid sufferer – both are fevered and delirious. So it was with the media at Bisuli.

Once Celia had been carried out of the arena, journalists fell over themselves in their eagerness to talk to, film or photograph any of the remaining actors in the drama. The hacks had been taught that a story was no good, even if it was exclusive, unless personalised with a quote or a piece to camera. Omar and Khaled had gone. Ayeb was nowhere to be found. Bill Wells declined to speak. Hope Kakwani was hunted down but preferred not to speak English, so was dropped. It was poor Major Mifsoud who was mobbed in French and Arabic. The feeding frenzy continued around him for a good hour till he walked away to supervise the migrants' onward journeys.

The media chaos was complicated by the fact that the foreign journalists at Bisuli were travel and leisure correspondents not political pundits. They suddenly realised they were covering much more than sun, sea and ruins. This was a complex story about migration, human suffering, typhoid and bravery against an unexpectedly tense political backdrop. There were Tunisian heroes and, best of all, an English heroine. Some of the younger correspondents saw this as a once in a lifetime chance to break a big story; from travel supplement to page one. They did not care how they behaved in the media scrum in the amphitheatre to get the people and the pictures they wanted.

With the long-suffering migrants in the background, a nervous BBC reporter tilted his head as he'd seen his seniors do and recorded to camera over the bubbling hubbub of noise:

'What began as the launch of a tourism project here at Bisuli in Tunisia, turned into a day of quite extraordinary drama. As Mr Abdelaziz Ayeb, one of the richest men in North Africa, was announcing his no-expense-spared development of the ruins of this Roman town, nine-hundred cheering sub-Saharan economic migrants walked into the amphitheatre, over there, unannounced. They were led by a brave thirty-five year-old Englishwoman, Celia Purchas, from north London. She made a most moving appeal for help for the migrants and then collapsed with the microphone in her hand. According to Dr Omar Ansari, a Tunisian doctor on the spot, she is suffering from a recurrence of typhoid fever from which she nearly died while she was quarantined in a makeshift camp with the migrants…'

Meanwhile, in the eerie calm of Tahar's untidy office, Celia had fully regained consciousness and was sitting on a worn, scuffed leather couch. An electric fan whirred quietly on a filing cabinet, ruffling the tissue-paper on a bundle of broken pottery. A blue, plastic crate full of labelled stones lay by Tahar's desk, disturbing a line of ants silently going about their business. A broad shaft of light from the one window illuminated the dust floating in the warm air. Alison was standing by the couch holding a glass of water. Her eyes never left Celia's face.

"I feel as though I've known you all my life," Alison said. "You can't imagine how strange I feel, now that I've caught up with you."

"I don't understand," said Celia.

Alison paused for several seconds. The only noise was the ticking of Tahar's office clock.

"We both love the same man," Alison said.

"You too?" said Celia.

"Yes. Obviously Sam talked a lot about you."

"How long have you known him?" said Celia.

216

"Five months or so. I met him in London last autumn after he came back from Tunisia. After your…"

"My what?"

"Your disappearance. At least that's the word Sam used. That's what he believed."

Celia shook her head slowly. Her green eyes glistened. She wasn't sure what drugs Omar had just given her but she felt stronger, more in control.

"So it was you who took my place? I might have known something like that would happen. I feared it would. He's a very attractive man."

Alison nodded. Celia continued.

"Attractive in the sense that one cannot avoid being drawn to him. He has a powerful pull, like a magnet with pins or paper-clips."

"More like being caught in a whirlwind as far as I was concerned," said Alison. "Things moved so fast with him. He would get carried away." She made an upward gesture with her arm and regretted it. The pain from her bad shoulder made her wince. She still hadn't done anything about it.

"But it takes two," said Celia.

"Of course. But I couldn't have stayed with him permanently without knowing what had happened to you. You were always in the background. Sam pretended that your disappearance didn't hurt him. But it did, you know. It hurt him a lot."

Celia stood up and walked to the window. The sun outside bathed Bisuli in the clear light that photographers love. Inside, a butterfly was trapped on the window and fluttered vainly up and down the glass. Alison stood beside her, looking at the beautiful insect.

"We nearly lost our lives together here, right here, just a few hours ago."

"What do you mean? What happened?"

So Alison described the accident, the vault collapsing, how far she fell, how Sam was trapped. As she talked, she could feel that Celia understood, was even forgiving – at least to a degree. A bond between the two women began to form. It was not just that there was a man common to both of them or indeed that they had both just looked death in the face. It was something unspoken, intangible but strong nevertheless.

"Why didn't he reply to my letters?" Celia asked.

"Letters?" said Alison.

"Yes."

"He never received them."

"My God. Major Mifsoud, the commandant, you met him just before the ceremony, he told me that if I hadn't had any reply, it was probably because my letters were intercepted. He was right. Poor Sam."

Alison sat beside Celia on the couch. She noticed how thin Celia was. Neither spoke. Both looked at the window and the exhausted, imprisoned butterfly.

"I don't know how to say this without it sounding odd or even patronising," said Alison, breaking the silence.

"But it's something I feel as a woman and I must say it because I admire you, I respect you."

She hesitated then turned towards Celia.

"Sam belongs to you and you to him. I know he loves you still," said Alison.

Celia put the back of her hand to her mouth as if to stifle a cry.

"Do you really think so?"

"I know it."

From outside the room came the burbling of low voices. A man was talking into a mobile phone.

Celia looked Alison in the eye. There was a trace of dried blood around her nose which Alison started to wipe away with the corner of her handkerchief soaked in mineral water. As she wiped, tears rolled down Celia's cheeks. She put her other arm on Celia's back and they embraced. They clung to each other for a long moment. When they separated, Celia wiped what was left of her tears away, smiled and said,

"You are so good to me. Why are you so good to me? I don't

218

deserve it. Thank you for telling me. Thank you. It's true that I thought of him all the time at the beginning."

"At the beginning?" asked Alison.

"For the first few weeks. Then when he didn't write…"

"Sam talked about you. I knew you were not only someone very dear to him. But a very special, very unusual person. When you disappeared, I was sure something bad had happened to you. I didn't know what. I had to find out. I visited your house in London. I contacted Malwood Films. I interviewed Rafiq and Ferid. Eventually, I discovered where you were."

Celia put out her hand towards Alison's which was resting on her knee. Alison took it and held it tight. It was cold and slightly damp.

"You're still feverish, Celia. The doctor will get you the right drugs, he told me. You'll soon be better."

"I must get better. I absolutely must."

She reached down for her bag from which she pulled her camcorder.

"I have many hours of film here. I have interviews with Cameroonians, Sudanese, Malians and with a wonderful Nigerian girl called Hope. I have film of the doctors working with the sick and dying, of people so traumatised they could scarcely speak, of people on the edge of breakdown. But there are wonderful moments, too. Even funny. My plan is to get back to London as fast as possible; to talk to Alfred Feldstein; to show him what I have and to show the world what is happening."

Without a moment's hesitation, Alison said "I want to help. I'm in a lucky position financially. There is nothing more useful than this that I could do with my money. Nothing would give me more pleasure."

"Thank you. Thank you so much," said Celia. "Like all films it's a risk. No doubt we'll be damned by the political right. We'll be pilloried for being polemical. And I don't pretend to have the answers. But first the problem has to be acknowledged, don't you agree?"

"Yes, absolutely. If the film makes any money, where should it go?"

"To all the Hopes and Mohammeds, to sub-Saharan Africa," said Celia. "But I don't yet know how."

So began a partnership which led to the production within the year of 'The Migrants' Tale', narrated and directed by Celia, produced by Malwood Films and financed by Alison Grainger and Alfred Feldstein. Celia's discussions with Alfred Feldstein in Soho were remarkable for the blaze of excitement they produced. Feldstein was moved to tears by Celia's account of her time incarcerated in the camp. Like most people living north of the Mediterranean, he only had the vaguest idea of the suffering of the migrants. And he, too, felt guilty for not having done more to find Celia. A film was a way of making amends.

He immediately saw the potential. It had human interest and suffering on a continent-wide scale. It was topical and true. It was quite different. He wanted to try the market for more politically engaged cinema. Who, after all, would have thought that a film about the slum children of Mumbai would have swept the board? When Feldstein saw the footage that Celia herself had shot at Bir Assaya, as well as independent film of the amphitheatre speech, he had no further doubts.

The final product incorporated footage of the misery from which the migrants were escaping, the unbelievable privations they suffered crossing the Sahara, the tragedies in the Mediterranean and the disgrace of the migrants' camps. Few films dealing with such awful documentary material could have had such box-office success. Few films had cost so little but saved so many lives. It was the long overdue wake-up call.

CHAPTER 22

The response to Celia's appeal that day in Bisuli was overwhelming. For many spectators, this was the first time they had been made aware of the plight of the migrants; the first time they had had to face up to what was happening in their back yard. It had come as a shock. There was anger at the way fellow human beings had been treated without their knowledge. Shame was a common reaction. Guilt a common feeling. There was no great surprise, however, that it had been kept secret.

A primitive but effective system for recording the offers of help was set up there and then at Bisuli. Details were taken down by Major Mifsoud's officers at trestle tables strategically positioned between the amphitheatre, press tent and car park. By the end of the day, about a hundred migrants had been promised mentors, foster families or even employment. The job of matching offers to individuals was then picked up and taken forward in the succeeding days by a team of hurriedly assembled officials.

Earlier in the amphitheatre, as the spectacle unfolded, Bill Wells had felt increasingly uncomfortable. Good taste was not an attribute automatically associated with him. Yet when he saw that something was in really bad taste, he recognised it. He thought the vulgarity of the ceremony – the diaphanous dresses, the naked girl in the conch shell, the fashion show, the sword fighting between centurions – was unnecessary, over the top, even for a showman like Ayeb. More importantly, he was disturbed by the reports he had had in London of the way Ayeb had used information from the Foreign Office for his personal gain. Ayeb had even sent him an embarrassingly gushing e-mail about mutually beneficial cooperation and about oil slicks having silver linings. If that message were ever to become public – and it seemed everyone's in-box was vulnerable to hackers these days – his career would come to a premature end. He had decided to distance himself from the man even before coming to the amphitheatre.

The dramatic appearance of the migrants and Celia's impassioned appeal on their behalf, eclipsed all else in his mind for days to come. He was doubly shocked when he learnt from a journalist who had been present, and with whom he lunched later in London, that the migrants had been herded into their camp at Ayeb's instigation. The man was not only ambitious but a criminal. He certainly wasn't a suitable Secretary General of the World Economic Forum. After his years of British party politics, Bill Wells was not entirely naïve when it came to character assassination. A quiet word dropped into the right ears at the next OPEC summit by Bill's Saudi friends ensured Ayeb's candidature did not succeed.

Hints that Bill dropped at Westminster and at party headquarters to the effect that if there were a reshuffle, he would not be averse to taking the Overseas Development portfolio, were equally effective. Unkind observers said there were no other takers for the job. But Bill was genuinely delighted. More quickly than he had imagined, and thanks in no small part to the favourable atmosphere engendered by 'The Migrant's Tale' and Celia's lecture tour to promote it, cabinet colleagues agreed to a refocusing of aid on Africa. Bill was proud of his One Point Plan for Africa: Investment. It was easy to remember and easy to promote. But it would take more than Bill Wells could deliver, more than one country could offer, to turn things around. Much more. But it was a start.

Bisuli never looked back after it hit the headlines. Tahar was deeply affected by the sight of the migrants and Celia's courage. He arranged for a group of migrants to stay on the site at Bisuli and provide ever-welcome manpower. The field kitchens, the sanitary facilities, the marquees were all put to full use.

The new attraction, and the most important from the archaeological point of view, was the sanctuary for the sick. Its restoration had been easier than expected. Stones had not been plundered, as was the case with so many other monuments. Kind sands, blown by the winds of the intervening centuries, had preserved it well, notwithstanding the deadly collapse of the roof. In 200 AD the place had been much used. Hundreds of votive objects testified to that.

The waters of the 'therapeutic' spring, which still filled the sacred pools beside it, were tested by the health authorities. As Tahar feared, they contained traces of the *salmonella typhi* bacteria. The public health people were mystified as to how this could be. Tahar told them that the water distribution system at Bisuli had not yet been mapped. All were agreed that it was vitally important that it should be. In the meantime, there was no question, the authorities said, of the public being allowed into the sanctuary.

But the most intriguing discovery only came to light when the statue of Febris was brought to the surface and examined by Tahar. At first he puzzled over the type of stone, which was darker than he expected. Looking more closely, where it had been chipped when the vault collapsed, he saw it was no different from that used elsewhere on the site. Perhaps then, he thought, there were either layers of soot from countless smoking lamps or a discoloured pigment. He sent a flake of the covering to Tunis for analysis and was surprised when the result was phoned through. It was ox-blood. The statue had had ox-blood poured over it for many years. When worshippers came here, did they bring animals with them for sacrificing to Febris? Or was the blood brought in separately? It was not immediately clear. The sanctuary had slept on its secrets for centuries and even now was unwilling to yield them up.

There were, in the end, no Romans in togas and no nudes at the baths. There were no gladiators in the amphitheatre and no slaves building new villas. No chariots clattered down the straight streets. No oil was pressed or flour milled. Instead, the ruins themselves invited visitors to imagine these things, and they did.

They came for Abdelaziz Ayeb at four in the morning on the thirteenth of April. He offered no resistance. Few people do at that time of night. It was a vigorous but correct arrest. The police arrived in numbers. A dozen plain-clothes men took away the contents of a fire-proof cabinet in his study as well as the files from two smaller cabinets. His computers were somewhat roughly put into the back of the police van waiting in the dark outside. Mrs Ayeb, who was sleeping in a separate room, was told to stay there, on her bed, by two firm policewomen while the rest of the house was searched. The code-name for the police operation was Icarus. Ayeb had been allowed to build wings and fit them but he had now flown too close to the sun.

The main accusation was conspiring against the State with named officials in the Ministries of Interior and Defence, including officers in the police force. He was also accused of the illegal detention of foreign nationals. There was never the slightest doubt that he would be found guilty.

After his arrest and with suspicious Tunisians watching, the government was obliged to act. Rumours flew around the internet, albeit in guarded language, that Ayeb's corruption was not an isolated case. A pseudonymous blogger writing under the name of *rompu.cor* was brave enough to write that 'the country was being bled to death by a coterie of unscrupulous individuals cleverly putting themselves above the law.' Within three days the authorities tracked her down – for it was a lady architect in Tunis – and had brought her in for 'questioning'. Within a week her licence to practice had been revoked.

The Ayeb arrest sent different signals to different people in Tunisia. The regime meant it as a warning to any individual who thought he could set himself up as a rival to the president. The brave but secretive dissidents saw it as proof that the rot had set in. However one looked at it, eliminating Ayeb from the scene was important.

Judge Ansari, no less, father of Omar and Khaled, was appointed to decide on the distribution of Ayeb's confiscated assets. As a first step, Ayeb's hotels in and around Carthage, were requisitioned, fully staffed, for the migrants. For the first time in their lives they slept between linen sheets, enjoyed hot showers and could eat their fill.

Money was allotted from Ayeb's personal bank account to buy them clothes.

It was explained to the migrants that come the summer, the hotel rooms would be needed and they would be flown back to their countries of origin. Predictably, a few decided to risk their lives with the people traffickers and took to the sea. Others accepted offers of apprenticeships on farms, in bakeries, as leather workers, potters or security guards.

The judge's most inspired decision was that one tenth of Ayeb's assets was to be dedicated to the upkeep of Tunisia's archaeological sites, with one million dollars reserved exclusively for Bisuli.

CHAPTER 23

When they returned to London after the dramas of the previous week in Bisuli, both Celia and Sam were looking forward to the peace and quiet of their respective homes. Yet the luxury of tranquillity was denied them. 'The Migrants' Tale' needed telling now. The tragedy was contemporary. Remedies were required right away. Celia felt strongly that the film would lose its power and political purpose if it was not made as soon as possible. Motivated by the migrants' plight and persecution, she did not have a day to lose. She knew as well as anyone how long it took for a film to be made. Alfred Feldstein used to say that even elephants pro-created more quickly. But this film couldn't afford to wait.

Negotiations were started by Feldstein to acquire rights to the recordings shot by TV organisations in the amphitheatre. Celia's camcorder footage from the camp turned out to be inspired. Celia and Feldstein were delighted to discover two screenplay writers with personal experience of Africa, to apply their talents to 'The Migrants' Tale'. Finding the storyline to fit the film together was not too difficult. The Nigerian teenager, Hope, was the obvious choice. Her poem, her face and her smile buoyed Celia up during her first days back in London.

However, typhoid fever, poor food and stress had taken its toll. Celia was far from fit for active service in the film industry. She knew that her GP was right in advising her to decompress, to convalesce, and to allow her body to rebuild its defences. Her parents, shocked by her loss of weight, had told her the same thing. But she didn't have the time to rest.

Each day was a struggle. She wondered where her strength had gone. Researching, talking to the international charities and agencies, writing and film-editing tired her out. The result was that she didn't have the space for Sam in her current life even though they lived within walking distance of each other. Of course, they could talk on the phone – which they did most nights at first – and there were texts and even e-mails too for a while. But she could feel they were drifting apart.

On his side, Sam thought that he, too, would be busier than ever because whilst still in Tunisia he had had a long e-mail inviting him to write and present another TV series, this time on Roman Africa. On his first day back he had already fixed an evening meeting to discuss it and was thinking of different approaches to the subject, of the various options for a six-part series.

At work there was a backlog of managerial decisions for him to take, or at least contribute to, as income for the museum dwindled dramatically from all sources. It was no longer a question of which projects could go ahead but whether any at all could. He was not, he had long ago realised, cut out to be a manager. He actually disliked the word. It had always surprised him that subject expertise was valued less than management skills in the organisations where he'd worked. The higher he went in the hierarchy, the less quality time he had for pure archaeology, for research, for the science. He sometimes felt that if he saw another request for a career review or a budget breakdown or a completed time-management chart he would explode.

He had only been back a week when he had the first of his headaches. To begin with he thought it was an allergic reaction to something or other – food, wine or even the new pillows he was using. The media reminded him it was the hay-fever season and talked about rising pollen counts, even in the cities, and how as the climate changed, it was going to become worse. But Sam didn't normally have hay-fever, so he eliminated that.

A couple of days later, he mentioned it to Celia.

"Try belladonna, it's excellent for migraines," she advised.

"How do you know? Have you tried it?" asked Sam, who was suspicious of everything homeopathic.

"Not myself, no. But friends have. Anyway, I'm not a sufferer. Presumably you've given up on ordinary pain-killers?" said Celia.

"Yes. They're having no effect. Today was particularly unpleasant though. I'd just arrived at work and was trying to fire up the computer when I found I couldn't see the keyboard clearly. It was all fuzzy. Not to mention the screen. I went to the wash-room and splashed my face with cold water, took a walk up and down the corridor and felt better. But a couple of hours later it started again. In fact the rest of the day was pretty much a write-off."

He paused then added, "I'm puzzled, Celia. A bit frightened actually."

"What are you going to do?" Celia replied. "Shouldn't you see a doctor?"

Had she not been so stressed herself she would have recognised this as a 'cri de coeur'. Later she realised she should have gone round to his place to see what the problem really was. But she was too wrapped up in herself, preoccupied with her deadlines and her migrants to sense there was something wrong.

Two days later when she rang as usual at bed-time she found Sam curiously aggressive and slurring his words. Admittedly it was late and she assumed Sam had had a glass of wine too many. He seemed a bit confused about when he had left work. Celia first understood it was that morning but then he seemed to be saying he hadn't been back for two days. She was reassured to hear him say that he was seeing the doctor the next day. "We're both tired," she thought as she put the phone down and switched off the light.

Doctors' receptionists receive little praise for their thankless job. When the experienced receptionist at the surgery took Sam's call, she remarked on his confusion to her colleague. Busy, thirty-something male patients were not usually confused like that. Something told her to alert the doctor setting off on his house calls that Sam hadn't shown up for his appointment. Sam was hastily added to the list and the doctor arrived in the late afternoon the same day. Answering his questions, Sam revealed that he had had an accident in Tunisia; that he had lost consciousness but was perfectly alright afterwards. Five minutes later, the doctor was on the phone for an ambulance.

Sam was lucky that his local hospital happened to specialise in brain surgery. As suspected, the scans showed a blood clot in the left hemisphere. By early evening the neurosurgeon was doing what he could in the first available operating theatre. Removing the clot took three hours of delicate surgery. The surgeon told Sam afterwards that he wished it had been diagnosed earlier. Craniotomy was never easy and the longer the clot was on the brain, the more doubtful the outcome.

Celia didn't discover where Sam was until, to her surprise, his phone was answered that night by his father.

"Is that Sam? No? Oh, I'm sorry. I must have the wrong number," Celia said, trying to make her bedtime call.

"No. This is Sam's father. Who is that?"

"Celia."

"Ah. Celia. Yes. We were wondering where you were. Sam hasn't been terribly good about keeping us in the loop. My wife had lost your number. In fact we came up from the Isle of Wight in such a rush, we left our address book behind. Anyway we weren't sure..." He was kicked under the table. "Well anyway...You obviously don't know what's happened."

"O my God! No, tell me," said Celia.

"He was taken to hospital in Hampstead this afternoon. Scans showed a blood clot on the brain. They operated this evening. He's in intensive care. Not come round from the anaesthetic yet. When the phone rang I thought it might be the hospital, though come to think of it, I asked them to ring my mobile number. We were asked not to come to the hospital until first thing tomorrow morning. We'll meet the surgeon and see Sam, though not to talk to."

"Is there a danger...You know... How is he?"

"We don't know yet, as I said. The surgeon will tell us how it went."

"I must be there. I want to see him. I know Sam would want me to be there."

The surgeon was Lebanese, immaculately dressed in a light suit and silk tie but with tired eyes. Courteous to a fault, he was also unexpectedly frank. He apologised for not having discussed the operation with Sam's parents beforehand but time had been short. He had been convinced that there was only one course of action to take and Sam was lucid enough to sign the consent forms. Accessing the blood clot was difficult, he said. Between the time of the scan and the operation, it had moved. The intervention hadn't been a moment too soon.

He said recovery would be a slow process. Sam would have to stay in hospital for some time after leaving intensive care, perhaps ten days: it depended on so many things. He would be six weeks off work and it would be three months before he would be able to drive the car and resume a normal life.

Sam's parents noticed how carefully he chose his words when they asked about brain damage. Much would depend, he said, on whether there were complications. Any brain injury such as this could lead to an impairment of brain function. He could become very distressed, realising that things weren't right. It was unlikely, but there might be speech problems. Speech therapy and physiotherapy would be available.

Celia met Sam's parents later in the hospital. For some reason, Celia found the experience unreal. She found her attention wandering. Sam's father's voice drifted upwards as Celia looked away from him towards the wilting flowers on the cloth-covered table in the airless relatives' reception room. It was such a shock and so sudden. She was trying to take it all in but couldn't. Sam was still young. He had so many projects in the pipeline. His identification of the fever sanctuary by all accounts was the biggest thing in the Roman archaeological world for a decade. How could this happen to him?

She was the first to admit that she had missed the signs of his illness. But how was she to know? The truth was that they weren't nearly as close now as they had been before she was stuck in Bir Assaya. She regretted it. But that's where they were at, Sam and herself. She had had only one thing on her mind since returning: to do something for the migrants, to make her film.

She phoned Alison before breakfast the next day with the sad news. Alison was still in bed.

"Are they sure it's the result of the accident in Tunisia?" Alison asked.

"It's highly likely, apparently. The doctor said that blows to the head were particularly difficult because the real internal injury mightn't show straight away."

"It's true his hard hat was damaged, so it could have been a big hit. We were both unconscious for a while. Can I see him in hospital? When will they know if there's any permanent damage?"

"I think the surgeon said that he shouldn't have visitors until he's out of intensive care. Except for his parents. I guess they will want to camp at the hospital until he's out of danger. As for permanent damage, I suppose we will find out quite quickly. Though the surgeon was very cautious about it."

"But there is a risk…?" asked Alison.

"Very much so, unfortunately," said Celia.

"Thank you for ringing so early like this. I still can't believe it. Please keep me posted all the time. Sam is such a special person, isn't he?"

"A special person. Yes. I must rush now, Alison. But I thought you would want to know. We'll keep in close touch."

Alison thought it odd that Celia wasn't more sympathetic towards Sam, more emotional even. She sounded so matter-of-fact, almost distant. How could she be so rational, so disengaged?

Once she had put the phone down, Alison sat up in bed, quite still, staring at the light coming through the shutters. She knew what she had to do but wondered how she should do it.

CHAPTER 24

D ozing under the duvet, Alison wished she was tougher. She wished she could say, 'I'm going straight round to that hospital to see Sam. I've something he needs to know.' If she found Celia barring the way to Sam's bedside she would brush her aside imperiously saying, 'It's me that Sam needs, not you.' And she would rush to where Sam was. She would be wearing the black flamenco dress she'd bought in Seville. The nurses would step aside and he would squeeze her hand to show he recognised her, even though his eyes were shut. And Celia would go away and he would be completely normal and everything would be alright.

When the alarm rang, she pushed the button but continued staring down the bed in a semi-trance, smoothing the bed-covers on either side of her hips.

Women who succeed, she thought to herself, like Celia, know how to shut out their feelings. Why was it, Alison wondered, that she didn't have that hard edge? She shunned confrontation. She doubted that she had the ruthless streak to make it to the top in business. And she had become worse and worse emotionally in recent days. Little things – a woman hugging her son outside the front door, an advert on TV, a piece of music on the car radio – would bring tears to her eyes for no apparent reason.

When she started her medical degree at Oxford she came to know a much older postgraduate who was teaching basic medical sciences at her college. They had mutual friends and the relationship was always platonic. They had kept in touch after she switched from medicine and he was now doing clinical work again. Alison phoned him about Sam, knowing he would be frank. He confirmed the risks of brain damage that Celia had mentioned. He guessed that Sam wouldn't be pronounced as being completely out of danger for two weeks after the operation.

Pacing up and down her kitchen, coffee in hand, Alison rehearsed the arguments for seeing Sam without first telling Celia. She could do just that. But she knew that in her present state, seeing Sam would reignite all her dormant feelings for him. She didn't feel she could trust herself. She couldn't see Sam on the sly or briefly pop in and out because this would be no ordinary hospital visit. It needed preparation. The time had to be right. Alison had to be feeling well. And calm. Not emotional. There should be no crying. Well, ideally no crying.

She wondered if Celia realised the sacrifice that she, Alison, had made in Tahar's office after her incredible speech in the amphitheatre. What was it she said? Ah, yes. "Sam belongs to you and you to him. I know he loves you still." It is difficult to be more generous than that, to hand over a man you love to a woman who loves him more and who is your friend. Not many women would do that. But she did in Tunisia. Now she regretted it.

Sometimes, Alison thought, sometimes even the best intentioned gestures come to naught. Or turn out to be wrong.

"I wasn't thinking straight. I must have been mad, mad, mad."

She pushed down too hard on the toaster's slide and broke it.

"Damn. Can't even make toast now."

She refilled her coffee mug and stared out of the window.

"I was wrong to have let go of Sam," she spoke aloud, to herself now. "I must find the courage to tell Celia what's happened. She is, after all, the person I most admire after Sam. I can't see Sam behind her back."

The hospital was insistent that Sam should not be allowed visitors for three days after the operation. Alison had time to talk to Celia. They agreed to meet for coffee at Celia's house.

As she walked there on a sunny summer morning, Alison remembered her first visit when beginning her search for her. She remembered the abandoned front garden, the dead Christmas tree and the actor in the basement flat. This time, although the tree was gone, little else had changed.

Celia opened the door wearing a pink shirt and a slightly flared skirt. Her hair had been swept back and sunglasses were planted on the crown of her head. She looked as pretty as ever, Alison thought, despite the creases round her eyes betraying tiredness.

"Alison, come in. How are you?" They embraced. "Why don't we go straight through to the garden? It's a shame to stay indoors on such a lovely day."

The back garden was as much of a mess as the front. The French windows gave onto an overgrown tangle of flowering bushes, straggly hedges and weeds – dandelions mostly. A couple of roses reached for the light and were taller than either of the women as they brushed leaves off two garden chairs. At least there was plenty of shade. The one spot receiving uninterrupted sunlight in the centre of the neglected plot was occupied by a red-painted barbecue on wheels, stained with blue and white bird-droppings.

"I haven't had the time to get down to this," Celia said, waving her hand at the jungle. "It seems to have gone mad in my absence. What with rushing back and forth to the studios and sorting myself out, there hasn't been a moment. I'm disappointed that houses can't look after themselves better. It's a bit the same indoors. The hot water's dodgy and according to my lodger downstairs, I could be sued for having slimy steps to the basement! Coffee?"

Celia had no trouble making small talk for another five minutes but still there was no mention of Sam. Yet he was in intensive care in hospital after brain surgery. Surely he dominated her thoughts?

"Thank you. With lots of milk, if I may," Alison said.

"Alison, I expect you want to talk about the film – the money side. You know, your confidence in this project has been invaluable. Having a financial backer like you has been a great comfort. As it happens, Mr Feldstein and I are going to have a big meeting about the budget on Monday…"

"No Celia, I've not actually come to talk about that at all. I've come to talk about Sam." She paused.

"I'm pregnant."

Celia put her coffee cup down with a clatter. She glanced towards Alison's tummy and saw for herself although she wouldn't have noticed unless she'd been told. Any bump was well hidden by Alison's loose blouse.

"I see," she said. "I suppose I should say congratulations. There's no doubt that it's…"

"No doubt at all about the father, no. It's due early next year."

"Well, I don't know what to say, what to think. Sam knows, of course?"

"No, in fact, he doesn't. That's why I must see him now."

Celia's brow furrowed slightly. She laboriously ate a biscuit and re-crossed her legs. The breeze moved the branches overhead allowing flashes of sunlight to flit across her face. They mirrored her emotions: bitterness, disappointment, jealousy, resignation.

"You know," she said, "what I experienced in that camp has altered me. My life's priorities were overturned and reordered. Finding happiness with Sam, or any man, no longer seemed the most important thing in my world. I thought all that would change once we left the camp behind. But it hasn't. Anyway, when I had no replies to my letters to him from the camp – and they were not easy to write or to send, I can tell you – when I had no replies, I guessed Sam had found someone else."

"But I told you, he never received your letters," said Alison.

"How can you be so sure?" asked Celia.

"Well, we were together much of the time, especially weekends, and I just would have known."

Celia smiled wanly. "People do change. I have changed." She threw away the remains of her biscuit for the birds and wiped crumbs off her skirt with her hand.

"Sam could not have found a nicer person than you, to be honest."

"You're very kind," said Alison. "I expected you to explode."

"I know that you will make Sam happy," Celia said. "I can't be angry about that. Anyway, I don't think I would have had the strength to give Sam all that he needs now as well as driving the film forward. It's more to me than just a film, you see. It's a solemn undertaking to the migrants, present and future, and it's also trying to set an agenda for governments. It's taking up my life. I've no energy left for Sam. You have my blessing with him."

Alison didn't know whether her tears were pregnancy tears, tears of relief or tears of joy. Probably joy, she decided.

When Celia closed her front door and Alison's footsteps could no longer be heard, she wept too. For minutes on end.

Two days later, Sam was moved from intensive care to a ward. He was at last allowed visitors and Alison did not delay. She arrived with roses. Not the scentless ones from the supermarket or the hospital florist but from a local shop which somehow stocked what Alison called real flowers. She spotted him at the far end of the ward, by a window. There was white sticking plaster on his head beside two large bruises. He was reading a folded news magazine held up with one hand and didn't see her until she was at the end of the bed.

"Sam, what have they done to your hair? I'll have to call you 'baldy'!"

He dropped his magazine, stretched out both arms and leant to the side of the bed where Alison was in order to embrace her as best he could.

"Alison, oh it's so good to see you! I was dreaming that you would come. The Romans were right. Dreaming works!"

"How are you, Sam?"

"I must be well otherwise they wouldn't have unhooked me from all those monitors! Seriously, I feel fine physically but a bit fuzzy sometimes up here. I'm sorry about the shaved head: it obviously shocked you. It shocks me when I look in the mirror. If all goes well, in two more weeks they'll let me out."

"Then what?"

"Probably stay with the parents for a bit, until I'm able to start work and so on."

"Sam, darling, I have some big news." She lowered her voice to a stage whisper. "We're going to have a baby. I'm pregnant."

Sam's face creased into a huge smile.

"Wow! I don't believe it! My God! Wonderful. I'm so pleased."

He opened his arms again and kissed Alison, once, twice, three times, then held both her hands and stared at her, wordless.

There were the inevitable questions from Sam as the news sank in. The patient opposite Sam had seen and heard everything and was smiling too.

"Nurse," Sam called out. "Nurse. How does one celebrate becoming a father in this place?"

"We don't have a lot of that on the neurology ward," said the harassed-looking nurse with an Irish accent. "They would know downstairs in maternity!"

"Champagne?" said Sam, to the nurse smiling still from ear to ear.

"Don't you dare," she said, "and you only yesterday coming from intensive care!"

"Let me see how you look," Sam said turning to Alison who was wearing a scalloped-neck embroidered blouse with puff sleeves and a summery skirt. "Is there anything to see? Oh yes. Just a little something."

"I was frightened," said Alison, "that you wouldn't be pleased."

"I'm deliriously pleased and above all surprised," said Sam.

"I wasn't sure about you and Celia."

"Ah," said Sam.

"So I went to see her. I told her I was pregnant. She took it well. Sort of gave me her blessing."

"She should have said that things have changed between us..."

"She did."

The Irish nurse approached to say that Sam should rest now. He was meant to be calm for a few days. She made it clear, in the nicest possible way that the visit had been long enough.

"Thank you for the roses, darling. I'll call you tomorrow."

CHAPTER 25

It was a blessing that on release from hospital a week later Sam's parents were in a position to be full-time carers. They took him back to the farm in the Isle of Wight.

Once there he became increasingly aware that he had slowed down mentally. He felt as if he was under a permanent light anaesthetic. He also began to have flashbacks triggered by random events. On the main road to Newport with his mother driving, they passed some road-works. A tractor was using an earth-borer, like a large corkscrew, to perforate the clay. They were halted by temporary traffic lights, so Sam saw the massive steel bit with its sharp, revolving tip plunge into the grey matter, grinding, churning, turning deeper and deeper until the tractor itself started to rear up when the drill could go no further. In the back seat, Sam shouted, shut his eyes and leant forward, groaning.

"Don't worry, Sam, the light's changed. We're moving on now," his mother said.

But when she turned round again, Sam was still wincing, rocking up and down in distress. When she put her hand out to touch him, Sam roughly brushed it aside. He was in his own tormented world.

There were other telling episodes. As the English summer blossomed, they would go for walks on the farm and on the downs above, where skylarks sang invisibly. Sam's mother noticed that he was disturbed whenever other people came towards him – ramblers, joggers, lovers strolling along the footpaths lined with may and dog-rose. Sometimes he would shy away from them like a startled horse. Sometimes he would out-stare them with feigned smiles. In case he felt self-conscious about his short hair and the scar on his head, his mother gave him a floppy hat. But he felt even more conspicuous wearing that, so he lost it.

Mistakenly, she thought occasional shopping trips might help him conquer his fear of other people. But if anything, they made him worse. They sat for an hour in the corner of a pub garden, overlooking a creek full of bustling yachts, rolling at their moorings, their rigging rattling. Sam turned his back on the scene, his screwed-up eyes hidden by oversized sunglasses.

The hardest day for his parents was on the first of June, an unusually hot day. There was a pleasant park, a safe and favourite place for families, next to the local supermarket. Herbaceous beds of geraniums and purple irises enclosed a pond and tinkling fountain. Fenced off behind it were swings and roundabouts for children.

Whilst his parents went shopping, Sam suggested he should wait in the fresh air on one of the wooden benches *('In fond memory of Arthur who loved this spot. Donated by his loving wife, Dorothy, 2006')*. There were just too many people streaming in and out of the store for Sam's liking. And Sam didn't have a role when shopping. His father was the master of vouchers, lists and offers. Sam's mother trundled the trolley between the banks of brightly-lit lettuce, own-brand butter and insidious three-for-two's. They were gone for the best part of an hour. How were they to know what a tinkling fountain would trigger in the injured brain of their son?

Sam could not say and did not know what made him step over the fence, sidle round the slide and jump on the see-saw with all his force. He'd chosen a descending end where a girl of six straddled the seat in new sandals and was licking an ice-cream cornet. Her little sister of five in a yellow blouse and pale-blue shorts, was propelled into the air on the higher part of the plank and cried out in alarm "Mummy, Mummy!" She managed to cling on to the handle in front of her and it was a miracle she didn't lose her balance.

"What the hell do you think you're doing!" the children's mother screamed at Sam. "Get off that see-saw!"

Sam didn't move, but kept one foot on the plank so that nobody was hurt. He looked back to the fountain, staring at it wide-eyed, then slowly turned towards the mother and said

"Sorry. I'm sorry."

"So I should bloody well think. Madman!"

With that she reached up for her younger daughter who by now looked terrified, and put her safely on the ground. She immediately clung to her mother's leg, sobbing. Her sister, ice-cream abandoned, joined her, clinging with sticky fingers to the other leg.

Another mother came up, with a cigarette in one hand and mobile-phone in the other.

"I saw him on the bench earlier and I thought he looked funny. That hair-cut and the big shades. I'm ringing the police. It's not normal to sit and look at children, is it? Not normal at all. That's why I'm ringing the police." She looked triumphant.

Numerous witnesses told Sam's mother he gave them the creeps. Or rather the woman with the phone did and the others all agreed. One described how she'd seen Sam in the sand-pit with his legs apart, pretending to hit a golf-ball. Another saw him imitating a monkey, trying to make the children laugh. By the time the police came – a WPC fiddling with the radio on her shoulder and a constable with ginger hair and an Isle of Wight accent – Sam was leaning against a tree trunk.

"We'll take some statements and then you'll accompany us to the station, alright?"

"I'm waiting for my mother," said Sam.

"A likely story. Pull the other one," said the WPC to nobody in particular as she flipped open her notebook and looked at her watch.

When Alison heard Sam's voice that same evening, she knew he'd had a set-back of some sort. He sounded depressed and upset. He knew that small things triggered strange reactions but could not predict them or stop them. Alison said she would come down to the Isle of Wight the next day. Sam's mother was delighted. She was feeling increasingly inadequate in the face of her son's bizarre behaviour.

In the first class carriage to Portsmouth, Alison was thoughtful. Her book remained unopened in her lap. She gazed languorously out of the window at the Surrey hills and the Hampshire woods. She had started to knit at home but felt self-conscious knitting in public. It drew attention to her distending belly. But since the carriage was empty, she wished she had brought it with her. It was good for the nerves, less demanding than reading. As for what people thought, she had been psyching herself up for her new role as a mother, perhaps a single one, for some days. She told herself that thousands of women were carrying children in far worse circumstances than hers.

On arrival, Alison was impressed by the genuine warmth of Sam's parents' welcome. They clicked. Sam was upstairs and hadn't heard Alison arrive which gave his father the time to say he'd spoken that morning to the surgeon in London who was not too worried by Sam's unpredictable behaviour. He'd come across this before. Over time – a few months – it would get better and in the meanwhile there was medication that would help. The results of the last tests he'd had and a further scan were excellent, he said. All the clinical signs were that Sam would make a complete recovery and could be back at work in six weeks or so. Alison was reassured.

In the comfortable farmhouse sitting room, she saw where Sam's inventive streak came from: his father. Her eye was drawn to four display cabinets strategically placed against the walls. She didn't have time to study the contents in detail but one contained an assortment of spinning tops and gyroscopes; another a collection of what looked like model, brass propellers for boats. The parents withdrew after a decent interval leaving Sam and Alison alone.

"We'll be in the garden should you need anything," Sam's mother called over her shoulder.

Sam was standing with one hand on the back of a tall chair. He was wearing clothes she remembered: blue linen shirt with two pockets, beige trousers and a crocodile-skin belt. In his free hand he was holding a small parcel wrapped in blue paper, tied with gold string. Little presents gave much pleasure to them both. They moved round the opposite ends of the sofa to meet seated in the middle, angled towards each other, knees touching.

"I'm sorry the police bothered you yesterday, Sam. What happened?"

"Random things – or maybe they're not random – set me off. Yesterday it was children falling through the air on a see-saw and a fountain."

"Of course. The sanctuary – Bisuli – the accident. Oh Sam darling. It's hard to forget, isn't it? I still have nightmares about the accident, too. I remember the roaring noise as the ground opened up. I remember the weird feeling as my legs had nothing to stand on. Like a rug being pulled from under me. Then nothing. I suppose I landed on my head but I'll never know for sure."

She saw Sam turn away, biting his lip.

"I worry that it might have affected our baby," she said. "I can't wait for my first scan next week. We must both forget about that accident."

"Yes, but can we?"

"Of course we can. I'm thinking positively. By the way, your father told me that your doctor now says you'll make a complete recovery. Back at work in a matter of weeks. That's fabulous news."

"Well, on that note, I have something to say."

He waited until Alison was absolutely still.

"Will you marry me?"

By the time Sam's parents had come back from the garden in response to his 'There's something you must see, both of you. Come quickly!' Alison had unwrapped the parcel with the ring, Sam had slipped it onto her finger and they were standing at the open French windows, arm in arm. Alison couldn't help her tears again and wiped them away with Sam's hand which she only released when he kissed her.

From somewhere inside the house a radio was playing. Sam heard the DJ say "Hope Kakwani singing *I dreamed today*' from the film due to be released next year and in which she features." A child's clear tenor voice – Hope's voice with its unmistakeable

African accent – floated over Sam and Alison towards the roses in full bloom and the green lawn beyond.

"I dreamed my village now was safe,
That wells were full of water,
That fields were growing with new life
And echoed with our laughter."

Acknowledgements

Writing a novel is surprisingly time-consuming. My first debt of gratitude is therefore to my family who have had every right to feel neglected. I thank them for their support.

I am grateful to many others for their helpful comments during the preparation of the book. I benefitted from expert archaeological comments from Michael Green and Liliane and Abdelmajid Ennabli. I thank Dr Raa Gillon for reading an early draft and Michael Cracknell, Sue Lee, Laura Macdougall, and Joan Byrne for all sorts of other help. If there remain any inaccuracies, it is my fault, not theirs.

I R
London 2012.

Lightning Source UK Ltd.
Milton Keynes UK
UKOW040046160612

194501UK00005B/3/P